"I have to get away from you," Trinity whispered.

"What?" He was staring at her mouth, as if trying to decode a foreign tongue.

"I'm sorry," Trinity said. Strangely enough, she meant it. She grabbed her backpack and bolted past him.

At least, that was her plan. But Cal leaned forward, his hand blurring out and closing around her upper arm. "Is this really what you want to do?" Hot breath on her ear. "I'm here to help you, honey. We can do this the easy way, or the hard way."

"I. Have. To. Get. Away. From. You." She enunciated clearly, so he could not possibly misunderstand. "I am dangerous, Eight."

"Don't call me that." Soft and reasonable. "You really think you're dangerous?"

You have no idea. How many are dead because of me?

Then again, a better word might be *toxic*. More precise.

She tested his grip, struggling.

"I have a mission." Analyses and percentages raced through her head. None of them added up correctly. How far had mental degradation progressed?

"So do I, honey." A little husky now. "And it involves keeping you out of their hands."

Dear Reader,

Plenty of people consider logic and emotion mortal enemies. Certainly Trinity, who readers will remember from *Agent Zero*, does. When does logic become monstrous, and when does emotion become pathological? The balancing point is different for every person. It was interesting to write Cal, whose casual exterior masks deadly seriousness, and Trinity, whose icy self-control is a survival mechanism, not a choice. The older I become, the more I find what you see isn't ever what you get.

Even the most logical or self-sufficient superspy sometimes has to rely on someone else. I hope you enjoy the story of how these two people come to rely on each other. I'll warn you, a great deal of this book takes place in the dusty desert, and I had to drink gallons of water while writing it...

Lilith Saintcrow

AGENT GEMINI

Lilith Saintcrow

HARLEQUIN® ROMANTIC SUSPENSE

Recycling programs
for this product may
not exist in your area.

ISBN-13: 978-0-373-27947-0

Agent Gemini

Copyright © 2015 by Lilith Saintcrow

This edition published by arrangement with Harlequin Books S.A.

For questions and comments about the quality of this book, please contact us at CustomerService@Harlequin.com.

® and TM are trademarks of Harlequin Enterprises Limited or its corporate affiliates. Trademarks indicated with ® are registered in the United States Patent and Trademark Office, the Canadian Intellectual Property Office and in other countries.

Printed in U.S.A.

Lilith Saintcrow has been writing stories since the second grade and lives in Vancouver, Washington, with two children, two cats, two dogs and assorted other strays. Please check out her website at lilithsaintcrow.com.

Books by Lilith Saintcrow

Harlequin Romantic Suspense

Agent Zero
Agent Gemini

Harlequin Nocturne

Taken

Visit the Author Profile page Harlequin.com, or lilithsaintcrow.com, for more titles.

For Mel S., again, because of reasons.

Part One: Finding Trinity

Noah Caldwell had good news, for once, so he didn't wait to make the daily report. When the brief codescramble of encryption was over, its whine through the earpiece enough to make him wince, he didn't waste time on niceties, either. "Bingo, sir."

"What?" Control sounded irritated, but that was usual. The past few months had been one irritation after another, and even Gibraltar Two getting off the ground with flying colors hadn't sweetened the old man's temper.

Caldwell himself was of the opinion that you had to be prepared to overcome obstacles to get near anything worth having, and it had served him well.

It got him to his major's acorn, at least, before he'd been put at Control's disposal.

And he'd performed well. He was Control's fireman now, rushing around the front to patch up holes. The chance for further advancement was very good—if he didn't screw it up. "We have a security breach."

"Where?" Control didn't waste time getting angry. If it was bad news, Caldwell would own up to it soon enough.

Still, Caldwell reminded himself to step carefully. His heart hammered. He shifted his weight fractionally, looking out through the smoked glass of the office wall at the banks of computers, shuffling paper, glowing screens and uniformed people drinking overboiled coffee, collating, speaking into ugly but efficient headsets or phones. The only difference between this space and a telemarketer's call center were the guards at the two doors, sidearms on display and their expressions granite-stony. "Beta Four."

"Pocula Flats." Control caught on, but not as quickly as he usually did. The old man must be tired—or worried. "That's—"

"It's our girl. The gamble paid off—now we have a location." Caldwell kept his tone even. The old man didn't like being interrupted, but would tolerate it in certain circumstances. If these didn't qualify, none did.

"If she hasn't already blown by now." The cigarette-roughened words rasped, even through encryption and auditory filters.

So Noah sprang his little surprise. "She hasn't. She didn't get everything she came for."

A long pause. Then careful, even and measured words. "How do you know?"

"Because that's how the trap was set, sir. I'm requesting on-site assets and full authorization."

Another short silence. There was a click—probably a lighter. "You have both. Don't screw this up, Caldwell." Control sounded weary, but also mildly pleased, which was a banner occasion in and of itself.

Agent Three, the crown jewel of the Gibraltar I program, was a high-priority recapture. And she had, after months of keeping just ahead of the game, committed her first mistake. All Caldwell had to do was bring her in alive, and his promotion, not to mention survival, was assured.

There were other reasons to bring her in, too. More…personal ones.

He still remembered her walking across a slick rooftop, gliding across ice like a panther, all fluid grace. Her wide dark eyes and her slim shoulders. He'd always liked blondes, and this one was a doozy.

"No, sir." Noah Caldwell hung up, smiling.

The cereal aisle was by far the best. Bright boxes soothed her—all standardized sizes, arranged with a clear plan, bright sugary kids' breakfasts just below adult eye-level, healthful blandness up top, the very bottom reserved for generics and other alternatives. The bags of generics in their bins were a little troublesome, you couldn't *quite* get them perfect, but a little deviation was to be expected even in the most smoothly running system. Instead of overheating over a natural law, it was better to build some tolerances into every complex pattern.

Even, and especially, the ones inside your skull. It had taken her some time to arrive at that conclusion, but it worked wonderfully.

Trinity ran her finger down a line of General Mills products—their finest corn-syrup-laden offerings—tilted her blonde head and narrowed her dark eyes slightly. Constant Muzak, bland and inoffensive, seemed louder when the store was deserted; whether it was a function of selective attention or the absence of warm round human bodies to soak up stray sound waves was an open question, saved for when she needed calculations to stave off shutdown. Fluorescents buzzed overhead, outside a city slept or dozed, and inside this concrete cube a rogue United States government resource broke down cardboard with mechanical grace, slicing with a box knife then applying just the right amount of force to snap any remaining tape as the headache returned and her ribs ached.

She'd slightly miscalculated the fall onto the trailer of a passing semi to exit the Pocula Flats installation, and perhaps one of her ribs had cracked.

The Gibraltar virus's strengthening of her natural healing processes would soothe *that* pain in short order, but the headaches were growing more frequent and nothing eased them. With enhanced metabolism, pain medication was burned through extremely quickly unless she took a massive dose of opiates, and the concurrent risk of being incapacitated was unacceptable each time she ran the relevant equations inside her skull.

Trinity suppressed a useless sigh. You were supposed to work down the aisle and stock as you went, not break open boxes by size and waste time going back and forth, but Trinity had calculated any time lost backtracking was made up when she heaved the already-sorted cardboard into the binder, where it would be turned into a tightly wrapped brick of recyclable plant fiber. Perhaps the binder appreciated her thoroughness, and she was certain she had more in common with its metal jaws and brisk movements than she did with Tengermann, the night manager, or even with her fellow stockers.

Her hands moved without much conscious direction, making sure brightly colored cardboard blocks were brought flush to the edges, each shelf arranged for maximum aesthetic pleasure. It…irritated her, to work slowly enough the other stockers wouldn't notice anything strange. East Felicitas, squatting like a surprise mushroom in the middle of parched heat-glimmering flats, drew from a labor pool large enough that a single woman with a disposable SSN could pass anonymously, and poor enough that most people were too exhausted to mind anyone else's business, too occupied with their own. This Sav-Mor Supermarket on the west side was the perfect cover.

Military employees and families from the Pocula Flats base—an hour's drive away, behind its razor wire and its two visible gatehouses—were the only reason this burg had swelled to its present size. Anyone who had the proper identification shopped at the PX; anyone who could afford it shopped on the north side of town, rarely venturing past the railroad tracks into the southwest quadrant, where the ranchero music blared, the street vendors clustered and the fields beyond the pavement held coyotes both human and otherwise at night.

It was Pocula Flats that Trinity was interested in. Not the training ground or the labyrinthine medical buildings, though the latter probably held something useful and was on her secondary list of objectives. She didn't care for the historical markers scattered all through the area or the scars of past nuclear testing, either, beyond wondering if radioactive waste still lingered in the air and what the Gibraltar virus would do when faced with such a stressor.

No, it was the highly secure northern quadrant of the base she had fixed on, with its ancient brick buildings hosting basement warrens of ceiling-to-floor file cabinets. It was time for the second and last try; the process of elimination meant the files *had* to be here. If she wanted to answer any of the questions crowding her before they were rendered academic by her own demise, this was her only chance.

"Yo, Alice!" Eddie appeared at the end of the aisle, next to the instants—instant oatmeal, instant breakfast, Pop-Tarts and other easy foods created for convenience. They were her least favorite, so she did them last before she dragged the cardboard back and returned to repair the damage done daily to the baking aisle. "Goin' on break."

Why tell me? I'm not a manager. She nodded, a single efficient bob of her head. Her hair, scraped back in a ponytail as usual, felt like straw—she'd stripped the black dye from the indifferently trimmed mane just prior to beginning this job. All dye eventually flaked free, her hair not accepting the color as a normal woman's would.

The patchy coverage such simple cosmetic applications afforded was protective coloration she may not need, since scrawny washed-out blondes were a dime a dozen. Camouflage was also afforded by the scratchy, stained red polyester vest and the jeans night stockers were allowed to wear. After all, nobody saw them except for blur-eyed insomniacs, addicts, or the occasional blinking, hair-mussed parent in desperate need of formula, diapers or an emergency bottle of baby Tylenol.

No customer took any notice of the muscle on Trinity's slim frame or the sloppiness of some of her coworkers. She was an invisible appliance, an anonymous drone, and that made it safe.

"It's cooling off out there," Eddie persisted. "You wanna catch a smoke with me?"

I don't smoke. Why is he asking? She spared him a single glance, from his shaggy head to his broad but softening shoulders, the top of his collared shirt undone and his sad, worn-down work sneakers splattered with rancid milk from the latest disaster back in the dairy section. He seemed to have more than a few problems with milk crates, racks and the eggs, as well.

His steady staring, his attention to her—they were both troubling. A surreptitious sniff gave her the news that he had showered before work and put on a dab of cologne—both unique occurrences. His pheromones held an edge—acrid maleness, nervous sweat, the metabolizing of the cigarettes he'd already smoked tonight—and a faint whiff of the microwaved turkey potpie he'd had before his shift warring with a cloud of burned coffee.

Every one of the stockers except Trinity drank gallons of boiled or sugar-laden, effervescent caffeine, and she had amused herself by calculating flow-through rates and uptake algorithms for a few days when she first started.

It helped keep her on track. Any calculation did. The deconstructing had slowed, or perhaps she was simply losing the acuity necessary to gauge its creeping progress. One more reason to hurry, but she wasn't finished planning yet. And if the past few months had taught her anything, it was that planning was indispensable, even if the plan had to be altered as soon as it engaged with reality.

It was a military cliché, but it had the advantage of being completely true.

"I have to finish this." She pitched it with care—just loud enough to be heard over the music, pleasant and neutral, her face stretching in the approximation of a smile most likely to seem unthreatening and regretful. "I'm behind."

"You? You're *never* behind." A little forced, nervous laughter. "You sure you don't want to? Just for a minute? It's a nice night."

His idea of a nice night was a hot, sterile breathlessness, with clouds of insects clustering street lamps and any mammal they could find in equal measure? The street lamps reminded them of the moon, probably, and the mammals were a rich food source, but understanding the insects did *not* manage to overcome the faintly sick unsteadiness Trinity was subject to when she thought of them.

Comprehension brought comfort, but no reduction of repugnance. The uneasiness was unwelcome and just another symptom of her decline.

"Gotta finish this." She took care to inject just enough of a drawl into the words to match the regional-local speech patterns. "Maybe later."

A rough raw pink of disappointment, like seeping, undercooked beef, spread through Eddie's scent. "Okay." He dawdled a little, but she went to work facing the instant oatmeals. He finally turned and plodded away. His chinos had a stain on the left side of the seat, shaped almost exactly like Florida.

Hopefully, it was coffee.

He was paying too much attention to her. She should quit here. But sitting in the apartment with nothing to calculate unless she turned the television on and began free-associating would only lead to… disturbances, inside her head or the rest of her body. Ones she couldn't pinpoint, even with the viral load she carried giving her vastly heightened control over autonomics and a dose of high-grade neuroplasticity.

The virus. A strange sensation rippled down her back. She was coping, and she had tied off every loose end she could. She was hiding successfully and about to make her third and final run to find the records. Before she deteriorated completely, she would at least know who she was. Or *had* been, before the Gibraltar virus and the induction procedure erased everything but faint, misleading cortical ghosts.

For a moment white light filled her head, the raw scrape of a throat screamed dry, restraints at wrists, ankles, waist, elbows, knees—

Stop. Remembering the induction was quite useless. *Control yourself.* Her sweat glands opened slightly. It took more effort than she liked to bring the various processes into harmony again. Homeostasis was such a delicate, difficult balance.

How did the uninfected handle such spikes in hormones, in internal activity, in sensation? How had *she* handled them before the induction? It was difficult to imagine when you had no memory for comparison.

Focus on the task at hand, Trinity. She redirected her attention, breathing deeply, and found she had placed a box of strawberry oatmeal in with the blueberry. The boxes were the same size, true, but it was a disturbing lapse, a bloodred blot in the middle of the blue.

She stood for a few moments, trembling in her serviceable hiking boots, before her hands moved to right it, placing the offending box with its own kind.

It was no use. She couldn't ignore the signs. Deconstruction was proceeding at its own insidious pace.

I am, she thought grimly, *running out of time.*

It was a simmering Tucson afternoon, the kind that should be spent inside with air-conditioning and a cold beer while you watched overgrown steroid-fed jackholes run into each other for your amusement on a screen you paid too much for. Preferably with some slow-cooked barbecue at the end of the day, and your girl cuddled against you on the couch while you watched sitcoms afterward. The good old American dream—cable, cholesterol and circuses.

Hold that thought, Gibraltar Agent Eight—or Cal, as he preferred, even though it wasn't any closer to the name he was born with—told himself and pretended to stumble as they shoved him into an alley.

Three men against an agent was close to a cakewalk. Even when the agent was handcuffed. Knee to the first one's groin, stamping down along the shin with a heavy boot-toe—steel-toed Docs were still the best—driving himself aside, *that one's got a knife, dammit,* shoulder into the knife man's stomach and skin tearing as he yanked his right hand free.

If you didn't mind losing a little flesh, handcuffs came right off. Zip ties were laughably easy if you had some freedom of movement, so was duct tape, but cuffs always meant blood loss. The knife skittered away, fetching up under a Dumpster; Cal's bleeding hand snapped up and there was a crunch as the nasal promontory broke, driving into the brain.

Oops. Steady on, Cal. Need one for questioning. Left hand whipping out, fingers folded through the now-free right-hand cuff to brace it, a strike to the third one's throat.

These were standard-issue goons, probably NSA fieldhoppers though their watches were wrong, in suits with the wrong wingtips for urban camouflage and sidearms they didn't dare use out in public. He'd waved himself like a red rag in front of them, and they'd leaped to snap the cuffs on him and get him off the street, probably to hood and zip-tie him while they called for backup.

Idiots. Getting all excited and moving to take him even though they probably had orders to call for backup *first.* But you got high-testosterone boys in a group, and their functional efficiency went into the basement once there was a bit of caveman exertion in sight.

Textbook closed-space combat, blond hair flopping a little in Cal's face since he'd needed to grow it out a bit for camouflage. Really, with the enhanced strength and speed, it was hardly fair.

Fair was for idealists, not survivors. A greenstick crack as he took out the first one's knee, spilling him on the alley floor, and the third was quietly choking. Big, bullish, brawny boys, probably ruthless and used to winning against defenseless civilians.

Definitely not used to fighting an agent.

A hollow *bong*—the third had kicked a Dumpster, the body scrabbling for breath. Cal sighed, stripped the still-twitching corpse—Number Two—of its gun and wallet, spent a few minutes making Number Three a little more comfortable and a little less visible from the street-mouth, then went back to the first. He got a hand over the man's mouth just as shock loosened its grip enough to permit screaming, got *that* gun away and examined the man critically. A real corn-fed wonder with a high and tight, little blue eyes way too close together, and he smelled like chili. The sweet-roasted edge of incipient diabetes lay under the taco-and-beans funk.

Thirty-five or thereabouts. Not too old for field-work, but metabolism starting to slow down. Still in good shape but had too much rye mash last night. That's alcohol metabolizing. A kaleidoscope of smell and sense impression inside his head. Sometimes

Cal wondered how he'd ever got along without the invaders in his bloodstream, spinning all his dials up to eleven. The initial illness had been goddamn uncomfortable—that was true enough—but the end result was better muscular efficiency, flexibility, problem solving and a host of other benefits.

It was a pity he hadn't come out of it with, say, Reese's ability to plan instead of what the eggheads called "tactical flexibility." But you made do with what you had, and what he had right now was a man to question.

"Hi," Cal said softly, politely. No use in shouting. "Let's keep this simple, okay? I ask questions. You tell the truth, you live."

His sides heaving, his eyes white-ringed, Number One still had the remarkable presence of mind to look over Cal's shoulder, probably thinking he'd get some help if he could choke out a yell. Cal sighed, shook his head, blue eyes darkening a little. "You want broken ribs, too? Come on, man. You've had a hard day. Just tell me what I want to know."

"What?" Number One choked, his voice high and squeaky. Maybe fear, maybe pain, both were pouring off him in waves. Cal's right hand smarted—the flesh was already sealing up. He might scar, despite the virus jacking healing processes into hyperspeed.

Wouldn't that be interesting. The longer he walked around with the swarmies in his bloodstream, the more interesting things kept cropping up. Like the headaches. "What's your initials, fella?"

Cal dug at the man's coat, found the badge holder and flipped it open. It looked legit, true, but looks weren't everything. "Aw, come on. You're not FBI. Your socks are all wrong. You're not NSA, either, those watches are outside your pay grade."

"In-indep-pendent," the man stuttered, and Cal's nape roughened with gooseflesh. *"B-b-b-bait."*

Uh-oh. Independent contractors, working in a major American city. Deniability and tactical flexibility in one nasty package, and getting the authorization to let them do anything domestic was a maze of paperwork. Someone was *very* invested in this. "Huh. That makes you collateral, then, doesn't it." Still nice and level. His entire back was crawling now. *If you're bait, sonny boy, I'm a lot closer than I think.* Like all good news, though, it had a lead lining.

Because *bait* meant trapjaws, too, nice and shiny and jagged, looking to close on him.

Cal glanced up at the alley sides and the slice of blue sky he could see between two six-story buildings, then back at the street, where a golden flood of pure-D Arizona sunshine was busy cooking everything stupid enough to try moving during the middle of the day. He wasn't sweating *too* much—temperature differences were a lot less likely to affect him now—and it took a second to throttle back the adrenaline dump in his bloodstream, everything revving down so he could think without the chemi-

cal soup of fight-or-flight fogging his mental processes. "Bait, huh?"

"Don't k-k-kill me," the man whispered. "OhGod,
don't kill me, dontkillme *please—*"

You get this close to me and survive, they'll *kill
you. Or make you wish you were dead in debriefing.*
Cal shrugged easily, every nerve screaming *Get the
hell out of here, man, what are you doing waiting
around?* "You're not here for me." Logical enough
to make even Reese proud.

"G-g-girl." Number One flapped his left hand,
and Cal's fingers were there, reaching under the
suit jacket cuff to feel tape and paper. "B-b-blonde
g-g-girl."

He yanked on it, and the photo—taped to the
shirtsleeve underneath for easy reference and sweat
proofing—crackled against his palm. "A girl, huh?
Didn't anyone tell you she had a boyfriend already?"
He grinned easily, and Number One's mouth fell
open as he cowered. Whatever was on Cal's face at
that moment must not have been pretty.

It didn't feel pretty from the inside, either. A cold
breath against his nape again warned him he was
running out of time and room. *Put him down. It's
kinder than what they'll do.*

Besides, jackholes like this had killed Tracy. His
hands ached with the urge, ached further with the
loss of skin, just two short moves and it would all be
over. He could even make it painless, if he wanted to.

One hundred and twenty seconds later, Cal peered

down from the roof above, the right-hand cuff already open and the irritating metal bracelets forgotten, as black SUVs clustered the alley mouth. More big brawny goons clotted the small space below, bundling up the two bodies and ushering Number One toward a quick ride to debriefing and maybe liquidation.

It would have been better to just erase the man, Cal told himself again.

Tracy's voice, soft and kind. *You're not as bad as you think you are, you know.*

Except Tracy was dead now, without ever knowing the truth: that Cal would be just as bad as necessary to get the job done. Right now, his job was finding another woman before these yahoos did. A woman who smelled like blueberry pie and sweetness, a woman who had neatly rescued Reese's girl Holly and then saved *all* their collective bacon, before vanishing.

A woman like that deserved some looking after.

More independent contractors, taking their orders from someone in government. If he watched closely enough, he might get a clue.

Hang on, what's that? He breathed softly, ignoring the sun beating on his back. A tall figure, dark hair not military cut but the rigidity of bearing suggesting some bootcamp, moving unhurried through the frenzy of activity. They'd probably take everything in the Dumpster in for scanning and analyzing, as well. *Hello, sir, who are you?*

No time to introduce himself to this interesting new player on the scene, even if he had the urge. There was a thopping of chopper blades, and Cal ran lightly across the rooftop, tar softening under his boot soles. It took a special kind of sliding to keep your speed across footing like this—you were liable to throw your knee out if you didn't do it right. By the time the helicopter arrived and began its search pattern, he was already in the car, almost running a stop sign the way they did down here, just slowing to a California roll with the AC blasting and the steering wheel hot enough to cook his fingers. A police scanner set under the dash crackled and burbled softly, and he had the picture from the guy's sleeve propped over the RPM gauge.

It was a woman with big dark eyes, her blond hair pulled too tightly back and little gold hoops winking in her ears. Unsmiling, she stared directly into the camera as if it was a mug shot, and the shape of her cheekbones was sweet enough to make any man's heart pound. She was too thin, the architecture of her neck clearly visible and her lush mouth pulled tight with what had to be hunger.

The scanner squawked—they were using some of the local resources, which meant he could infiltrate and hop one step ahead of them, again. It also meant they were very, very close to the prize, and getting closer all the time.

Cal let out a soft breath, not quite a whistle, and rolled his window up since the AC had finally stopped blowing more heat into the car and started doing what it was supposed to.

Now the only problem was getting to the girl before *they* did.

There was someone in her aisle. Trinity suppressed a scratching feeling behind her breastbone— it was not *rational* to be irritated at a bundled-up figure who had shuffled in from outside to stand in front of the tuna-fish shelves, staring at the cans as if the fate of the world depended on picking the right constellation of ocean trash and dolphin meat.

Homeless. Female. Thirty-five or a little older. The scent—ripe and almost rank, a woman who tried unsuccessfully to keep herself clean against great odds—rode a draft of chilly air, and Trinity's head cocked slightly. It was far too warm outside for the bulky parka and knit cap the woman wore, not to mention the layers of sweatpants tucked into high-laced hiking boots caked with sand and quite possibly some animal scat. The boots were also much more worn than Trinity's and had been mended with duct tape.

Trinity dropped the box of pickled asparagus— the people on this patch of dusty earth seemed to crave a truly prodigious amount of the things—just hard enough to make a noise, but not hard enough to crack any of the jars.

The homeless woman didn't even flinch. Trinity's nostrils flared slightly—copper adrenaline, nervous sweat, but no hint of any drug, illegal or otherwise, metabolizing on the homeless woman. Then again, if she was deconstructing, could she trust that her sensory acuity would remain, or—

That was the trouble with this sort of work. It was not nearly challenging enough to keep her from what could be classified as *worrying*, a fruitless endeavor if ever one existed, and that probably hastened the deconstruction.

"'Scuse me." Shuffling footsteps. The woman was coming closer, her head bobbing strangely. "'Scuse me, 'scuse me."

Adrenaline, cortisol, other substances to prime her for combat—Trinity throttled them back, watching as a flushed, pitted face swam into view under the knit cap. Bloodshot blue eyes and one shoulder hunched much higher than the other. *Scoliosis. Malnutrition. Her teeth are rotting.*

Had the virus saved Trinity from this fate? There wasn't any way to tell. She did not fold her arms or straighten. She simply stood, as the woman hitched herself closer and closer. For a moment or two she had thought it a feint, the woman a government asset sent to pinpoint while others closed in. Then she discarded the idea as vanishingly unlikely, only a 1.2 percent chance such a maneuver would be tried in this setting.

"Got a cat," the woman stage-whispered. "A cat. Yes, a cat."

Trinity stayed very still. If the other woman kept

approaching on this vector, they would collide, but there didn't seem to be any need to step aside just yet. No further calculation she was capable of seemed to apply. *Not a threat. Ankles swollen—edema? No, the shape is wrong. What is that?*

"For my cat," the woman whispered and winked, her face screwing up into a map of sunstruck wrinkles and peeling. She altered her course by just a few degrees, passed close enough Trinity's eyes threatened to water at the smell, and she suddenly realized what the bulkiness around the woman's ankles was.

She has cans of tuna fish in there. Another swift glance, calculating. *Three on each side. How interesting.*

"Hey!" Tengermann's piping tenor echoed off the floor, the shelves, bounced back down from the light fixtures. *"Hey! You!"*

Trinity watched, mildly attentive, as the night manager, in his pressed white shirt and black slacks, bolted past her. The heels of his prissily polished shoes left long streaks on faded blue linoleum-over-concrete. The homeless woman scuttled for the front doors with amazing rapidity, given her decrepit condition, and just as it seemed he was going to catch her, Tengermann slipped on an overly shiny patch of linoleum, careening over an endcap—boxes of soda cans and a middle stripe of two-liters, all full of carbonated chemical sludge the people here drank instead of water.

Considering the quality of said tap water, it was

probably a reasonable choice. Trinity began calculating how many of the cans would explode with fizz when opened, her brain seizing on the problem as vastly more complex and entertaining than the pickled asparagus, and watched as the homeless woman made good her escape. The doors opened, whooshed closed behind her, and Tengermann struggled out of the nest of boxes and two-liters, his face beet-red and his right eye rapidly puffing shut.

Cynthia, the night checker, openmouthed, stared at him; there was a low snort an aisle over—Eddie, but he didn't sound as if he was in pain.

No, Trinity realized Eddie was trying unsuccessfully not to laugh. Cynthia's mouth twitched; she tucked a strand of frayed, frizzed, reddish hair behind her ear, her worn face lighting with a brand of amusement possibly close to schadenfreude.

What a lovely word. And completely applicable. Finding a word that fit perfectly in a proper slot was a deeply satisfying event.

Tengermann finally bounced to his feet. Nobody moved to help him; he spun angrily on one heel and fixed Trinity with a hot glare, though his battered face—one of the two-liters must have fallen on him—somewhat detracted from any quelling force said glare would possess.

Funny, he looks like Bronson. A jolt of recoil against her wrists, the man's body sagging—

Trinity pushed that aside. Free-associating about

the man in local control of Division's Midwest section was useless. After all, Richard Bronson was dead.

Just one of many murders.

"God*damn* it, Alice! You let her get away!" Tengerman yelled.

Irrational. She watched as he stamped back down the aisle toward her, fuming. *Ah. He feels his authority has been threatened. Next comes anger.*

Petty tyrants, really, were all the same.

He halted just inside her personal space, probably thinking to intimidate her. Trinity realized she was smiling just before he did; his face went through several shades of fury and finally settled on something close to apoplectic.

Another precise, beautiful word, she mused. The world was full of them. When they fitted into their proper slots, the satisfaction was almost intense enough to be physical.

"You *let her get away!*" he fumed, pointing an accusing finger, its nail darkened with an arc of dirt, at her. "You will be *written up!* What do you have to say for yourself?"

He constantly berated his underlings about hand washing and proper procedure, yet allowed a great deal of grime to accumulate on his own digits. "Apoplectic," she murmured. That was an absolutely correct word for his expression, his flushing cheeks and throat.

"What?"

I did not mean to say that. Calculations sparked

and flowed inside her skull, a delightful shivering. She heard herself speak, as if from a great distance.

"I quit." Her hands were already unbuttoning the frayed polyester vest with flying ease. The magnetic name tag, with its peeling sticker saying *Alice* because "corporate" hadn't sent a permanent one yet, clicked slightly as she shrugged out of the sad little garment. "You are a man of little intelligence and even less personal hygiene, and you bore everyone who has the misfortune to speak to you. Also, your habit of demanding unpaid overtime is against local, state and federal labor laws, and the interest you display toward teenage girls who enter this store is nothing short of repugnant." She had the vest in a ball now and flung it at him, an accurate toss that hit him in the midriff. He blinked, his mouth ajar, working like a fish's, and the free association—*tuna fish, cat, man, fishmouth*—pleased her even more deeply for a moment before she turned to walk away. There was an exit near the cardboard crusher; she could easily step out and away, vanish into the empty lot behind the store, catch a bus on Salterello Street and go back to her hide.

None of them had ever noticed that she carried no purse. The address given on the job application was false, the phone number a now-defunct prepaid cell. When she vanished from here, it would be permanent.

"You can't quit!" Tengermann yelled, her crumpled vest at his feet, but she was already at the end of the aisle. Eddie stood by the dairy case at the very back of the store, slack mouthed with wonder—another fish of a man, she debated telling him that his longing for a female partner would have a 38 instead of 3 percent chance of being satisfied if he would wash his clothes a bit more thoroughly and stop eating microwaved meals. *"You can't quit. Who will do this aisle? Alice! Aliiiiice!"*

I am not Alice. No, she decided, Eddie likely would not take her advice, however solidly phrased, with anything resembling disinterested calm. The doors to the back swung as she pushed them, and the crusher was dark and silent. She paused to gaze at it for a moment, perhaps saying goodbye, and continued over ground-smooth and shiny concrete with no fiction of customer-friendly linoleum over it. Drains set in the floors were marvelous places for insects to hide, and sprinkled liberally with poisons every week by the silent, squat women Tengermann called *Janitorial*, as if they were a country unto themselves.

Trinity realized she was running just as she hit the back door at a third of the speed she was capable of, judging the impact needed to throw it wide. Her stride lengthened as she blurred across the back parking lot, empty except for locked Dumpsters since the produce delivery wouldn't show up for another hour. A hop and a leap, a breathless jolting down a slight declivity sprayed with herbicide and other poisonous substances every few months, and she was in the fields beyond, the hot night a bandage against her eyes before her pupils flared, adapting much more quickly than a normal's.

Why did I do that? It was a departure from her careful cover. She had planned to simply not show up after she carried out her second run on the installation.

This altered her situation somewhat. Her hands shook, even as she forced her body to carry her smoothly, quickly, over hard-packed dirt, through scrubby stands of yellow waist-high grass and thorny trash bushes. Not because of the deconstruction.

No. For a moment she had considered stepping forward, striking Tengermann in the solar plexus, and then, as shocked lungs struggled to function, a quick knuckle-strike to his larynx, crushing it. Standing over him as he choked to death, as the Muzak blurred and tinkled through the empty aisles.

This is not deconstruction. It is something worse.

Trinity put her head down and ran faster.

It was amazing what you could get away with when you carried a clipboard and wore a lanyard with a laminated card. There was also camouflage to be considered—business casual only went so far, and most places you couldn't wear a shoulder holster if you expected to slide through unnoticed.

A midsize police station was one of the exceptions. Wear the right beaten-down shirt, slightly yellowed under the arms, the loosened tie with its artful ketchup stain, the ill-fitting suit jacket just barely matching the pants, and good brogans, polished but not *too* carefully and worn enough to say *I've chased a couple dickheads down, yes, I have*—do that, and you could slide through almost as if you were invisible.

The real trick here, just like anywhere, was to *move* as if you belonged. With a weapons-grade virus messing around with your mitochondrial DNA and giving you incredible control over your autonomics, you could even *smell* right. Not that any of the normals around you would notice on anything except a subconscious level. Most people operated straight from the subconscious anyway. The greater proportion of a normal's calories were expended on *not* thinking, numbing themselves or working to earn a paycheck that would go toward further mindlessness.

Normal. You even remember what that feels like, Cal?

He'd been working the small towns within striking distance of major centers around military installations, especially the big black hole of Cranston and its satellite, Pocula Flats. This particular chicken-fried burg, Felicitas, was large enough that the cop shop wasn't a tight-knit family affair, which was all to the good. The clipboard and laminated ID got him in; keeping his head down and moving like a cop did the rest. His rumpled suit was detective-worthy, even if his hair was a bit on the long side. A couple of the uniforms glanced at him, glanced again and marked him as "one of those Vice idiots"—especially as he was in much better shape than most—and kept going.

The midmorning rush worked in his favor, too.

Finding an empty office with a working terminal was the difficulty. He frowned at the clipboard, his skin alive with the consciousness of being in enemy territory. Just enough adrenaline and cortisol to keep him sharp, control over autonomics keeping him from sweating too much. All the same, he had to let a little moisture out—blending in was the name of the game, and too dry was worse than too damp. Cal caught himself wishing he was more like Reese—that dark-haired linebacker-shaped bastard could *plan*. He probably would have a smarter way to catch the girl, instead of the fishing Cal was doing, following the hunters to find the prey.

Reese and his girl, Holly, were in Mexico, last Cal had seen, and this particular mission was all his. He tended to just pick a beat and dance to it, and most of the time it worked out pretty well.

He was hoping this was one of those times.

Two plainclothes guys in a hurry burst from a locked door at Cal's ten o'clock; his instincts tingled and he moved, catching the heavy reinforced metal before it could swing shut. He was through in half a second, letting it close behind him, and his nose caught the pepper musk of adrenaline. Excitement riding the drafts of air-conditioning, a mental image of dogs straining at a fraying leash.

Interesting. What's this?

At the end of the hall was a hurriedly constructed fishbowl, desks pushed together and cubicle walls hastily erected to give some idea of organization, not privacy. An expectant hum—people working the phones and hunched over keyboards, and precious few of them looked like cops.

Especially the two goons in front of a leaderboard display, one with his hands clasped behind his back and the other...

Cal paused, his pulse spiking before he clamped down *hard*, his pores slamming shut. It was close and muggy in here, despite the AC. Sweat, burned coffee, several smokers behind on their scheduled puffs, a couple that had skipped showers. A rich simmering stew full of information both usable and otherwise, but there was too much pepper in it.

Normal people smelled washed-out, faint olfactory shadows. It was only other agents who hit you in the nose and the back of the throat like good curry or better whiskey. You could mask your scent a little bit, ameliorate it, if you kept yourself buttoned all the way down, but it was difficult and often not worth the energy.

This was the one time it *was* worth it, and he was a little out of practice.

To top it off, Cal realized he was horribly exposed, standing there like a dumbass. He looked back down at the clipboard—different shades of pink and yellow paper covered with meaningless squiggles, stolen from a copy shop's recycling bin, just like the broken clipboard itself. He kept moving to the side, hoping he wouldn't cut across a current of air that would alert the other agent.

Which one is it?

"Hey!" a bespectacled girl with a pile of messy chestnut hair called. "I've got her!" That hair, kept in place with a couple pens thrust through its sloppily coiled mass, looked as if it was about to eat her head whole. She was so pale she probably bathed in sunscreen, and her wire-rimmed glasses twinkled cheerfully.

All eyes fastened on her, which was just fine by Cal. Because all of a sudden, a picture flashed onto the board, the digital projector humming, and the blonde woman haunting Cal's head these days stared over the fishbowl, her hair slicked down and darkened on either side of her gaunt, pretty face, as if she'd just bathed. She was even thinner, and that mute pain in her gaze was deadened by the poor quality of the image.

"How did you override the projector?" one of the idiots looking at the board began to protest. "And how did you—"

"Simple. I went digging." Spectacles Girl beamed. She had a cute little heart-shaped face, and Cal decided conscious effort had been made to tie her wildly curling hair into some sort of elaborate shape. It had failed dreadfully, though, and she smelled as if she hadn't bathed in a couple days, a rich brown intoxicating scent that was nowhere near agent-strong but still a little pleasant.

Except it wasn't what he *wanted* to smell, that blueberry pie and sweetness he'd only managed to get a single lungful of before they escaped the installation in Utah.

Huh. Cal kept going, finding an unused desk and dropping down, spreading his papers out and assuming the tired, beaten posture of an office grunt. *Don't look at me. Let's just see what's happening here.*

"See," the girl continued as the two men from the front of the room bore down on her. "If she's been in the area for a few weeks, she needs money, right? Everyone's gotta eat. So I went looking around new hires and turned up a list of SSNs that had just been pushed through for W9s. Lo and behold, look!"

One of the men, a lean blond spit-shined number with dark eyes, whose entire bearing shouted *military*, firmed his mouth up and leaned over the girl's shoulder. "What the hell's *that?*" He pointed, but quick as a snake, she slapped his hand away.

"Don't touch the monitor. Anyway, I ran the SSNs and I found one that hasn't even been *issued* yet, just obeys the algorithm so it didn't trigger any flags. It's attached to a supermarket out on Fresney Highway and Saltarello. Right on the edge, a whole lotta nothing, and—"

"The picture's from a grocery store surveillance camera." The other head honcho, dark haired and ramrod-straight, spaced the words out evenly, almost

robotic. His affect was incredibly flat, but Cal had a
sudden sinking sensation. "How did you access it?"

"I have my ways," Spectacles Girl intoned myste-
riously and glanced at the blond, who had to be the
decision maker. "Say, what's she done, anyway?"

"Weren't you listening? Better for us not to know,"
a bearded twentysomething male at the desk to her
right piped up. "Dude, how did you string into an
intranet?"

"You never worked in a grocery store, did you,
Mike." It wasn't a question. Spectacles rolled her
eyes and stretched, pushing her chair back. It must
have rolled over the blond's foot, because he yelped
and hitched backward, and Cal took in all the information on the screen in two swift sipping glances.
It was arranged like a PowerPoint presentation, for
God's sake. Spectacles Girl was an overachiever.
"They're easy to crack. I thought this was going to
be *challenging.*"

Cal stayed where he was. His pulse kept trying to
spike. He stared at the leaderboard, a thin, beautiful
woman's face in pitiless detail, not a flaw or blemish
to be seen. Right next to it, a map of Felicitas's west-
ern side, a shiny little arrow over a grocery store. It
blinked between street map and terrain display—
even the ass-end of New Mexico was sat-scanned
by the private sector these days.

"Miss Frasier." The blond winced as he put weight
back on his foot, and his hand fell on her shoulder

as she started to rocket out of her seat. "Where are you going?"

Her mobile, expressive little face twisted up in disgust. "To the little girls'. You've been on us all morning, I haven't taken a single break, and unless you want me to find a corner and drop trou, you know? Besides, Sartino said that if I found this one for you, I'd get a plea."

"Ah. Yes." The blond let her go, but Cal didn't like the flicker of expression crossing his face.

Not my problem. Worry about your mission, Eight.

The other agent was almost certainly the black-haired guy next to Blondie. That dark head had come up, nostrils flaring, and what were the odds this was the figure he'd seen in Dallas, moving through the scurrying of independently contracted security goons like a shark through a flock of minnows? Lazy and graceful, for all his rigidity.

Cal's throat had gone dry. His peripheral vision registered a flicker of motion—Spectacles getting up, bumping her chair so it spun neatly between her and Blondie. Cal stared at the woman on the screen, willing his heartbeat back to a reasonable pace, keeping his respiration nice and just-shallow-enough. It was her.

It was Three. *Trinity.* She'd bumped into Cal in the corridor, all of them fighting for their lives, and everything inside him had turned over *hard*. If this was how it had been for Reese, no wonder he'd gone to hell and back for his girl, Holly. They were pretty disgustingly blissful, the two of them, and it was Trinity who'd sprung Holly from Bronson's clutches not too long ago.

Since then Cal had been on her trail, and now he had a clear shot. It looked as if she'd need his help, too.

He still couldn't look away.

"Peace out!" Spectacles Girl called cheerily and stamped down the hall Cal had slipped through.

Blondie glanced at the black-haired agent, who immediately glided in her wake. The rest of the workers were either busily tapping at their own keyboards or watching Blondie for their marching orders.

"All right," Blondie said. "We have a direction. Blue Team, pick that up and shake it. Let's see what falls out. Red, you guys keep turning over the other rocks. This might be a dead end."

Not goddamn likely. Spectacles Girl, if Cal was any judge, was way smarter than Blondie.

"Mr. Caldwell, sir?" This from a lean, harried-looking guy with two days' worth of stubble on him and sunken dark eyes. "There's a call on the, um. This line."

Blondie-Caldwell stalked across the room and hooked the receiver up. *"What?"*

Cal scraped together the papers, tapped them together on the clipboard and rose like a ghost, heading for the hall.

"Sir." Caldwell's tone changed abruptly. "Yes, sir. Sir."

Getting a chewing-out, boy? What are you doing using local resources this openly? That's against protocols, as far as I know. Too much information dispersal, too much entropy introduced into mission operations. It was a puzzle, and one he didn't like the look of. They shouldn't have been this hot after her after months, not with the rest of the program going down in flames and Bronson dead.

Unless she'd done something to pop up on the radar again. Or if she was valuable enough to warrant this kind of outlay.

The black-haired gent was indeed the other agent. His smell overlaid Spectacle Girl's, and something about the two made Cal's nose tingle. They were *almost* complementary. A slight acidity marred the other agent's trail, a burning like electrodes, concrete and pain. Why did Blondie have him on the girl? The virus on Black Hair would perk up and notice her big-time, and she probably smelled mouthwatering to him. It was a recipe for trouble.

Don't worry about it. Get the hell out of here.

"Hey." A whisper-yell. "Hey, who's that guy?"

Uh-oh. Cal made it to the door, hoping it wasn't a two-way lock. It opened, and he was out in the other corridor, strangely deserted. There were shouts in the distance, running feet, and he hesitated on the verge of breaking cover before his ears told him they were going the other way.

"Stop her!" someone bellowed, and then a female voice rose, a cry of effort that turned into, of all things, a phrase Cal recognized from childhood.

"Kowabunga, dudes!" Spectacles Girl screamed, laughing, and glass shattered.

What the hell? Cal shrugged internally, turned the other way and got going. If she wanted to provide a distraction, he wouldn't complain.

He felt the sudden need for a little grocery shopping.

The urge to curse, reined in, still tingled in Noah Caldwell's throat, just like Control's displeasure had scorched his ears. He did his best to swallow both and regarded the single best asset he had with a level glare. "Well, Bay?"

The black-haired man, tall and broad shouldered, had a very deep voice, but none of the words carried more stress than the others. "Miss Frasier has escaped, sir."

For the love of... "Great. Well, the cops can grab her. We can't be bothered. We have an address for the target."

Caldwell's neck ached, and Bay didn't ask for instructions. That meant either he had a question, or he considered moving after Agent Three to be a stupid move.

Bronson hadn't listened to Three, which was probably why she'd escaped. He'd treated the most exciting advance in intelligence history like his own personal secretary, even sending her to fetch his cheeseburgers from the intake desk.

Bronson, in short, had been an idiot, and Caldwell did *not* want to follow in his footsteps. All the same, he sighed heavily before shaking the tension in his fingers out. "What?"

"Miss Frasier is an asset. We were to retain her." Agent Bay didn't fold his arms or shift his weight.

The hacker girl was only an irritant, and one easily swept under the rug. "The cops caught her once, they can catch her again. Don't tell me you're fond of her." The Gibraltar II virus was supposed to be stable, without the mutability that turned the first iteration into the Gemini virus and caused this entire headache in the first place. The first round of Gibraltar males had sooner or later showed increasing emotional noise and finally ended up hitching themselves to "complementary" women—the geminas.

Thirty percent of the Gibraltar II males survived the induction process meant to strip emotional noise from them, and if they could get their hands on Three as well, they could figure out *why*. At least, the civilian eggheads could. Male and female agents with greater strength, smarts and endurance, high mission fidelity, and absolute loyalty to America and apple pie were the goal.

The current problems were just roadblocks. Obstacles.

"Sir?" Bay looked mildly puzzled. Of course, he didn't have a clue about the others.

Caldwell restrained himself for the umpteenth time that day. The Frasier bitch had almost broken his foot, running her chair over it. "Never mind. Look, get that printed out. I've got to scramble more resources. I hate working in halfass little burgs like this. Do up a capture plan for her and for our primary. We need the primary for study. We'll tie off Frasier if we have to."

"Yes, sir." A strange look ghosted over Bay's emotionless face and was gone as soon as it surfaced.

Caldwell had already turned away, too busy to notice.

She woke in the long, stuffy time of midafternoon, when anyone with any sense would be taking a siesta. The ceiling fan spun lazily, its dust and cobweb-grimed motor strong and patient even under years of neglect. Anemic puffs of oven-hot air brushed Trinity's bare skin—white cotton panties and a silk camisole worn not for modesty's sake, but because if she had to move, she would be at least half-dressed. It was simply too hot to follow protocol and sleep fully clothed.

Any moving air was better than none. These apartments did not boast air-conditioning, and consequently, only the desperate gathered under their patched roofs that leaked when the gullywashers came through. However, the manager took cash and asked no questions, and the steady stream of those who didn't wish much scrutiny provided a certain protective cover.

For a few moments she lay very still, facedown on the narrow, stinking bed. The light was wrong—she had set her internal clock to wake her at dusk, and it was far too bright. Heavy gold painted the shades, the sun fingering persistently, wearing its way in photon by bleach-scouring photon. Everything faded under its steady assault, and then there was the dusty wind, not moving fast enough to cool but just quick enough to sand down every surface with apathetic dust.

Not like the forest, giant trees hung with sheets of green, moisture sinking into every crack and surface, mold and mildew filling every crevice while she ran, the backpack on her shoulders and her mouth dry with terror...

For a moment she could almost, *almost* remember something important from before the induction. Just out of mental reach, flickering and taunting the way dreams inevitably did upon waking. A name, perhaps, or an image from her former life. Then it was gone, a chill running up her lightly sweating back on tiny, icy insect legs.

Danger.

She slid swiftly off the bed and reached for her faded, broken-in jeans, folded and placed within easy reach of her carefully calculated landing spot. A thin white cotton button-down over the camisole, her fingers flying as she knotted the two sides of the shirt above her midriff—that would provide her with more carrying space should she need it, and trim her silhouette. No gun, because she had removed it to the cache since she didn't want to wear it to work and had calculated that leaving it until just before she ran her final penetration of the military base was the safest and most efficient option.

She was still unaware of what, precisely, had roused her.

Paranoia? Perhaps. Not enough data to arrive at solid percentages. Her body was already moving, the cold, logical part of her watching, simply bemused, as she often was, by the impotent scurrying of a biological unit that would perish in a relatively brief span of time anyway.

That was the downfall of pure analysis. With a wide enough focus, any event seemed insignificant.

Even a human life.

She grabbed the black nylon backpack, ran a critical glance over the inside of the tiny room with its tiny, hideous attached bathroom—the smell from the drains alone was enough to give anyone unpleasant dreams—and its yellowing, naked walls. Shrugging into the pack, making sure her pockets were loaded and tugging her bootlaces, listening intently.

Run through it.

First, what she could see. Just the inside of the dingy little room, its filthy blinds, the ceiling fan turning lazily. There had been flypaper festooning the ceiling when she first entered this room, but she'd taken it down. Let the little disease-spreading nuisances come in, if they wanted to. The sound of their scratching and struggling as they starved to death high above was a distraction. Simply an irritant, nothing more.

Then why did you—

She shook the thought away. Nothing against her skin but soft, perfectly worn cloth, different than her work outfit and much more comfortable. She gapped her mouth, tasting the air—bitterness, her body reminding her she was metabolizing whatever fat reserves she'd managed to accumulate two towns ago. She would need to begin a gorge pattern soon, unless she wanted to start burning muscle instead. The trouble was, consuming food took too much time that could be allocated to other purposes. Elimination was similarly troublesome, but much more urgent.

Focus, Trinity. A deep inhale, then several short chuffing ones to acquire the maximum amount of airborne data. The baking scent of open air, dust, feces both human and animal—this particular place housed dogs as well as humans, even the poverty-stricken needed something to care for—and cheap, burned food that could be prepared on a hot plate or in a tiny microwave. Something else, too.

There.

A single thread of sweat, determination, gun oil, exhaust—not from any of the ugly jalopies managing to wheeze out one more trip around the block but from heavy, well-maintained engines. If not for the indifferent weather stripping, she wouldn't have smelled it.

Last but certainly not least, wrong notes in the sleepy stasis of afternoon. A baby cried—there were even children in this forsaken place, but this particular tiny biological unit was off its schedule by a good half hour, even accounting for the variables of a small digestive system and heat-induced fussiness. Doors closed softly, a scurrying hustle on the backside of the building, and Trinity thought for a moment of sliding out through the small window in the bathroom. She had spent some time making certain it would open, for just this occasion. The idea that perhaps someone would use it to enter mildly interested her at best. She was confident in her ability to dissuade a normal criminal from any attempted assault or theft.

She was already moving. The locks slid back— she had oiled them not too long ago. The doorknob, grease-sweating metal, turned softly and quietly, and she was outside in the blistering heat. Her ears perked again—soft engines, idling a few blocks away.

Preparing for engagement or starting their sweep? She turned to her left and set off down the row of doors—they were all closed. On most afternoons, even in the searing heat, they would stand open to allow some air circulation, as long as at least four people clustered in the doorway to protect whatever faintly valuable items lay inside.

Not today, though. Some collective unease had withdrawn them, anemones retreating into shelter.

Around the corner of the building, into uncertain, simmering shade. More engines that didn't belong, some even in the empty lot to her three o'clock. Stealthy creaks riding odd currents to her straining ears. How much of it was her, simply suspecting, and her senses, sharp as they were, obeying a psychological instead of objective directive?

The normals know it, too, Trinity. Stop second-guessing.

There. The rickety ladder, its bottom half rusted away but the rest of it solid enough, hanging off the side of the building like a scab. It was too high to be reached even with a Dumpster dragged underneath—if you were normal, and your genetic information hadn't been modified by an experimental virus that had, in the end, turned out to be dangerous and unstable.

Trinity picked up the pace, her hiking boots providing just enough grip, and leaped. Calculations over, it was time to perform, and for a blessed moment the whirl of prediction, counterprediction, data, analysis and static ceased. Feet kissing cracked pavement, coiling, exploding into a leap, not for the ladder but for the Dumpster opposite it. Landing, the metal lid flexing *just* enough, and taking off again, back across the narrow space but with significantly more height and velocity. Catching the rungs, pushing herself up, and she was over the top before the Dumpster lid stopped quivering. The chain-link fence behind the Dumpster rattled slightly, but that couldn't be helped. A hammerblow of sunshine, her pupils contracting, and she heard booted feet stamping in unison.

She cut across the roof, much more data pouring in now from every sense, collated swiftly. *Basic surveillance ring. Drug bust? I didn't think there was enough traffic here to warrant this level of resource expenditure. Is it a random sweep, perhaps?*

Sirens blared. Flash grenades banged, and screams began below.

The casualty percentage was likely to be low. Still, she was aware of a tightening in her chest that was not the body's response to sudden activity. She couldn't hear the baby's plaintive cry or any of the other children who grew like weeds in barely hospitable cracks around here. How often had she wondered what their lives would be like, cut short by violence or backbreaking work, or survived until a frail old age spent in the same grinding poverty—

Too many variables, and the fragility of such beings lodged in her throat during long, bleak midnight hours while she paced the bedroom and planned.

Focus, Trinity.

She realized it wasn't a drug raid or a random enforcement sweep just as the other agent blurred up over the edge of the roof behind her—he had used the same ladder. Trinity snapped a glance over her shoulder, and her mouth filled with copper. She couldn't see much, just a shadow moving with the spooky blurring speed of a virus-soaked male, and for a moment blackness closed over her vision as all analysis left her and the naked calculus of survival took its place.

It's him. It's Eight.

Only his name was no longer Eight, and he was no longer working for the government *or* the military. He'd gone off the rez, he called himself *Cal*, and Trinity was absolutely certain of one thing.

He wanted to kill her. With an agent's strength and speed, he no doubt could—if she let him get close enough.

The scanner under the dash squawked and burbled—they were coming in hot, and there was all sorts of chatter Cal didn't like, call signs that were out of place in a town this size. Someone was calling for eyes, which meant a chopper, and Dispatch had split into three to handle the sudden spike of traffic. He was too far away, parked in the shade of a Coca-Cola billboard, focusing through the modified binoculars—he'd managed to get to a cache after finding Reese and Holly in Sinaloa, and it was good to have some real kit again. Nothing *they* could trace, nothing they could leave little telltales in, just clean professional hardware.

All the hardware in the world wouldn't help if you

were too late, though. He'd been well on his way to the supermarket out on the highway and Saltarello when the scanner began telling him something else was going down.

She went up the side of the squat crumbling faux adobe like a lynx up a tree, all power and grace. A mop of flowing honey hair, not scraped back in a ponytail—Holly said she'd dyed it, but it looked like the natural color had won out. He remembered that, the threads of gold in her mane under pitiless fluorescents, as she saved not just Holly but all of them from Bronson, blurring across distance with an agent's speed, the roar of gunfire as she neutralized the man who would have shot them all in the back.

Jeans, a backpack, hiking boots, a button-down that clung to her as if it was poured on. She was *fast*, dammit—less muscle bulk to move around meant more speed, and women generally had better re-action times anyway. He watched her cut across the rooftop, swearing under his breath, and a second blur slipped across his field of vision.

It was the other agent, the black-haired sonofabitch from the station.

"God*damn* it," Cal breathed softly. Even in the shade, with all the windows down, it was a dry sauna in here. Alternatives began clicking over inside his brain; he kept visual on her as long as he could. The scanner erupted—*target acquired, hold positions, do not engage*, all telling him that it was up to the other agent to bag her. Why?

Doesn't matter. Think fast, Cal.

He dropped the car into gear, stuffing the nocs into the backpack on the passenger seat. A sharp right turn, bouncing briefly up onto pavement, and he heard through the scanner that she'd broken to the north, down the back of the building and aiming probably for a tangle of jam-packed poverty-stricken streets to lose herself in. If she'd been in place, she'd have reconned thoroughly; homeground advantage might be effective versus the agent but not so much against the cops. They had numbers on their side.

Cal mashed the accelerator and the car leaped forward, smoking the wheels into a left-hand turn. He'd had time to study the layout from the high ground; this particular avenue should bring him around to the north, just outside the police ring.

Christ, they've got SWAT vans. Maybe from the base or imported from County? Feathering the brake, everything inside him turning cool and calm now that it was time to *do* instead of think and fret. He ignored the short, surprised burp of a siren behind him, houses flickering past in a blur of washed-out dusty colors, the only bright spot a new trampoline in one weed-choked yard. Part of him listening to the scanner, decoding its awkward static.

"Shots fired, shots fired!" someone yelled, and more noise poured out. No chopper just yet—why not? Had she moved before they were ready? She was a slippery one, fine instincts or maybe paranoid; Cal had needed every ounce of training to keep up

with her. So close, he was *so damn close*, and if he could cut across her path he could tangle pursuit and maybe, just maybe, scoop her up himself and get to know her—

The scanner screeched again as a flicker of motion darted from his left. She nipped between two police cruisers, bouncing between them to get height, and leaped, the chain-link fence rattling as she monkeyed for the top. On the other side, she dropped with lithe grace and kept running, and if not for Cal's own reaction speed, he might have pasted her with the hood of his nice blue Chevy. As it was, he laid on the brakes and didn't even see the other agent dropping down behind her before the impact.

SMASH.

Windshield starred with breakage, the body tumbling away to the side as Cal whipped the wheel, physics deciding according to her own jealous laws that the tires wouldn't blow *just* yet, Cal caught a flash of white that was the other agent's shirt. The car righted itself with a shake, the agent's body tumbling away in the slipstream. The scanner was full of more chatter he didn't like, now—more resources scrambled in, and it looked as if someone over at County had got their panties in a wad over "jurisdiction," that perennial stumbling block.

Enough confusion that she could slip free, maybe, unless she was unlucky or just stopped running.

"Suspect in custody!" the scanner blared. *"This

is Dakota one-five-one, we've got her, she's down, I repeat, we have her cuffed!"

Cal did the math, came up blank. *What the hell? Did someone really collar her, or was that—*

D-151 sounded very young and very excited. *"We've got her! She ran right into me! Uh, ah, we're gonna need an ambulance, and—"*

This wasn't in character for her at all. Either she was slipping, which was interesting...

Or she'd deliberately allowed herself to be caught. Why?

Who knows? Get out of here and ditch this car before that chopper arrives. There was one good thing about this mess, though.

At least now he knew where to go to collect her. He'd have to move even more quickly now, and he needed a fresh set of wheels.

Dammit. I hate stealing cars. Tools to get the job done, sure, but he often thought about insurance hassles and missing work for the owners when he grabbed one. It didn't *stop* him—that moral flexibility Division liked so much in him made sure of that—but he still sometimes felt a little bad over it.

Of course, there was an alternative in this particular situation.

Cal sighed heavily and cut the wheel, bouncing to a halt behind an abandoned Popeyes. *I hate getting arrested, too.*

Choices, choices. But then the scanner started to

crackle with some very interesting news, and Cal's eyes narrowed as he listened, the sedan's battered hood ticking a little.

Looked as if he wasn't going to steal a car after all. At least, not yet.

Agent Bay—*short for Beta, you're our new version*—lay on hot concrete under an unforgiving glare just like the lights shining in his eyes when he woke up without a name. The blue sedan had come out of nowhere, Bay's concentration narrowed to pursuit of the target's mop of honey-colored hair, and the first stunning impact was dreamlike. He tumbled, rolling loosely, arms protectively curling around his head, hitting concrete with stunning force. For the first few moments nothing hurt, shock and adrenaline sealing away the nerve impulses that meant *something is very wrong.*

Internal injuries? Cranial swelling? Perhaps. He tried to move, to shake the stunning noise of concussion away. *Get up. Target acquired, target fleeing.*

He made it to hands and knees, vaguely aware of blood filling his mouth. Spat to clear his throat. A great rolling breaker of pain came; he realized ribs were broken and froze. More muscular contractions would pull the breaks apart or cause more agonizing feedback. He had to remain still, to let the virus work at accelerating natural healing processes.

Attention turning inward. Lungs and cardiac

muscle uninjured, lung function impaired because of rib breaks but no punctures or scraping. Spleen damaged, other internal traumas, the emergency responses of cells clustering and blood clotting swiftly. The worst would be getting the rib breaks smoothly sealed. Did he have a concussion, too? He couldn't tell yet.

His legs twitched. *Hairline fracture: left femur. Pelvis unharmed. Tibial fracture, too, hematomas everywhere.*

Sirens. Voices. He ignored them. Something else occurred to him.

Who had he been chasing? Not the chestnut-haired girl who smelled so enticing.

Why was he thinking about her? She wasn't part of the mission. All that mattered was the mission. *Fidelity*, they called it. *Semper Fi.*

Where was that from?

He grayed out under the assault of pain and plummeting blood pressure, a dangerous moment or two of shock before his control reasserted itself and several functions kick-started, sealing off rips and fractures, cells swarming to repair, energy from small fat stores yanked out of storage and applied to the most critical wounds.

He was lifted onto a stretcher, ignoring the activity around him as he held to life with all the strength his violated, virus-soaked body could muster.

The mission. He had to remember the mission,

but the image of the chestnut-haired girl with her wire-rimmed glasses, running and laughing as the police station's front window shattered, wouldn't go away.

That's my mission. Finding the woman. But which one?

The blonde and her rasping, unhappy scent full of smoke-terror faded. The other woman—he found the name in a dusty mental corner as EMTs barked medical terms at each other, the sting of a needle in his arm and the jolt as the ambulance jerked into motion. *Frasier.* Odd name for a woman. *It's Fray,* she'd announced to the room at large, *but don't get attached to me, I'm not staying.* Confident, rolling her chair back over his handler's foot, the smell of her blotting out everything else in the world.

That was, he decided with relief, his true mission. The woman. Find her.

Now that he'd figured that out, everything became easier. He was vaguely aware of argument among the EMTs, *which hospital, his vitals are stabilizing, get out the paddles, no, look at his heartbeat, he's fine—*

It didn't matter. Agent Bay, short for *Beta*, had a clear goal in sight. In order to find her, he had to first become ambulatory. Afterward, he would utilize the avenue most likely to lead him to her. Possibly his handler. He would make that decision when he could think again. The primary aim was decided.

He settled himself to heal.

* * *

The arresting officer, a crew-cut corncob with big raw hands, did not manhandle her, at least. He frog-marched her toward a cluster of bright lights and dusty official vehicles, and she let him. She went quietly into a black trailer with far too few air vents attached to a black, diesel-grumbling SUV too clean to be part of the police fleet, handcuffs savagely tight only because the young officer was overexcited and soaking in adrenaline. This was probably the most TV-like event he had ever been part of, and the emotional arousal and sharp pepper of a clean male was pleasant insofar as it blotted out other smells. The kid, fresh faced in his dun uniform and spanking new crew cut, almost climbed into the trailer with her, but an older officer—county SWAT by his uniform—yanked him aside and began dressing him down. The van door slammed, sudden darkness only broken by the glowing furnace-slits of air vents. A diesel engine roared into fresh thrumming life, and she calculated the likely temperature of this little metal box by the time they reached anywhere air-conditioned.

The result was depressingly high. Even the horse trailers in this deadly hot part of the country were better equipped. Clearly she was of less value than an equine at the moment, or they judged any heat damage to her as acceptable. Or, most likely of all, they intended to transport her to one of Felicitas's stations and put her in a holding cell.

Which was exactly what she was hoping for.

First priority: getting out of the cuffs. She wriggled, ignoring pain as ligaments stretched. He hadn't taken her backpack, the excited little boy. Hadn't even searched her for a weapon, perhaps assuming a woman wouldn't be armed. Either way, he was in for some trouble when his superiors found out.

The entire trailer jerked, began moving forward. She thudded against the sidewall and slid down, no betraying sound wrung from her even though the pain was a bright red blossom. She strained her ears some more—nothing but wind against the side of the van, tires humming and her own harsh breathing as control over respiration slipped. The concentration needed to keep her breathing calm was better allocated to maximizing blood flow to aching areas as she applied pressure. Zip ties or duct tape would be better—the shearing force necessary to break either was relatively low, if one had time and some freedom of movement. But cuffs were not an insoluble problem; she had her right hand loose in short order.

The driver hit the brakes, and Trinity let herself continue forward until she hit the front panel, in case they were listening. No window there, either. The temperature had already ticked upward; she plunged her right hand into her backpack. Stupid, not stripping her of gear.

Her skin chilled, a reflex—it had been so close. If not for the blue sedan appearing out of nowhere,

Eight would have caught her. No doubt he would see it as justice.

Moritz. That was her name. The civilian. Bronson had given the order to tie off all civilian loose ends, and Trinity had calculated the parameters herself. It had not been as easy as some of the others, since Eight had been extremely careful to cover his tracks. Unfortunately, Trinity was better at digging than most were better at burying.

Eight had been captured, Tracy Moritz—undoubtedly his complementary gemina even though the reports hadn't shown any viral load in her yet—killed, and without Trinity, none of it would have happened. She had found the betraying wire transfers and noted the precise location of Eight's emotional noise.

Trinity shook memory and fruitless unpleasant thoughts away. A few moments had the cuff off her left wrist as well, and the driver accelerated again. She had one foot jammed against a wheel well, though, and didn't move much. She dropped the cuffs so they would clatter, a good cover for her real location, and reached again into her backpack, searching.

Her internal map calculated trajectory, what she could tell of speed and the layout of Felicitas. Sirens around them—the van had flanking protection. There was a thopping—a helicopter. It couldn't be *them*, Division wouldn't send these novices to collect her. At least, if Division was fully on-site, she would have restraints at wrists, ankles, knees and elbows, and probably be tranquilized to boot. She should know—she had generated, ordered testing and double-checked the transport protocols herself.

Perhaps there was an APB out—Division could have cast their net wide, but why on earth would they want to alert her or risk her going even deeper into cover? She hadn't calculated that Eight would return to them, either, but perhaps they had refined the induction process and rid him of troublesome emotional noise.

If so, he probably wasn't chasing her for revenge, merely to return her to Division's fold. Which was small mercy indeed.

A frenzy of second-guessing was not helpful. She was *in the dark* with a rushing noise. The gleams from the slits in the walls were not good, either, because her eyelids were fluttering, making the sun's glow a weak, uncertain strobe. It reminded her of things best left locked away in the darkest recesses of memory—first the greenness of the forest, then the induction table, cold and hard. The straps, rasping against ankles, wrists, elbows, hips.

The *needles*.

The van wallowed up a slight rise, Trinity still wedged between the front right corner and the wheel well. Struggling to keep from hyperventilating, to keep the fear-chemicals from flowing. Her fingers found the top of the pill jar; she squeezed and rotated, ignoring the ache in her wrists. It was only a little skin lost, and she had far larger problems at the moment.

The pills moved under her fingertips, tiny tabs; she tweezed one out and got the lid back on, palmed the pill to her mouth as the driver hit the brakes again. They were almost to the freeway—the slight rise in elevation and the pattern of turns told her as much. The flanking vehicles had peeled away, as had the helicopter noise.

Well. This is interesting.

She settled herself to wait as the pill dissolved. She had four left; it would have to be enough. After a few moments the potent chemical burn began, spreading down her throat, her arms and legs relaxing into the rhythm of the van bumping over indifferent paving. She exhaled sharply, heart rate and respiration evening, and for the next two hours she was even more immune to physical pain or the creeping destabilization, her analytical capabilities given a boost and any other responses suppressed. She'd been told the pills worked with the virus, not against, and she consequently had much more control over their metabolizing. She still didn't know what was in them, and the records she had managed to glance through hadn't helped, either.

It didn't matter at the moment. Now she could think, her eyes shut to close out distractions. *Begin analysis. Eight is here. How long will being hit by a car slow him down?*

Not very long. He'd tracked her this far; he wasn't

likely to let small problems like broken bones or internal bleeding get in his way. Any agent was possessed of near-miraculous healing abilities, the virus both aiding and allowing the body to supercharge natural recovery processes, taking care of its host. His only problem would be getting the bones set before they fused and he had to rebreak. Then, if he was conscious enough to see where they'd taken her, he would come to the police station and pick up her trail—which was, really, why she had let herself be captured by the corncob officer.

A holding cell she was fairly certain she could escape. Another agent was a completely different proposition. There was only a 13 percent chance Division had reacquired him and set him on her trail—a comfortingly low number.

Her name was Tracy Moritz. The pill hadn't taken full effect yet. A queer, urgent, piercing sensation went through her, high on the left side of her chest, striking through ribs. *Tracy Moritz. She's dead, Trinity. You ran the numbers, you told Bronson.*

What was that sensation? It was increasingly uncomfortable, to say the least. She breathed, filtering out the smell of diesel fumes and waiting for the dip-and-rise to the left that would tell her they had turned onto Blecher Street, the most logical route to the downtown station house. It was irrational to brood on the Moritz woman.

After all, she wasn't Trinity's first murder. Or her last. Certainly other hands had wielded the weapons and pulled the triggers, but it was Trinity's analysis and calculations, not to mention planning, that had sent the teams out, given them protocols and analyzed returns. Bronson asked, the soulless machine that was Agent Three answered, and that was that.

She identified the sensation just before the dip-and-rise curve to the right of the interstate on-ramp. It was what others spoke of as "shame" or "guilt." The induction was supposed to remove all traces of such things and leave only logic. As soon as she named it, the feeling began to fade under the pill's cold, creeping clarity.

They were taking her north and west, onto the freeway instead of to one of the Felicitas station houses. Why? Trinity braced herself, cracked her eyelids and examined the bare interior of the trailer again. It was time to plan, and she unzipped the backpack a little farther. She might even escape this without giving her opponents a chance to shoot, but it would require careful thought.

How strange, she thought as her brain once again became the perfect machine, deconstruction halted for a few precious hours. *My cheeks are wet.*

She discarded the sensation as irrelevant and took a deep breath. Sooner or later, they would have to open the doors.

When they did, Trinity would be ready.

He almost missed the black SUV and the trailer, almost didn't notice the one wrong detail. There was no APB out for his car, and that bothered him. Then again, jalopies with cracked windshields were common as the cold, and the hood wasn't that bad, just scratched, and had anyone seen him hit the other agent? Cal listened to the scanner with half an ear— some jurisdictional borderlines being fought over, the dispatchers confused and given conflicting orders, everything snarling and tangling. In the middle of that came the news: the cop who had bundled her up and tossed her in a trailer had disappeared along with some of the out-of-towners, and the suspect? Gone, whisked away.

Felicitas being the size it was, a couple comments were made about all this juris-my-diction crap, and a gruff, brusque voice from someone high up on the local food chain leaning over a dispatcher's shoulder came on to tell them to mind their goddamn mouths.

Cal listened while he drove, and his plan—to go downtown and spring her from a holding cell— evaporated like cheap beer. The Ford's engine idled a little choppily as he waited at the freeway intersection for a lumbering oil truck to heave its way past, and the black SUV and trailer slid across his field of vision like a bad dream. He blinked, and there it was—good old Texan blue-black-red, instead of the scarlet and yellow of the New Mexico license plates. If he hadn't been listening to the scanner, he wouldn't have known to follow it, and if he hadn't been paying attention, the plate might have gone unnoticed.

What the hell? Why…

To an agent, two and two didn't always make four. Sometimes they made five or even eight hundred fifty-three, and this was one of those times. Cal wasn't a planner, like Reese—he openly admitted as much. What he prided himself on, however, was being a tactical savant, quick to take advantage of any, well, advantage. Even one as simple as plain dumb luck.

I cannot be this lucky. Except he was, and he hit his left-turn signal. The light changed, he turned smoothly and stayed well back, hoping the rattling in the engine wasn't a bad sign. That big wallowing SUV ahead of him would need a lot of fuel, especially when pulling a trailer and heading into the wind, and when they stopped, Cal could open up the back and get his hands on her.

Trinity. They'd called her Agent Three, Holly said, but she preferred Trinity. *They did something to her*, Holly said. *She looks bad. And she's… I don't know, but she's hurting. Inside.*

The thought of that brave fragility—because it took guts to help Holly in the first place and even more guts to keep running—poured tension down his arms, and the steering wheel groaned slightly as his fists gripped. Just those few minutes in the hallway, under fire and smelling that wonderful, mouthwatering, absolutely drenchingly beautiful scent pumping out through her pores, had pretty much knocked him ass over teakettle. It meant the little swarmies in Cal's bloodstream liked her, too, and that was a bonus.

She thinks you want to hurt her, Holly had cautioned, but that was ridiculous. He wanted to *find* her, that was all. The goddamn virus wouldn't let him rest until he did. Reese was lucky, finding his girl so early in the game, and anyone could see Holly thought the world of him.

Was that what he was hoping for? He tried to imagine the unsmiling woman in the photographs trembling, looking up at her rescuer with those big dark eyes. In person, she'd been cool and efficient, but those eyes of hers could knock a man out into the black, and he could remember the thin gold hoops in her ears, her practical shoes, and the unconscious, beautiful grace as she slipped through a door and vanished after shooting that ass Bronson.

She shouldn't have had to do that. Cal should have done it, because sure as Shinola, Bronson had sent the teams that killed Tracy, and directed every step of the game afterward.

And he'd seemed like such a hatchet-faced nonentity at the time. Maybe he'd just been the man on the spot, but sitting across the table from him during debriefs had given Cal the idea that Bronson *enjoyed* sending out kill orders.

There was a difference, Cal had finally decided, between killing when necessary and killing because you liked it.

Once they cleared the tendrils of Felicitas's

sprawled fingers, the freeway was a ribbon heading for the horizon. Cal turned the scanner down and drifted through heatshimmers on pavement behind the SUV and trailer, his eyes narrowed against the glare and the wind roaring through the windows, and spent a few moments wishing the windshield wasn't so distinctively broken.

That brought up an uncomfortable thought: hitting the other agent with the car probably hadn't killed him, any more than it would kill Cal himself. The program had been wound down, but maybe they'd brought Black Hair in and given him the chance to round up strays? Not likely, with the Gibraltar virus mutating and the men who carried it suddenly getting hard-ons for very specific women. A twist like that made an agent go domestic and start prioritizing things like a girl and their own lives over things like orders, percentages and mission fidelity.

Or it could be that this agent was a new kind, since he smelled so off-kilter. Reese had theorized that they'd find a way to get rid of both the mutation and the emotional noise, or learn how to send the agents out to pasture in some way before the emotional noise became overwhelming. You could, theoretically, just keep agents away from women, but the simplest solution was often the most difficult to actually put into practice. Women were everywhere, civilian or military, and you couldn't help but breathe them in.

Which brought up another consideration. If not

for that fume of smoke and black metal covering Black Hair, he and the spectacled girl would have been complementary, and Black Hair would eventually be looking at just the situation Cal was in now.

That was Black Hair's problem, though. Cal's was sticking to that trailer and its cargo.

The SUV accelerated. Had they twigged to pursuit? Engaging them on the freeway was a bad idea. But no, it just settled back into a steady seventy-two miles per. Cal eyed the gas gauge, listened to the Chevy's ailing engine under the roar of the wind and wondered if he'd had all the good fortune he was going to get for the day.

What do you say, Lady Luck? Give me one last hurrah? I've done all I can here.

Luck, like a woman, doesn't stick around for those who don't bother to do all they can to keep up. For those who do, though, she sometimes stretches herself to the limit.

Two hours later the engine was still making that noise, but the trailer, looming ahead of him like a whale in the light traffic around the much bigger urban sprawl of Cuartova, flashed its brake lights and slid to the right, majestically. There was enough traffic to keep Cal from being noticed, if he stayed with the flow.

What the hell are they doing? The "Rest Area 1 mile" sign flashed by, and Cal breathed a term of surpassing, wonder-filled profanity.

Looked as if someone had to empty his bladder.

Which gave him a perfect opportunity. He kissed two fingers and rapped the hot dash, a little habit left over from his high school days, and hit his blinker to move into the right-hand lane.

This part of New Mexico was a whole lot of absolutely nothing, even with the smogshimmer of a city in the distance, a diseased heart drawing all the traffic toward it. Low scrub, sagebrush and rolling heat, endless reels of barbwire along the side of the freeway as if anyone would be stupid enough to veer off into the wilderness.

Whoever was driving had to be desperate or insane, because a rest stop that close to Texas wasn't likely to be maintained with any modicum of bleach or even simple soap. A hole in the ground might be more sanitary, and the smell would lead even a normal to suspect that was what most people chose over the low brick building bearing COWS and BULLS signs on indifferently painted sand-bleached doors that hung dispirited on either side of a concrete walkway swimming with trash.

The parking lot was deserted except for a couple big rigs simmering at the far end, their drivers either napping or cooking up whatever chemical cocktail would get them another few hundred miles down the road. The blue Ford coasted to a stop, the scanner turned all the way off, and Cal opened the door, unfolding himself, seemingly paying only a little attention to the SUV and trailer. His peripheral vision was very good, and he could see the damn thing was padlocked shut.

Christ, it doesn't have air-conditioning. What if she's not in there, and I've wasted all this time?

It didn't bear thinking about, so he shelved it and looked at the brick outhouse. Even from here, it reeked. The wind veered, hot and rasping like a cat's tongue, and from the simmering black-painted trailer came a thin thread of impossibly golden scent.

Holy... The words fell away, because the SUV's doors were opening, and Cal's lengthening strides had to get him into the strike zone *now*.

Two big slabs of beef, both with nicely tailored suits and shiny wingtips, coming out of the SUV. Both of them had shades on, and everything slowed down.

"'Scuse me!" he called, just loud enough. "Hey, I'm wondering if you can help me? My radiator's a little messed up."

"Sir." The man-mountain on the passenger side, his crewcut menaced and Butch-waxed into motionless terror, put one hand up, palm out. "I'm going to have to ask you to step back."

"It's my radiator!" Cal said cheerfully. "I thought I was going to have to flag someone down, but here you are! It's lucky, you know?" *That Escalade's got air-conditioning.* An unfamiliar heat in his belly, flaring up like paper tinder. Putting a woman in a closed-up trailer like that and driving her through a Southwest scorcher—were they trying to kill her?

"Sir, I'm going to have to ask you to step back," the passenger repeated, and Cal's brain was already clicking through the next few moments.

A slight forward bounce, his hand whipping forward, the strike blurring solidly home into the solar plexus. One more gift from the virus—you got so sick you thought you were going to die, and if you survived, you found out normal people were moving through the world on half speed at best, and that the borders of "physically possible" had been pushed way, *way* back.

And their limits made more elastic.

Passenger Beef stopped cold, his mouth falling open as shocked heart and lungs struggled to function. Cal was at close quarters then, his hand flicking out and divesting the big guy of his service piece. A .38—he was a traditionalist, and also an idiot, but that ceased to matter because the driver had started to realize something was wrong.

Fortunately, said driver—just as big as Passenger Beef, though with a crewcut not quite as shiny and a pair of bright yellow nylon socks visible because one of his trouser legs had rucked up from being crushed against the seat—had been intent on hurrying across the concrete strip to plunge into the malodorous hell of the BULLS side of the rest station. Which meant Cal was on him before he'd even finished turning around, and the greenstick crack of a neck breaking was lost under the rumble of traffic from the freeway.

He glanced at the semis parked at the other end of the rest stop. One corpse, another soon-to-be-corpse needing to be questioned if possible, both of them needing to be frisked—but the trailer was just sitting there, getting hotter and hotter with each passing moment.

You jackasses. He bent, swiftly feeling for anything like keys. "No way to treat a lady," he muttered and headed back to the SUV. Passenger Beef, sprawled half in the knife-edged shade, made a short grunting noise as Cal approached, but his face was rapidly purpling. It was almost a mercy, and the drumming of the man's heels on the concrete as the last nerve impulses fired wildly. This one had a ring of keys, and Cal glanced up again. Nobody here, just those two semis in the distance, dots of sagebrush, the faraway smog-cloud of Cuartova and the dry fine dirt. He might as well have been on the moon, but that could change at any moment if some yahoo decided chancing a rest area out here was necessary. Or if one of the semi drivers had seen anything amiss through the heat ripples over pavement.

You're not so bad, Tracy whispered in his memory. Her sunny smile, standing at the front of the classroom, a chorus of children's voices following hers obediently. *Not as bad as you think.*

"Plenty bad enough," Cal muttered and glanced over the key ring.

Time to get the lady out of hock.

* * *

Hours of hot, breathless calm, the road going by a few feet below Trinity's head as she lay wedged on the rumbling metal floor, enough air sliding through to puff against her face and the metal not as hot as it could be. Heartbeat slowed, respiration shallow, metabolic processes dialed as far down as she could get them and still retain a soupy half-consciousness. Hopefully, she would still have some drug-supported clarity when they opened the back door—if they weren't simply driving in circles waiting for her to mummify in here.

Two percent chance they would choose something so inefficient. The machine inside her head barely hummed, calculating that number. Someone had snatched her from the police. This seemed sloppy for Division, but perhaps they had been forced to move with whatever resources were on-site? That would mean they'd traced her to the supermarket somehow.

The thought of Tengermann being interrogated caused a tickle in her throat, one she suppressed as the trailer slowed. Spread out on the floor, she had maximized friction to keep her from sliding around too badly, and the deceleration was gradual enough that she didn't move.

Come back online or stay down? This half-conscious state conserved energy and made reasonably sure she would still have some active residue from the pill when she was prodded back into alertness. If she brought herself back now, she would perhaps burn some of that precious clarity for no true benefit.

The trailer bumped to a stop, and the thrumming of the diesel engine died. After so long, it was almost a shock. She inhaled smoothly, rising to three-quarters conscious, slowly, ever so slowly.

Sounds of movement. The faraway hum of traffic. Empty air around the trailer—the temperature began to rise again. She would need fluids soon; dehydration cut physical effectiveness in steadily mounting percentages the longer it was endured. She began to calculate the exact volume of water she would require based on her last weigh-in, and wonder if she should add a salt tablet to the equation, when a scrape of metal brought her up into full singing alertness.

It was the padlock on the back of the trailer clicking open and the bars over the door unlatching. Trinity tensed as her entire body roared into readiness, a flush of sweat all over her, her body realizing she needed all its resources *now*, fight-or-flight chemicals dumping into her bloodstream in precisely calibrated ticks. Just enough to sharpen her and ready her for combat, not enough to turn her into a blind mess.

The door was heaved open, late-afternoon sunshine scorching, Trinity's eyes closed so the sudden light didn't blind her while her pupils obeyed the imperative to shrink so she could open them more quickly than a normal's.

She had intended to stay still and sprawled until one of *them* climbed in to bind and drag her, but someone hopped lightly into the trailer, making the shocks bounce. A familiar smell—male, musky, agent-intense and terrifying—rode the faint whoosh of fresh air into the close confines, and her fight-or-flight chemicals were no longer calibrated. They flooded her, a copper taste filling her mouth.

It was *him*. It was Eight.

How was irrelevant. The only thing that mattered now was survival.

The feverish flow of calculation boiled away in a nuclear flash of white terror, and she was barely aware of moving as he bent over her, her lips peeled back in a snarl and her leg pistoning out. One boot sole caught him, not in the groin but high up on his thigh, and he huffed out a pained little grunt of surprise.

Get past him, and run. That was the simplest directive. She was past caring if it was the most efficient one.

"Hey! Ow!" He sounded surprised, wasting breath as she scrabbled and thrashed, trying to get her feet under her. He pitched forward, almost landing on her, a sudden deadfall weight. He was going to grab her, snap her neck perhaps—it was the most efficient way, so she kicked again, clawing at him when he tried to trap her in a bear hug. "*Hey!* Calm down, woman!"

Everything turned red, and Trinity erupted into

blurring-fast motion, wriggling in the only direction she had left, toward the front of the trailer and striking out with fists and feet. He slapped the strikes away, freely sweating as well because he had to work to keep her trapped between him and the floor. She clawed a long furrow on his face and scrambled back, *away*, freeing her legs with a violent twist.

Her back hit the front of the trailer with a hollow boom, and he curled up to his knees, pushing her backpack—she had intended to leave it there while she dealt with whoever opened the door—aside. She had no weapons but body and brain, and now she regretted leaving her gun behind. Acquiring another wouldn't be difficult—this was America, after all—but it looked as if she wouldn't get a chance to do so.

She certainly wouldn't be able to get her hands on one to help during the present situation unless *he* had one and she could somehow disarm him.

He stayed on his knees, watching her as her legs moved a little, trying to propel her backward through the metal wall. Her breath came in harsh swells, and she tried to analyze his likely next attack. His psych profile didn't indicate any sadism, but an agent was trained to do the job with whatever tools were required—did he want to talk to her? An admission of guilt?

"Hey." He spread his hands, as if he wasn't tense and ready for action, should she attack again. "Calm down. I'm here to help. It's Trinity, right?"

Her head tilted slightly, taking this in. Her hair

fell over her shoulders, an irritant but not a critical distraction. His pulse was up, respiration, too, and it was difficult to think with his smell filling up the trailer. It was a...pleasant...aroma, she decided, even as her hands patted lightly at her pockets, searching for anything likely to help her now.

He was much larger and had the advantage. Trinity was dehydrated, exhausted, even though the virus would be quietly turning fatigue waste into energy, and much smaller, though quicker and coldly determined to survive.

"Hi." He smiled, a familiar sight from the taped interviews and debriefs she'd analyzed for Bronson. Blue eyes, warm and welcoming, his entire manner calm and easy. A rasp of golden stubble along his cheeks. "Trinity, right? I'm Cal."

Endless analysis. She knew his file, had read his psych evaluations. What could she use? Emotional noise was a factor here; what was he thinking? She should be able to predict.

Unfortunately, brutally deep, wine-red fear fogged and clogged the machine in her head.

"I know who you are." Her own throaty whisper surprised her.

"I'm not here to hurt you." Even and calm. Blond hair longer than it had been while he was in the program, and the navy T-shirt straining his broad shoulders added to well-worn jeans as good camouflage. He didn't have a hat, though. His smell didn't alter. Most people knew on some level when they were lying, and their pheromones shouted it, not to mention their respiration and pulse rates. The exceptions, of course, were certain sociopaths—and agents, with their very good control over autonomics. "Okay? I am *here to help*."

Help? "Chasing me across a rooftop is helping?"

He looked puzzled for a moment, then shook his golden head. "That wasn't me."

Does he think I'm stupid? Also, irrelevant. She edged half a step sideways, testing, and stopped dead when he tensed, his broad shoulders turning hard as iron.

And yet, his tone dropped. Level, soothing. "Look, you know Holly, right? Reese's girl? She told me you thought I was after you to hurt you. I'm not."

Trinity absorbed this. She had seen Holly Candless herself not so long ago, down in the sinking stink and filth of Sinaloa. Candless had appeared well and whole, and Agent Six's emotional noise over her had blossomed into something that seemed...

Trinity couldn't find the word, even though she knew there was a proper one that fit. Each second that ticked by was a second less of the precious clarity she had from the pill, and it also put her at more of a physical disadvantage. He watched her, blue eyes narrowed but friendly, and she let out a long, shaky breath.

"You can't possibly expect me to trust you." She took care to make the words just on the edge between flat and conciliatory.

"Yeah, well, I just liquidated the two idiots who were driving you around in a locked horse trailer. And I'm about to offer you some food, and maybe a cold beer, and transport out of this neck of the redneck woods. Will that earn me a little trust?"

"Why would you do that?" It was *not* making sense. Analysis shifted inside her head, a whole new, unsettling constellation forming.

His smile widened a little, became lopsided. Trinity watched, fascinated. She'd never seen that expression in person before, only on screens. It was… pleasant…to have it directed at her. Perhaps that was part of what the profile insisted was his "interpersonal charm."

"You smell good," he said quietly. "You smell *really* good."

The absurdity of it hit her. Trinity shook her head. "I'm not a gemina."

"A gemiwhatsis? Oh, yeah. That." The smile, no longer lopsided, crinkled the corners of his eyes, and his stubble was more tawny than gold. He was lion-coloured and had a big cat's lazy grace. "We'll figure that out later. For now, though, you think we could get out of here? Sooner or later someone's going to want to stop, and my transport's had a hell of a day. Plus, I'll bet you want some water, right? You're probably thirsty. All you have to do is come with me."

Basic interrogation protocol. Offer your target aid, play the good cop. She knew the drill, but was not prepared for how effective it was likely to be in her current state. So she hedged. "Where?"

"Does it really matter? But since you're asking, we'll head into that city a few klicks away and find a hide for the night. And that beer. Do you like beer?"

"I don't know." Trinity went even more still, calculating options. Then he did something very odd.

Cal reached down, slowly, and picked up her backpack. He zipped it closed and slid it along the floor toward her.

She snatched at it, careful not to overbalance, watching him the entire time, tense and ready in case he struck. "You aren't with Division?" *Would he tell me if he was?*

"Nope. Not anymore. I'm a free man, honey, and I'd like to stay that way. Can we get out of here?"

She had assumed, all this time, that he knew of her involvement with the Moritz woman's death.

If he did not, he might *conceivably* be an ally. For the moment, at least. "You're going to have to back up."

"Okay. But can you give me your word that you won't bolt?"

My word? It was a very strange request. It outright assumed a level of trust. "Provisionally, yes."

He just nodded and moved backward, an awkward toe-and-heel-and-knee shuffle, and she realized he was trying to appear smaller. Less threatening.

Perhaps he thought she was less likely to bolt if he did so.

She edged forward, dried sweat cracking on her skin, crusting in crevices. The trailer's floor was dusty, and her hair was full of that thin, fine grit. She forced herself to analyze, to consider the problem from every angle as Cal hopped out of the trailer with easy fluidity, landing soundless and gilded in the sudden flood of light. The scratch down his cheek from her nails was already closing up.

His healing factor had accelerated. Just like hers. Interesting.

Trinity eased forward just a little more, and her peripheral vision caught a flash of blue. She glanced—it was the same car that had struck the agent behind her.

Perhaps Eight was being reasonably truthful. Trinity's shoulders slumped a fraction. She measured distance, probability and her own resources, and arrived at a strange conclusion.

I might as well.

It was enough to make Cal believe in sheer dumb luck. She was *alive*. Her hair, not pulled back, was full of golden highlights burning in the westering sun, her dark eyes actually a very deep mossy green, and she was so thin he could almost count her ribs under her button-down and tank top. But she was ambulatory and breathing, and got in the passenger side after he moved his gear, clutching her backpack like a schoolgirl and keeping her knees well clear of the now-silent scanner.

She was just like a stray cat—big-eyed, distrustful and twitchy if Cal moved too fast. The blue Ford started again; he eyed the gas gauge dubiously and dropped it into Reverse. When he moved his arm, as if to put it over the back of her seat, she flinched away so quickly her upper arm hit just below the window, hard enough that it rocked the entire damn car. "I'm just backing up." Very quietly, firmly, as if her fingers weren't on the door handle. "Okay?"

She swallowed once, nodded. Her skin was flawless cream, but her cheekbones stood out alarmingly. No gold hoops in her ears, but the tiny hurtful mark of piercing on the tender lobes. Dried sweat covered her, and she emitted waves of that glorious, mouthwatering scent. Everything in him tightened up a notch. He hadn't expected this.

Sure, he'd kept going, knowing he had to find her. He hadn't actually *expected* to. It should have been like everything else in his entire life—just enough good to get him to care, then a door slammed in his face and a kick to the gut.

He got them on the freeway with no trouble and decided that yes, they were going to make Cuartova on the eighth of a tank the Ford had left. She rolled her window halfway up and just sat there, staring straight ahead, an aristocratic profile marred only by an already-yellowing bruise spreading up one side of her thin neck. Someone was going to have to feed her some cheeseburgers.

Guess I'm nominated. He tried not to think about whatever had hit her to produce that bruise, because that thought did something funny to his insides. It was what the program called *emotional noise*, and that was dangerous. He was going to need all his wits to get her to calm down—and keep them both out of the government's clutches. *Division*, she'd said. He'd just heard it called *the program*. It was as good a name as any.

First things first. They needed distance, and she needed water. He rolled his window halfway up, too—the sun had dipped lower in the sky, almost blinding him even though the visor was flipped down. His fingers found the Evian bottle and he fished it up from under his seat.

She still didn't move, pressed against the door on her side, staring, almost vibrating with tension. Traffic was beginning to get heavier, and he hoped they weren't going to get trapped in anything resembling a rush hour.

He'd asked Lady Luck for too much already today, and been answered with too many affirmatives, to risk it.

"You're thirsty, right?" He kept one hand on the wheel, settling their speed at a solid sixty-seven to match traffic flow. "Here. I've got a couple more, but we don't want you getting sick."

That got a response. She turned her head slightly, studied him with that solemn expression. He returned his attention to the road, and after a few more of the white-painted stripes had unreeled to his left, his hand was suddenly lighter. She cracked the top, sniffed it cautiously, took a sip.

Jesus. She didn't even trust a sealed bottle of water.

This, Cal thought, *is probably going to take some work.*

Two and a half hours later, Cal slid his backpack off his shoulder, slung his duffel into a chair and glanced at her. The motel was clean, at least, and tomorrow he'd find better transport. The Ford was making a wheezing sound he didn't like—he never thought he'd live to see the day a Ford didn't run until its doors fell off but started complaining after a little bump and some high speed.

It had gotten them this far, though. That was good.

One queen-size bed covered with a blue rip cord spread, snow-white pillows, a bathroom that didn't reek, a spindly table and two chairs.

Trinity, silent, gaunt and grave, tiptoed behind him. She hadn't said a damn word, not even when Cal asked her if she wanted bacon on her burger. She carried the bag of fast food as if it was full of something unspeakably foul, and the drink carrier balanced in her other hand still held two huge, pristine chocolate milk shakes.

She hadn't even taken a sip.

It bothered him. There was some kind of cosmic law about sneaking the first few sips off milk shakes. You just *had* to.

"Yeah, why don't you set that down." He got the door, glancing out into the half-empty parking lot—nice and serene, no breath of pursuit. The mess at the rest stop had probably been discovered by now. They should have kept going, stopping only to pick up fresh wheels, but she was paper-white and moving like an automaton. That marvelous scent of hers—right now it was like a hot blueberry crisp, bubbling just from the oven, perfectly spiced—held an edge of fiery caramelization that was her body cannibalizing reserves.

You could do that for a while, with the virus helping, but it wasn't optimal.

By the time he got the door locked she had laid the two bags and the drink carrier gently on the table and retreated to the wall near the bathroom door, putting her back to it and staring.

What the hell? "Aren't you going to eat? I can tell you're hungry." *I can flat-out smell it on you.*

She didn't respond, just studied the curtained window as if it was the most interesting thing in the world.

Cal sighed. "Look, you're not in the military anymore, all right? Come on over and get some chow. Why do you think I got two of everything?"

A flicker of expression, finally, across that lovely face. "I…" The word was a dry little cricket, and Cal started digging for yet another water bottle. Stopping to get gas had involved buying another dozen liter-bottles of Evian, and she hadn't bolted. "It didn't occur to me."

Oh boy. Training was harsh for a male agent, even with the virus helping. He didn't think it was milk and cookies for a female, either, but her reactions were...unsettling.

"Yeah, well, come on over and pick your milk shake. I'm not going to poison you, for Christ's sake."

"Then what precisely is your intention?" Even dehydrated and too thin, her lips were amazing. They looked very...soft.

That was the exact right word.

"Um." *I didn't think much past getting you someplace safe.* "Well, maybe we could talk a bit."

"Talking is dangerous." But her shoulders eased, and she slid her backpack off. She was covered in dust, but it only burnished her, made that flawless skin and those high sweet cheekbones shine all the more. Tentative relaxation bloomed through her scent, as well.

Yeah. Just like blueberry cobbler, with some vanilla ice cream swirling through it. Which just happened to be his favorite dessert ever. His mouth was outright watering. "Why did you think I wanted to hurt you?"

That banished any relaxation, but she took two delicate, doelike steps away from the wall. "Bronson."

"You think I'm mad because you shot him? I'm

only sorry I didn't do it myself. Come on, this won't stay hot."

A fractional shake of her head, heavy honey hair swinging a little. "I...worked...for him."

Aha. Well, that makes sense now. "We all did. Why don't you sit down?" He pulled out the chair with its back to the curtained window, his skin crawling at the thought of sitting in such an exposed position. But it would mean she could take the more secure chair, and that might help. He sank down and began divvying up the food, his hands shaking just a little.

This wasn't at all how he'd expected this to go.

"I...planned. And analyzed. Threat factors, mission percentages, exposure ratios—"

"Yeah, well, I went into the field and liquidated targets." Cal's mouth was dry, so he took a shot of chocolate milk shake. He set the water bottle precisely where she would reach for it if she sat in the other chair. "We weren't just having tea parties out there, honey. We're even." *Or not even, because I did the actual killing.*

"My *name* is Trinity." Was that a ghost of irritation crossing that wan, pretty little face of hers?

He'd got a reaction, at least. It cheered him immensely. "Hi, Trinity. I'm Cal. Want to have dinner with me? I mean, I know it's too soon to tell if it's anything deep or meaningful, but I feel this *connection*, you know?" *Dammit. Mouth going. Must be nervous.* Girls hadn't made him nervous since the day in high school he first figured out he could make them laugh. It might not have gotten him frequently laid, but at least it got him *attention*, and that was good enough. If you were patient.

Cal had found, much to his own surprise, that he was a reasonably patient man. Attention sometimes got you lucky, too.

She didn't even crack a smile. She did lower herself in the other chair and stared at the food as if she had no idea how to unwrap it.

"Go ahead. You don't have to say grace or anything."

She reached for the milk shake. "*He* ate like this." A small shudder ran through the first word; there was no mistaking who *he* was.

Bronson. Who had always reeked of fast food and clogged arteries, the sweet-roasting of oncoming diabetes and the flat wet ratfur of lies and bureaucracy. Sometimes a breath of a different perfume had reached Cal across the table in debrief, and he'd wondered at it. Why it made his mouth water. Why any smell on such a pile of blubberous paper-pusher would give him any reaction at all, much less *that* particular one.

It wasn't until the corridor, under fire and face-to-face with *her*, that he'd guessed why.

"I always wondered," she continued, "what these tasted like." She stared at the frosted plastic, her winged eyebrows tightening just a bit and that mouth of hers slightly pursed.

Jesus. "You've never had a milk shake?"

Her thin shoulders hunched a little. She was so controlled, so precise, the tiniest movement was like a shout. "Not that I remember."

Something else that Holly had said occurred to him. Cal munched a mouthful of fries, giving himself time to think it over. "So…what *do* you remember?"

"Waking up." She took a sip of milk shake, and a strange expression floated over that otherwise-serene face. "On the table, after my viral loads had stabilized and I had survived the induction process."

Oh. Cal's jaw threatened to drop. "Induction?" He'd heard the term, once or twice, from the medical personnel. All their scraping and poking, tolerance tests and function tests—they'd probably done those to *her*, too. Or even more, since she was a female agent. Reese had a heavily redacted agent file that said *female*—maybe it was hers.

It was a hell of a thing to think.

She nodded, once. A slight dip of her chin, and for a moment something flashed in those dark, dark eyes. "They succeeded in stripping me of emotional noise. Unfortunately, the process proved fatal for every male Gibraltar candidate, even agents carrying a full and initially stabilized viral load." A longer sip of milk shake, her throat moving as she swallowed, and Cal shifted a little in his flimsy chair.

Just looking at that tiny movement did interesting things to him. That smell reached right down and pulled on every string a guy was led around by before he started thinking with the big brain instead. And those big wounded eyes of hers... Jesus. She was downright dangerous. "Wait. You're saying—"

"I told Ms. Candless." She unwrapped her burger with quick grace, poked at the bun experimentally with one finger. "She asked me about *feeling*. I do not feel. I calculate, I plan, I assess. I have no emotional noise."

"You don't, huh." He considered this. "Why are you running, then? Seems to me the odds are pretty much stacked on their side. Division's."

"Not necessarily." She poked at the bun again. "Is there any nutritive value to this?"

"Empty calories, but you need them. Are you going to eat?"

She glanced at him, a troubled, tentative look as if she expected him to yell. For a second he was back in the hallway again, the popping and zinging of live fire, her smell riding the air and everything in him narrowing to a single, small point. She thought she had no emotional noise?

From where he was sitting, it looked as if she was wrong. Right now, though, she was back to stray cat, and he got the idea the next few moments called for some very, very careful handling of this shy, beautiful, too-thin, finely tuned agent.

"I smelled you on him." It wasn't the best thing to say, but at least it kept her interacting. "On Bronson."

She straightened a little. "That's why you asked

him if he changed his cologne?" A smear of dust on her cheek made his fingers itch to smooth it away.

"You heard that?" If they'd been hiding her behind glass all that time...he'd been so close, close enough to touch, and never knew it.

"Debriefs were taped." She didn't shrug, but he got the idea she wanted to. Under the button-down and the camisole, she was braless. He could tell, because the sudden coolness of air-conditioning in here caused certain...reactions.

"Very voyeuristic." He hadn't felt this breathless since he'd been a teenager. Christ.

That flicker across her wan, beautiful face again. Irritation? Or was it the ghost of a smile? "Protocol. Agents meeting face-to-face was discouraged, but I had to analyze, and that was the best way. Besides, I am...*was*...high-value, having survived induction."

Was? "Was?"

"I suspect now they are simply tying up loose ends. However, several aspects of this particular situation are troubling. I must analyze."

"Well, eat first." He watched her apply herself to a French fry, then another. She chewed as if it wasn't an enjoyable experience, but she did seem to like the burger. At least, she finished it and looked a little wistful as she surveyed the empty wrapper.

He made a mental note to get her two extra-bacon next time and decided there were a great many things troubling *him*, too. Like how the hell he was supposed to deal with a woman who said she didn't have feelings. It was like a bad country song, except they were both in it together, and Cal had a chance to make up for everything. All the lies, the pain, the fighting, the blood.

If he didn't screw this up, it would be a miracle.

The real questioning started much later than Trinity thought it would, as she was neatly folding the wrapper from her burger and smoothing the greasy, empty fry packet. Cal simply balled his own packaging up and dropped it into the grease-stained bag, finally turning his attention to the dregs of his milk shake and examining her critically. "So what were you doing in Felicitas?"

She concentrated on making the wrapper's creases nice and sharp, then deconstructed the fry packet. It was of more solid almost-cardboard, and its topology was interesting. She filed the problem of the machine responsible for its construction away for later analysis—it was always good to have something in reserve. Without a problem to dissect, she was uneasy. "I have to go back," she said finally, carefully.

"Oh?" His sandy eyebrows rose. His face was even and regular, and far more mobile than it had appeared in the debrief tapes. Living color was different, so to speak. Now she could understand why he was thought handsome. There was a certain regularity of features that was pleasing enough, but it was his seemingly unguarded attitude that would draw an interrogation subject in and coax them to reveal more than they should.

She kept glancing at his expression, smoothing the burger wrapper. So far, he seemed remarkably even-tempered. "Yes. Recent events will, at least, lead them to calculate that I won't return to that area. Which improves my chance of success."

"Success at what?" He sucked at the straw, the reluctant fluid in the bottom of his cup gurgling, and set the milk shake aside. "You might as well tell me."

Why? "I have to." Very simple, in case he didn't understand. Surely he was intelligent enough to understand it was a given parameter if she bothered to voice it at all.

"Why?"

"I have to find…" She shut her mouth, abruptly aware of the risk. Should he somehow guess she was involved with the operation that had brought him in and liquidated Tracy Moritz, warning him of her plans was an error.

"Find what? Something in those old military installations right next to Felicitas?" He shook his head. "No dice. You're with me now, honey, and we're heading for a safe location."

"And where, precisely, do you calculate either of us would be *safe*?" She found herself rolling the fry packet up, but it was too thick to do so neatly, and a rasping went up her back. His presence was oddly soothing, she decided, but the packet was extremely displeasing in its current asymmetry. "Given the chance of infection or, more likely, unacceptable information dispersal from either of us, Division will want to disinfect as thoroughly as possible. It's only a matter of time."

"So we go over the border. Hook up with Reese and Holly, and—"

She was already shaking her head. "And endanger Ms. Candless, as well as draw attention to ourselves? Unacceptable."

"Which part? Endangering Holly or drawing attention? You're kind of cute."

What? She blinked, and he reached across the table, sliding the burger wrapper away.

He unfolded it, eyed it critically and then began to fold again, fingers deft and gentle despite calluses from combat and training. "You don't want to endanger Holly, who has Reese to look after her, so that's a nonissue. And you're already thinking for both of us. That's good. I'm a tactical sort, not much of a big planner. It's good to have that on my side."

Your side? "What exactly do you think—"

"Here." He held it up. Trinity blinked. He'd folded the wrapper into a…what *was* it? "It's a crane."

She studied it further, then saw the resemblance. "I see." She took it back, his fingertips brushing hers. For some reason, the slight touch felt overly warm. An agent's metabolic fire, perhaps, but the heat slid down her arm in a decidedly odd way. "You simply fold it in the right sequence, the angles all fall into place. Interesting."

"You can do all sorts of animals that way. Turtles. Dogs. Unicorns."

"Unicorns are imaginary." Still, the marriage of topology, paper and animal forms was very ingenious, and pleasing. You could probably perform such an operation just about anywhere, and the calculations would be a welcome distraction from just about anything, especially that activity labeled *worrying*.

Cal ducked his head a little, smiling oddly. "Then a rhino, maybe. It would probably look like that if I tried. All I can do is a crane, I learned it in grade school."

Trinity glanced at him, returned to studying the folded paper. Why did he look amused? Was it camouflage? What was his purpose? She slid the rest of her trash into the bag and looked at her empty milk shake. She would have to try more of them—semi-liquid, high in sugar, with a small amount of protein, they would be useful when she forgot to eat and needed simple, stomach-soothing, easily digestible items for short-term energy.

Cal took the empty cups, tossed the rubbish into the receptacle near the dresser. An ancient television squatted atop the cheap dark wood, right next to a mirror that showed the dingy paint and the fabric-covered headboard bolted to the wall. Once, it might have been a vibrant blue. Now it was a muddy beige, and Trinity decided she had no wish to calculate the rate of color loss.

"Go ahead and take a shower," Cal said, not moving from near the trash can. "I'll keep watch."

At least he didn't forget that she might want one, as Bronson often had. Then again, Trinity was no longer taking orders. There was a fresh set of clothing in her backpack, and the idea of being clean again was immensely appealing.

It wasn't until she had turned the water on in the narrow, faded but clean bathroom that she realized she had implicitly accepted Eight—*Cal* wouldn't betray her while she sluiced dust and sweat away. Bathrooms were vulnerable points, one's guard nearly always dropped. She calculated the odds of duplicity, the percentages of likely unpleasantness and her desire for cleanliness, before deciding it was an acceptable risk.

When she exited, scrubbing at her hair with the one towel allotted for her use—assuming an equal division of resources—he was at the window, peering out through a space between the dust-stiff, pineapple-yellow curtains. "Looks clear," he said without turning. "You want to watch while I take mine?"

"If you like." She pulled her backpack up onto her shoulder and approached the window, expecting him to move. He stood very still, though, only stepping aside when she nervously halted just outside close-combat reach.

"I didn't mean just this second." But he took the sodden towel and disappeared into the bathroom.

I could leave now. Trinity peered through the

curtains, as well. In an urban area with reasonable density, she could vanish and return to Felicitas. It was too soon, but nobody would expect a solo penetration of the base at this point, would they? There were other factors to be considered, though—she needed rest to recover her full range of effectiveness, and escaping Eight might prove to be easier than she had previously assumed, if he was ignorant of her guilt and still suffering some manner of emotional noise. She was still calculating when the gush of the shower halted, and she decided resting in place was the strategy most likely to restore her to efficiency, and escape would have to assume a lower priority for the moment.

Even if that strange rippling sensation all over her was intensifying. She labeled it as *irritation*, perhaps, or *nervousness*. Her cheeks burned.

Deconstruction was proceeding.

Trinity lay on her back, stiff and tense. Her breathing, deep and controlled, might have fooled a normal man into thinking she slept. A warm lump of grease and calories in her stomach had restored some of her resources, but she was still tired.

Eight had told her to take the bed and folded himself down near the door, propping his head on his duffel. He seemed to fall asleep instantly as well, breathing and pulse dropping rapidly, but she distrusted appearances. He was an *agent*, just as capable as she was of staving off fatigue and waking instantly to deal with a threat.

Or with Trinity stepping over him to ease her way out the door.

The pills were in her backpack. Four left. She had intended to take one before her final attempt to infiltrate the Felicitas installation. If she found her records, the three that remained would be enough for her to trace whatever she could of her former life. If, that was, the records held useful information, which was a 20 percent chance according to the variables she could list. However, so many other factors remained cloudy, that wasn't a fair estimation.

A sigh worked its way out of her, a completely natural physiological loosening of tension. Strangely enough, Eight's breathing paused as well, and when it resumed, relaxation spread through his scent, too, musk and a faint blue tang. The fast food did not make his scent greasy, as it had Bronson's. Instead, it gave it a slight sheen, oil on healthy tanned skin. Unfamiliar comfort threaded through Trinity's bones, her muscles turning to liquid one by one.

How strange. A profound soporific effect? Was it in the food? No, no chemical I can trace. Besides, he hadn't had a chance to tamper with it.

The folded crane was still on the table, a lonely sentinel.

Still wondering what this pleasant new sensation sprang from, and if it was a further mark of cognitive degradation, Trinity fell asleep.

* * *

A woman's breathing, in the dark.

Cal lay with his head on his duffel, inhaling greedy gulps of that marvelous, mouthwatering scent. She was here, and safe, and this time, he was going to do better. He was going to do it *right*.

Quit thinking about it.

Except he couldn't. It was like sleeping on the broken-down brown couch, knowing that behind the bedroom door Tracy was dreaming, snug in her own bed. After the virus, he had trouble letting go enough to get any real rest. Tracy's one-bedroom walk-up had been his solace, and he could still feel every lump and worn-out spring in that damn couch.

He'd been wandering aimlessly one autumn evening, doing some recon around his own spic-and-span, expensive hide masquerading as a banker's almost-penthouse, the one the government certainly had tabs on, and his ears perked at the sound of a scuffle. Around a corner and in an alley, a soft sound of pain, and he'd put the male attacker down before he quite realized what he was doing. The dark-haired victim, sobbing brokenly, told him it was her soon-to-be-ex-husband. *The police...oh, God, the police...*

Turned out the husband didn't want to be ex and, in the time-honored fashion of selfish losers everywhere, had decided that if he couldn't have Tracy, nobody else would, either.

Cal, at the time, only felt a little irritation that he'd

involved himself—but then she insisted on going to the hospital so they could photograph the bruises, and one of his civilian identities was used up just like that, a Good Samaritan witness to intimate-partner assault.

Then she had to go and be kind to him. *Let me buy you coffee. It's the least I can do.*

She was a fourth-grade teacher and good at her job. Her calm, firm demeanor never cracked in the classroom, but outside the school she was a mess of nerves. She was ripe for a rebound relationship with a rescuer, but Cal decided to take it slow and easy, since at any moment he'd be called out of the country to do some dirty work for the powers that be. And really, it would be taking advantage of a vulnerable person—double, since he was trained to infiltrate, to capitalize on uncertainty, to play another human being like a harp if he had to. All part of the job and ridiculously easy with the viral benefits.

It seemed kind of…cheap, to do that just to get laid.

Now he wondered if he shouldn't have been so reticent. He slept on her couch, since she was terrified the ex-husband would show up again. Cal could have told her he wouldn't—one of the benefits of being an agent was being able to scare the crap out of jerks who thought hitting a woman made them manly. It only took two sessions with Cal before the ex decided to head out for greener pastures, namely, Alaska.

If Tracy was still alive, Cal would have been checking on Richard Moritz fairly regularly, to make sure he was staying a decent distance away from her. Ironic, that Cal himself had turned out to be the thing that got her killed. A statistical outlier, so to speak, considering how domestic violence cases usually ended.

He concentrated on his breathing, but the memories had decided it was time to come out and play.

It was usually so easy to compartmentalize. To sometimes even half forget the blood and the dirt, the sound of snapping bones or gurgling a last breath, and just be—well, just be "Tracy's friend." She hadn't asked many questions, thought he worked in international banking, and though her hormones often shouted that she was very aware of him, she kept her distance. He'd even grown to enjoy the dance and congratulated himself on keeping her hidden, shaking off any potential tails before he visited her. Just like a training exercise.

Stupid, thinking they wouldn't notice.

Going off grid to pay off her dead parents' foreclosed farmhouse for her—well, he'd arranged it carefully, structuring it as an insurance payout from a maze of fictitious companies, and her face when he gave her the news and the clear-and-free title had been a study in wonder, soothing some deep aching he hadn't even known he was feeling.

After about fifteen minutes, though, she'd remembered caution. *Why are you so good to me?* A little suspicious.

Because you make me feel human, he'd almost said, but had just shaken his head and said something else. Now he wished he hadn't. Useless to deny it—he'd been thinking about going off the rez even then, leaving the whole welter of killing and bloodshed behind.

Then it had all gone to hell, and Tracy was dead in the flames of that pretty little farmhouse. He didn't even know if they'd shot her. Two teams with submachine guns, all to bring him back. He'd been nerving himself up to tell Tracy everything, but where did you start with something like that? *Hi, I'm actually infected with a supervirus, I do dirty work for the men in office, Mom and Pop and apple pie exist because I kill and kill and kill. Let's elope!*

That would have gone over *real* well. There was no way to make that pill palatable.

Trinity made a soft sound, a sleepy murmur. Cal took a deep breath—if he could smell the hard edge of tension and stress boiling out from his skin, she could, too. How long had it been since she'd really rested? She'd gone out almost as soon as her head touched the pillow.

Come on, Cal. Don't lie to yourself.

That was the trouble with being able to nudge people in the direction you wanted them to go. It was so damn easy, and you couldn't shake the persistent feeling that maybe, just maybe, you were subconsciously doing it because you were a shell of a human being. A killing machine who already suspected something was very, very wrong with him even before the suits came and fetched him from basic, telling him there was a way he could serve his country, he was perfect for it, his measurements—though they never said of what—were optimal. He'd gone along, fat, dumb and happy, letting them scrape and swab and take blood.

Then he woke up after almost-dying of the Gibraltar virus with abilities that made James Bond look like a pissant poser.

In the end, though, it hadn't saved Tracy. It hadn't saved anyone that Cal could see, just spread death and destruction everywhere.

Like a disease.

Trinity made another soft sound, tossing and muttering. Cal exhaled, soft and slow, forcing his pulse to come down, too, tipping the hormone balance into *relaxed* instead of *chewing on old mistakes*.

They didn't tell you that control of the autonomics couldn't make you a machine. Just because you could keep your pulse down didn't mean you didn't *feel* it.

The grief was a sharp sweet candy, and he sucked on it all through that long night, sliding in and out of restorative slumber whenever Trinity moved. Around 3:00 a.m. she was awake for a while, and Cal kept his silent watch in the dark, his own breathing not altering. Did he think she couldn't tell, or was he hoping she could?

Didn't matter. Only one thing was for goddamn sure. He was going to make certain *this* woman stayed alive.

Because if he failed, Cal would be gone, too. Either sliding off the edge mentally, or physically, because he was sure she was for him what Holly Candless was for Reese, and that man wouldn't quit going until his girl was safe.

Cal thought that was a good way to be. It was decent, at least. Better than the alternative, which was cutting everyone loose and going down into a black hole of rage that had been his companion for most of his life, the rage he covered up with easy charm and deceptive mouthing off. He'd thought Tracy was his last chance to use that fury for something good.

Now he was hoping like hell he'd been wrong.

He didn't wake her at dawn, and her internal clock misfired again. It was well past checkout time when Trinity jerked into alertness, sitting straight up on the bed and reaching for a gun that wasn't there as Eight swung the door closed and locked it again. How had she not heard him leave?

Or had he left? She spun for a moment between confusion and certainty, analysis gridlocked by sleep still gripping several of her bodily systems.

"It's all right," he said softly. "Just had to pay for another day."

She shook her head, her hair spilling over her shoulders as she had never allowed it to do while on base. It was longer now; she needed a trim to keep it within regulations—if she wished to do so. That was a question for another time.

Trinity rocketed to her feet, amazed at how deeply she had rested. While welcome, it was *not* usual. "It raises the chance of being traced by 15 percent if they have grids running, and—"

"We don't have to stay another *night*," he pointed out. "Just a few more hours. You needed the rest."

"Wastage of funding." A shiver ran through her. "Assuming your available resources are comparable to mi—" Her mouth worked for a moment. *Don't tell him how much you have, that is an irreparable breach of classified knowledge.* The inside of her head clicked and shivered, her pulse spiking, her breathing quickening.

Oh, no. Stop. Stop it.

Deconstruction was accelerating. She clung to analysis, desperately seeking to remember any of the list of things she had prepared for such a moment, questions her brain could seize on and use to stave off the impending storm. *Think. Think, damn you!*

Movement. She struggled, her elbow meeting something with a crunch, and was lifted off her feet, effectively trapped. She inhaled to scream, an ineffective strategy but the urge was undeniable…and the cry vanished, evaporating in her throat.

Darkness, because her face was pressed into

something harder than flesh should be but softer than the wall. Padded chains around her—no, not chains. Not restraints, either. Unfamiliar calm swamped her, soothing the ragged edges of analysis and adrenaline. Her breath made a hot, damp spot against it, and it was dark because her eyes were closed.

Trinity went limp. The black wave of panic receded. It smelled *safe*, musk and male and a faint tinge of something she could only classify as *blue*. Scents didn't have colors, of course, unless one factored in synesthesia—

That line of analysis stilled itself when she took a deeper inhale. It was wonderful, to have the machine inside her head simply *stop* for a few moments. Behind her eyelids a greenness bloomed—moss-hung trees, the holy silence of a cathedral broken only by a drip or two of water, a campfire glittered, and for a moment a name trembled on her lips. Something starting with *A*.

"Shhh," he said softly. "It's okay. Nothing here's going to hurt you." A rumble from his chest, communicated through her forehead and cheekbones. "It's all right."

Control over autonomic and semiautonomic functions returned. She slowed her runaway pulse, inexplicable clarity settling inside her skull, as if she had taken another pill. *Strange. Is it... Hmm. Why does he... How...*

"Okay?" He spoke into her hair and inhaled just afterward. A shudder went through them both, or maybe just through him and communicating into Trinity's smaller frame. She just reached his shoulder; it was truly novel to feel so enclosed and not claustrophobic. "Nothing's gonna hurt you, honey. I promise."

Hurt me? Her lips moved. "Pain can be controlled." How could he make such a promise, that nothing would hurt? It was meaningless.

"Some of it." He didn't let go, even when she moved against him, a slight twitch expressing her desire to step away. Instead, he inhaled again, a deep breath whistling in her hair. Oddly, it sounded as if his nose was stuffed, and something warm trickled against her scalp.

Trinity smelled copper and moved again, trying to tug herself free. He didn't let go, and an odd contest ensued, Trinity wriggling and pushing, Cal trying to keep hold of her. She had to use more force than she liked to extricate herself, and when she glanced up at his face, pushing her hair back, her fingers found a damp spot on her scalp.

Cal's patrician nose was bleeding. Now she remembered her elbow smashing into something, obviously his face. A queer tightening sensation prickled all over her. "I…I *hit* you."

"Yeah." He stared at her, those blue eyes gone distant. He'd shaved, and the cleaner line of his jaw was marvelous in its precision. Blood dripped on his navy blue T-shirt. "Got me a good one. It's okay."

The warm spot in her hair was his blood. Trinity's entire body turned cold. She had not been in complete control; the strength and speed of an agent were dangerous. She had assumed, so far, that degradation and deconstruction would be physical as well as mental, and her strength and reflexes would decay enough to represent no danger to civilians.

Now she was faced with proof that she might be wrong.

She took two deep breaths. Cal's gaze was fixed on her, a swipe of his blood simmering on her cheek. Her hands fell, limp white birds.

"I have to get away from you," she whispered.

"What?" He was staring at her mouth, as if trying to decode a foreign tongue. According to his file, he could speak at least four languages other than English, but—

"I'm sorry," Trinity said. Strangely enough, she *meant* it. She hadn't wanted to hurt him. Her knees loosened, a fraction of a second before she could drop and roll, grabbing her backpack and bolting past him.

At least, that was her plan. Cal leaned forward, his hand blurring out and closing around her upper arm. "Look, let's just—"

Training took over. *Snap.* She struck again, quick as a snake, driving her fist for his throat. His reflexes were agent-swift; he bent back, dropping his weight, and caught her wrist, deflecting the blow just enough. Trinity went loose, expecting his next move to be a kick, her knee coming up to deflect as well and her balance thrown off when he didn't take the chance.

Instead, he stepped sideways, a swift dancer-graceful movement, pivoting her. He lifted her again, as if she weighed nothing, her back to his chest, and Trinity kicked fruitlessly. *Stop. Conserve your energy.*

"Is this really what you want to do?" Hot breath on her ear. "I'm here to help you, honey. We can do this the easy way or the hard way."

"I. Have. To. Get. *Away.* From. You." She enunciated clearly, so he could not possibly misunderstand. "I am *dangerous*, Eight."

"Don't call me that." Soft and reasonable. "You really think you're dangerous?"

You have no idea. How many are dead because of me?

Then again, a better word might be *toxic*. It was certainly more precise.

She tested his grip, struggling. His scent had changed again. Darker, a little aggression, healthy effort on a very healthy male. Judging by the insistent nudging against her lower back, there was a certain amount of excess blood flow. Perhaps it was diverted from his brain.

That might give her an advantage. "I have a mission." Analyses and percentages raced through her head. None of them added up correctly. How far had mental degradation progressed?

"So do I, honey." A little husky now. "And it involves keeping you out of *their* hands."

"Why? There is no profit to be—" The differences shading through his scent were making it difficult for her to think.

"It's not about *profit*. Jesus, what did they do to you?"

What is that? She tried to quantify the change in his tone. It took a moment, but she found the proper word.

Disgust.

Trinity closed her eyes against a brief lance of pain spearing her chest. Perhaps she'd pulled a muscle.

He was disgusted by her lack of control. *It is to be expected*, she told herself coldly. "I am deconstructing, Agent Eight."

"Don't call me that."

"Does it disturb you?"

"*Disturb*'s not the word, *Three*."

It was perhaps only fair. Still, the word set off a cascade inside Trinity, and he had no warning, not even a breath of change in her own scent. She pitched sideways, bending farther than a normal human could and using his grasp on her as a fulcrum, her sock foot kissing the wall and giving her even more leverage as the unexpected angle twisted her free. The bed shuddered as she dropped, rolling, her hand flashing out to grab her backpack. Lunging up, her feet kissing the wall again—it was so *simple* when you could calculate force and trajectory. She leaped, bouncing off the bed again and bolting for the door, the window was too risky. She would heal quickly, yes, but—

Crunch.

They went down in a tangle of arms and legs, and Trinity brought her knee up sharply. Usually such a maneuver dissuaded a man, but it hit him in the stomach instead of its intended target. A short huff of breath was her only reward, and they rolled, ending with Trinity wedged between the wall and a male body much heavier than her own. Her mouth crushed against his shoulder, his T-shirt ripped away, and Trinity *bit*, worrying at fever-warm flesh. *How undignified.* Now, *there* was another appropriate word.

Cal hissed in a breath. More blood, a splash of copper filling her mouth. The treacherous lassitude from his scent swamped her again, and Cal made another soft, inarticulate sound. After a moment, Trinity recognized it as a *laugh*.

"Oh, man," he said, almost crushing the breath out of her. "Man oh man. You're feisty."

She clamped down once more, her jaw aching. He laughed again.

Pain can be controlled.

"We can tango until you get tired, honey." Still nice and soft, but with a hiss behind the words. "It might even help work off some of that stress."

Red heat bloomed inside Trinity. She thrashed wildly, until the idiocy of exhausting herself in this fashion occurred to her. She went limp, working her teeth free, and it wasn't just Cal's scent that held a darker edge of arousal now.

That's not supposed to happen. I'm supposed to be immune to anything like this. Everything inside her was whirling, breaking apart. "Stop...*stop* it..."

"It's just getting interesting." He didn't move. "I am not letting you get yourself caught."

"I...*deconstructing*..." Her throat turned to a pinhole. She couldn't *breathe*.

"You're wound too tight, that's all." His respiration dropped, his pulse slowing, too. "Seriously, woman, you have got to calm down."

Black feathers beat at the outer edges of her vision. Trinity's eyes rolled back in her head, and she did the only thing she could.

She shut down.

Part Two: On the Run

Cal finally realized she'd passed out, limp and quiescent against him. He lay there for a few moments, smelling her and the tang of his own blood. She'd bitten him a good one and struggled desperately. Flexible and snake-quick, he had a hard time keeping ahead of her, but he'd managed this once. Those big eyes of hers, soft wells of pain, just about drowned him.

I am deconstructing, she'd said in that throaty, choked tone. Great. Well, what the hell did that mean to her? Or to him?

He had no clue. Unless it meant scrawny-thin, jumpy and looking so lost and lonely it was enough to turn a man inside out? What other clues did she give?

Induction. I don't feel.

Didn't look like it from here, though. Looked like she was struggling to cope with emotional noise and not having much luck. He moved slightly, peering at his shoulder. She'd gotten a mouthful. If he was normal, he might scar, but the wound had already stopped bleeding. He didn't have to worry about infecting her with the Gibraltar virus, either. Any idiot with half a nose could tell they were complementary, just like Reese and Holly, their scents overlapping in a pleasant haze.

Great. He had blood all over him and was lying on the floor with an unconscious woman. All it needed was the police busting the door down to make it a comedy.

Nah, let's avoid that, okay? It was nice to imagine she was lying asleep in his arms, safe at last and willing, as well. He forced himself to move, very slowly, getting untangled. Getting his feet under him wasn't difficult. Lifting her wasn't that bad, either; even though she was deadweight she was oddly frail. What had she been eating?

Christ, she hadn't even known what a milk shake was. Of all the things Cal hoped Bronson was burning in hell for, it probably wasn't high on the list— but he could put it on, just because.

She'd slept on top of the covers, had barely dented the pillows. He laid her down, arranging her hair— this close, he could see the fine feathering of blond at her temples, the thick streaks of honey and paler highlighting, a natural sun-bleach job someone would pay a great deal for in a salon. The strands were silken-slippery against his fingertips, and he had to outright *make* himself back away.

Cal carried one of the chairs to the bedside, dropped into it and studied her while he could.

Those beautiful cheekbones. And without her stiff conscious watchfulness, he could see what she'd look like when she relaxed. She was a lot smaller than she looked while awake, and so fragile it made his chest hurt.

I have to get away from you. I'm dangerous.

Did she think she was going to hurt *him*? Good Lord. She had to know what he was trained for, had to have seen some of the reports from his missions. And she thought she could—what?

Damage him? That was a laugh. It was kind of... well, *strange*, to have someone worried about him that way.

It didn't take long. Ten minutes at most, before she stirred, respiration and pulse rising. He tried not to imagine she was waking up after a completely different series of events.

She flexed her fingers, then her toes.

"They're all still there," he said as gently as possible. "Do you often have panic attacks?"

Her eyes flew open. She curled up to sit, and Cal tensed, but she didn't bolt again. Instead, she hugged herself, palms cupping her sharp elbows, and regarded him steadily. "Shutdown." That sharply pretty face was blank now, and her voice just as emotionless. Only the shadows in her eyes remained. "Necessary to protect against deconstruction."

"You keep using that word." Cal kept himself on the edge of the chair, ready. "I'm, uh, not sure what it means to you."

"Full-blown cognitive degrade. Irreversible damage." Her breath caught. "A risk with induction. Any emotional noise is a symptom to be reported immediately. I did not."

Now, that was interesting. His own respiration was trying to match hers, breathing with her, trying to force her to calm down. "Why not?"

She shook her head fractionally. Hadn't anyone noticed how she curled around herself? How fragile she looked? "I am unsafe. Deconstruction is fatal. I have very little time before I die or am recaptured, and I wish to spend it in my own fashion."

"Huh." He scratched at his hairline, blood crackling on his face. His shoulder burned pleasantly. "Interesting."

"So, you agree this is the best course of action."

What? "Nope. I didn't say that at all."

She bounced to her feet, a clean, economical movement, and Cal found himself standing as well, his booted toes right in front of her sock-clad ones. His arms tingled still, remembering cradling her. She didn't back down, though it was probably uncomfortable to crane her neck like that, looking up at him. Her chin jutted a little, and he almost lost his breath again. She was goddamn gorgeous with that defiance humming through her like electricity through a high-tension wire.

This close, he could see fine threads of color in her irises, the thick masses of gold in her hair. She was too pale to tan well.

Imagining her in a bikini was something else, though.

"You are far more intelligent than you like to appear," she said finally, almost primly. A slight pinkness blooming in her cheeks. Even prettier.

You think? "Maybe that's just my charm."

Another flicker across that lovely face. He was getting good at seeing them. They were small and quick, but they were definitely there.

"Consequently I am forced to the conclusion that you understand perfectly well I am a danger to you."

Maybe just to my pulse. Jesus. "Are you, now." He didn't bother sounding impressed.

"Please." So softly it threatened to send a shiver down his spine. "Agent—*Cal.* Please."

His nose was full of thick bloodsmell. It was probably a blessing, because if he was this close and breathing her in while she said his name and looked up at him like that, he might agree to anything she wanted. The moss green of her irises, so close to his own, and then there was the tank top clinging to her as if it wanted to distract him.

It was doing a damn good job, too.

"Your chances are better with me." Why did he sound breathless? And *Jesus*, but his clothes were too tight, and bloody besides. He needed a shower. Hell, he needed an ice bath. "Right? A trained agent. One *they* couldn't catch."

"You were caught."

"I *let* them get me." *With Tracy gone I didn't care. But I'll be damned if I'm going to let them get their hands on you, too.*

A slight movement, her shoulders raising and dropping briefly. A shrug. She probably didn't believe him. "I have a question."

"Shoot." He almost winced at using that expression. The way the day was going, someone might end up squeezing off a round or two at them.

Those big eyes of hers, wounded and vulnerable. "Why are you doing this?"

Oh, *dammit*. "You, ah. You rescued Holly."

"Out of self-interest." An immediate whipcrack of an answer. This close, though, and with an agent's acuity, he could see the small changes in her expression.

Immune to emotional noise, hell. She was *soaking* in it. No wonder she was confused. Her mouth was tempting him, too. He kept glancing at it, at the exact shape of her lips.

Slow and easy here, Cal. "You were thinking they'd get around to tying you off, too, right? You could have just walked, you didn't have to help

Holly. But you did. You even saved Reese and me. Bronson had us cold." *He would have shot both of us in the back, put Holly down, then put a round through my skull and Reese's just to be sure. Can't heal from that.*

Immediate denial, her hair swinging heavily as she shook her head. "The odds of your survival were high, given the situation."

He shook his head, too, then wished he hadn't, because his nose ached and a final, warm, thin trickle of blood eased down his upper lip. He didn't move to brush it away. "He knew enough to put us down, then put a round in our heads. You went out of your way to help us."

"After I helped hunt you." Two bright spots of color in her cheeks now, not just pink. He was getting through.

Maybe. So he decided to throw out a question of his own. "I kind of wondered why you only winged me, at the cabin. You deliberately warned us."

With the flush, he could see, again, a little of what she'd look like without that pale severity all the time. He was going to die of heart failure once she really relaxed around him, if she ever looked at him that way and said his name and—

She raised her chin a little more. "I didn't mean to hit you."

So that was *her.* Neither he nor Reese had been able to figure that one out. "See?" His hands itched, wanting to cup her shoulders and pull her close. The smear of blood on her cheek, drying rapidly, bothered him, too. "It was a ricochet. You shot wide, and we weren't caught in the hole."

"But you *were* caught!" The flush deepened still further.

"Emotional noise," he said and tried not to grin like an idiot. "They try to get rid of it, but they can't."

That was the wrong thing to say. All the color and animation faded, doors he could almost *hear* slamming behind her eyes. "They did with me."

"You only *think* they did." He stopped, considering this. Something nagged at him, and a moment later, she stiffened, too. The little tingle of *trouble coming* crawled up and down his back, digging in its tiny cold fingernails. Silence stretched taut between them. Just when he was getting somewhere, too. "Get cleaned up."

"Do you think…" Her tongue darted out, wet her lips, and Cal lost every battle he'd ever thought of fighting with himself. He leaned down, his hands closing around her shoulders, and kissed her.

Confusion. The taste of copper, his mouth on hers, then his *tongue* was there, probing for entrance. She had a brief flash of…something, perhaps revulsion? *How unsanitary.*

Then a different feeling. A warmth, a softness, all through her. It was fascinating, the overlapping textures, and there it was again. The cessation of the scrabble, scrabble, scrabble of calculation and planning. His skin somehow muted the frantic motion, and even the coppertang of blood was no deterrent.

Stop it, some faint, fading rational part of her called, but Trinity barely listened. It was, instead, the sure consciousness of danger that dragged her out of the wide, deep, fascinating peace. As soon as she moved, Cal broke away, and Trinity found out he was breathing just as heavily as she was, and for the first time in a long while her head didn't hurt.

How odd.

"Get cleaned up." Cal's hands at her shoulders, not bruising or gripping hard, but definitely tense. He stepped back, knocking the chair over, and straightened his arms, holding her at a distance. "Make it quick. I, uh. There's something wrong."

What? It was difficult to orient herself. The room was full of that simmering smell the two of them made, with its deep blue tint, saturating her pores. She blinked several times. This close, she could see the faint line on his cheek where she'd raked him, already looking thin, white and healed. His lashes were sandy, too. He was more than handsome, from this angle.

"Yes." Her throat was dry. "I… We should separate."

"What?" A pained, quizzical expression, and it made him look…what was the proper word? She couldn't think of it.

It didn't matter. Perhaps he had not heard her clearly, so Trinity decided to recap. "This reduces

our percentage of efficient cooperation. It is a distraction and lapse in safety protocols." She rid herself of his hands on her shoulders simply by turning,
and cast around for her backpack. "Thank you for
the milk shake."

"What the *hell*?" As if he still didn't understand.

Trinity stepped into her boots, lacing them with
quick jerks, tying swiftly. Her backpack was by the
door, and a lick of flame lit itself in her core when
she thought of how it had arrived there. "Should I
be captured, I will do my best not to disclose your
location or implicate you in any—"

"Oh, no, you don't." He shook his hands out,
loose and ready, an agent's quick, graceful movement. "We're going to go into the bathroom and get
cleaned up. Then we're getting fresh transport and
blowing this town. Together, in case you still haven't
figured that out."

Yes, she decided, the proper word was *irritation*.
"This is not—"

"You want to end up on the floor again, sugar
pop? *Try me*." His hair wildly mussed, dried blood
in his stubble and his eyes burning blue, he looked
extremely irritated, as well.

Trinity could not blame him. Cold logic seemed
to infuriate many people unfortunate enough to
brush up against her. "Are you threatening me?"

His reply was a short negative that sounded remarkably obscene, and Trinity hurried for the bathroom. He had a valid point—rinsing off the blood

was a necessary move. Then, she told herself, she would simply escape while he tended to his own hygiene.

Unfortunately, he kept the door open and merely washed the blood off, changed his shirt and was ready to go while she was still hurriedly repacking her upended bag. She had paused to scoop up the grease-spotted paper crane from the table.

The worst thing was, she began to suspect he was right and that her chances of survival were higher with his cooperation.

Until, that was, he found out about the Moritz operation.

Ninety minutes later, Cal shook the man's hand and thanked him kindly while Trinity stood aside, her hair pulled back and a pair of large, cheap sunglasses tinting the entire world amber. Cal hooked an arm over her shoulders, casually, even though New Mexico heat bounced off pavement and used cars in every color crouching obediently around them. She could break away and start running, perhaps—but that would be incredibly inefficient.

She told the small niggling thought that perhaps she didn't *want* to move to go away, and it went, quietly.

"A honeymoon car, huh?" The salesman, his wide greasy smile not reaching his cold-coffee eyes, scratched under his bleached, sweat-stained ten-gallon hat. "Road trip's one way to do it. You picked a good 'un."

"I sure did," Cal said and bent to nuzzle her hair. Trinity blinked—the salesman had likely meant the car, but Cal was playing the part of a newly married man. *Just stand there and look pretty*, he'd told her. *I'll handle the rest.*

So far, she had to admit he was doing admirably well. This would take them farther, with less chance of unwanted attention, than a stolen vehicle.

The salesman, his suit wilting fast, kept babbling, and Trinity stopped listening. She scanned for threats as Cal laughed easily, diverting suspicion, smoothing the waters. His file indicated a high degree of interpersonal ease and an uncanny knack for ingratiating himself.

It seemed both were functions of his tolerance for what they called "small talk." Which was just another way of saying "the useless spending of breath and time hooting back and forth about nothing," as far as she could see.

I never liked empty words. The thought jolted her, and she made a small restless movement, almost immediately controlled. *Wait. I remember...*

Any chance of stilling herself and turning inward to follow the thread into the mists of pre-induction was lost when Cal took her flinch for a signal. "Well, we'd better get going. Thanks, Tom."

"Thank *you*, Brad!" The salesman was all too glad to get back into the air-conditioning and heaved himself away over the softening tarmac. Cal let out a soft breath and glanced down at her.

"Sleazy, isn't he." Pitched too low for the normal to hear, and he pulled Trinity along. "Get in, let's get out of town."

She let him pull her along toward the blue Chevy pickup he'd spent precious time bargaining for. "Why did you give him the extra money? It was not included in the—"

"Bribery, honey. Standard operating procedure when you can smell the greed on a fat slob." He opened her door—less a gentlemanly gesture than a security one, Trinity thought—and glanced over the lot, still uneasy. "The other two we looked at were lemons. This one isn't."

"Ah. He's selling substandard vehicles." It was a pleasure to learn another complex skill, and negotiating through the buying of a used car certainly qualified.

"Shh." He closed her in the truck. Even with the window down it was extremely warm, her skin prickling as her internal temperature regulated. When Cal slammed the driver's door and turned the key, more heat roared from the dash. By the time he found the freeway, though, cold air poured through the vents, and the windows were rolled up, keeping the slipstream at bay. "Those shades make you look like a movie star."

It was quiet. The enclosed space meant every

breath was full of that tranquilizing smell. He turned the radio on very low, and something that had to be music came tiptoeing out. It was all about how a dog had left its master, with twanging guitars. The second verse was about how a woman had left the singer.

Was that more irritation, pushing her teeth together and leaving a bitter taste on the back of her tongue? It was. The singer's voice grated, whining on and on, and she longed to reach for the buttons and force the radio to cough up something less trite and meaningless.

"You okay?" Cal glanced in her direction, and Trinity nodded, with what she hoped was a neutral expression. The idea of kicking out the window and escaping the noise was intensely tempting. Even the thought of likely damage ensuing from such a maneuver, since the vehicle had achieved freeway speed, wasn't enough to completely rule out such a desperate course of action. She began to calculate speed, densities, the probabilities of different bones breaking with different angles of impact, and the pressure eased a bit.

Unfortunately, the next song was just as whining and ugly, and Trinity's hands, lying obediently in her lap, tensed.

"Something's bothering you."

Is it obvious? She shook her head slightly, hoping he would pay attention to the road.

"I can't help you if you don't talk."

"I do not recall requesting your *help*." *In fact, I seem to remember not wanting it at all.*

He nodded slightly, as if she'd said something profound. "You seriously expect me to just let you go back there and commit suicide? Really?"

If you knew what I've done, you would probably try to hurry my demise along in whatever way you could. Her teeth refused to unclench. The singer this time was female, warbling what she no doubt thought were heartfelt and empowering words about a cheating ex.

Cal leaned forward and snapped the radio off. Trinity almost sagged with relief at the ensuing silence.

Then, five minutes of blessed peace and quiet later, he flicked it back on again.

Trinity's hands curled into fists.

"Let's see what else is on, shall we?" He punched the scan button. An advertisement for a furniture store. A wailing of ranchero music that wasn't half-bad, but the accordion was out of tune. A pop anthem. A religious station—something about the blood of the lamb. Trinity outright shuddered, a small, betraying movement.

Then, like a gift, liquid solace flowed from the speakers, and Trinity relaxed all at once. It was that best of sounds—Bach's *Goldberg Variations*, each note precisely measured, a soothing mathematical tapestry, every single tone in the right place. She let out a soft breath, tucking her hair behind her ear, and Cal's hand moved slightly, stopped.

"I think we'll just listen to this," he said. "Hard to get classical out in the sticks. Mostly it's country."

Was he engaging in small talk with *her*, too? "I noticed."

"Yeah, well. Next time actually open your mouth and say something, okay?"

"What?"

"Guys aren't good at that small-detail stuff."

She reviewed the past few moments of her mental footage and decided she still didn't understand. "At...classical music?"

"No, honey. At figuring out why a woman's gone all stiff and smells like anger."

"I apologize." Was that what he wanted? He didn't sound accusatory, but most males preferred a female to be constantly apologetic. Bronson, and later interactions with civilians, had taught her *that* much.

He kept his eyes on the road. "Don't. It's kind of cute. Definitely like a movie star."

What? Trinity decided silence was called for and stared out the window at the gently rolling taupe that passed for landscape. Tough green blots of sage dotted at random intervals, and she found, somewhat to her surprise, that she had no urge to calculate the availability of water and precipitation patterns from them.

She was also smiling.

* * *

Alexandria Fraser considered herself an easygoing person. Most people in the world were just doing their jobs, even when their jobs involved silly things, like Agent Sartino's. The FBI could be tracking down terrorists or something, instead of making life hard for a girl who just had some very specific talents she used to keep herself fed and clothed.

The talents weren't strictly *legal*, but so much of legality was just convenience for the Powers That Be, and Fray treated them as such. She hadn't hacked the account numbers and PINs to use them for nefarious purposes, she'd just been *bored*. It was sort of ironic that she'd been caught for that instead of anything else, and further ironic that Sartino had offered her a plea in return for helping catch someone. *A slippery customer*, he'd said. *Don't screw this up, Fray. I want to help you.*

The question of why a straitlaced FBI agent would go out of his way to help *her* was solved when Fray took a look at his personnel file and found out he had an estranged daughter. Also, some digging had turned up memos from Sartino's boss, telling him Fray was now the military's problem and not mentioning her escape from Felicitas's biggest police station.

Seems as if she'd pissed that blond bastard off. Served him right for being so smarmy, resting a hand on her shoulder, staring at her breasts and generally acting like every sexual-harassment cliché rolled into a single human male. Plus, he'd been dodgy about why they were looking for the woman with the strange eyes.

Fray took a sip of her nonfat cinnamon latte and glanced over the coffee shop's interior. She had a good view of the parking lot, too, simmering under a southwest sun. Cuartova had been within driving distance, large enough she could find some tech, and she could strike for the border if things got seriously hazy. There was money and a new identity waiting for her in Mexico City, but why use it before she had to? She'd been moving steadily ever since escaping the station; now she didn't want to chance a border crossing without cogitating things through a bit.

The first step was getting plugged in. Finding Wi-Fi wasn't difficult in any urban area; it was a pity she couldn't return to some of her old haunts. She missed real bagels and even caught herself missing the subway's rumble and grind. Driving everywhere was a wasteful drag.

The fresh new laptop, without any of the mods that made her old one so useful—if she wasn't keying in the codes on a regular basis, it would scramble and lead any investigator down a merry tangle of arcane electronic paths—sat glowing innocently at her. Fray's fingers itched to get back into her old stores, download some useful software and get cracking. But she had to think about things before she leaped this time.

Point one: blond Major Caldwell and his black-

haired goon. The goon obeyed his orders roboti-
cally, unquestioningly, and Caldwell obviously had
a whole *hell* of a lot of pull not just with anything
military but with local and national law enforcement. Not like there was much difference, with the
military giving surplus out to John Q Riot Control,
but still.

Point two: Alice Wharton, the blonde woman
with the strange eyes, had used a social security
number that obeyed the algorithm; she'd been working at a crappy little grocery store; and she was a
matter of national security. Her flat, indifferent stare
had bothered Fray until she realized why—it was
the same as the black-haired goon's look.

Point three: Fray's own escape hadn't provoked
an APB; neither had the hunt for Alice Wharton—
which was obviously a fake name. They didn't want
the public to know they were searching for her, and
Fray herself could easily end up vanishing if she
wasn't careful. Agent Sartino had been told to forget
the whole thing—it was in other hands now.

It all added up to something very dodgy indeed
going on. That made Fray's nose tingle and her fingers itch. She adjusted the black bandanna over her
wildly curling hair, crossed her booted ankles and
fidgeted a little bit before stilling, staring at the new
laptop's screen. It darkened—in power-saving mode,
even though it was plugged in.

She'd been thinking about this for too long.

Was curiosity a good enough reason to get further

involved? Or was she already in too deep as a result of Major Caldwell, the Sexual Harassment Wonder?

Because point four on Fray's list was the fact that she could find Caldwell's birthplace, some of his transcripts and a paper he'd written in college, but nothing else. He'd been scrubbed pretty efficiently, and so had the Wharton woman. Not only that, but the scrubbing was protected by some weapons-grade firewalls. Caldwell pretty much vanished electronically as soon as he entered the Army, which was *not* normal and had to be recently retroactive.

Something big, something *huge* and something centering on a lone woman working in a supermarket. They wanted to pick Alice Wharton up and make her vanish, and Fray knew enough about governments to tell that was not a good position for a lone woman to be in.

Fray sighed. She was already in it too deep; she wasn't going to risk the border *just* yet. She took another sip of her latte, savoring the tongue-burn of extra cinnamon syrup, and cracked her knuckles, one at a time, relishing the ritual.

The first step was to get better software loaded onto this virgin laptop.

The next was to begin digging harder.

Fray got to work.

The sense of danger receded with the Cuartova skyline. In a big old-fashioned gas-guzzling piece of rolling iron shaped like a pickup, they were as anonymous as barbecue or dust. A thin, pretty woman with large sunglasses distrustfully perched on one side of the bench seat, a good old boy with just the right faded jeans and chambray work shirt driving on the other. The only thing wrong was the classical music filling the cab—or maybe not, maybe there was a poet-cowboy out here somewhere.

And, of course, there was the dusty, battered backpack the pretty woman hugged as if it was a flotation device.

The radio burbled, a tinkling cascade of piano music coming to a halt, and Cal squinted. He had a lot to chew on and not much mouth to put it in. Her scent, rich gold and blue, was filling up every corner of his head, and a few corners that had nothing to do with rational thought.

What had he expected? A grateful, doe-eyed version of Tracy?

Except it had been easy to move Tracy from place to place. She'd been normal and predictable.

Stop thinking about that. Jesus. He shifted a little on the bench seat. This woman was smart, strong and determined. He hadn't thought about what he'd do when he found her, and he especially hadn't thought about the fact that she might have her own very definite ideas about what she wanted and where she was going.

It didn't help that she was so goddamn fragile, and powering through regardless. *That* was bravery, and it turned his guts cold to think of where it would end up. Especially if she figured out all she had to do was stand close and ask him nicely, and he'd be powerfully tempted to go along on whatever fool idea she'd concocted.

Think about something else. Get her talking. "Hey."

She didn't reply, staring out the window. He was pretty sure she wasn't ignoring him, though. Her silence had a sort of listening sense to it.

"I've been wondering." That was true—he'd been wondering a lot of things. "Why are you all set on going back to that base? You were in the area for a while, got a job and a good hide. What's in there that you would stick around so long?"

No reply. She hugged the backpack a little more tightly, that was all.

"Must be something that requires a little time to extract. Something you can't just dive in and grab."

That earned him a single, extraordinary glance, those dark eyes open and vulnerable for a fraction of a second. Outside her window, the sere, thirsty landscape flew by. The truck had good tires, and the engine was in better shape than anything else on the lot—which was why he'd settled on it. Better to buy and pay cash, use yet another disposable identity for the paperwork and change the plates later if he had to. Finding the right dealership was half the problem—you wanted sketchy enough, but not *too* sketchy, and respectable enough not to be the first place a questioner would nose around.

She didn't bite, so he added a few more words. "And if it's something you're so interested in, it probably has to do with the agent program. Which means it's likely something I'd be interested in, and Reese, too."

That got a response. "Agent Six." She really did have a very nice voice. A little husky, and not nearly as flat and toneless as he'd first thought. Like warm honey, smooth and sweet. "He had very low emotional noise, until he met her. Ms. Candless."

I'll bet. "Holly. Yeah, I can relate." Seeing the two of them together was enough to make you gag or say *awwwww*, and Cal was never sure which. Reese didn't show it as much as Holly did, but just the way he stood when she was in the room spoke volumes. There was nothing Reese wouldn't do for that woman, and if he was feeling anything like the way Cal was, well, he had a helluva poker face.

"And you met...Mrs. Moritz. During her divorce."

Hearing her say that was interesting and chilling at the same time, sort of like something walking over his grave. The fire, the screaming, bullets chewing every cabinet, blood on his hands when they brought him in. "She was a good friend."

"Friend?" Just the faintest hint of disbelief.

"Yes, friend. You jealous?"

"No." Sharp, curt little word. "Simply inquiring, since agents tended to go native with female...

friends…once they reached Gemini stage, instead of the initially stable Gibraltar virus."

"So Gemini's unstable?" That would be pretty unwelcome news, considering he was counting on the virus to keep them both functioning.

"Not precisely."

He waited, but a full mile went by and she didn't say anything else. So he bit. "What do you mean, not precisely?"

"The Gemini mutation—where Gibraltar ended up in every male agent, given enough time—is complementary. For the virus to be completely stable and its benefits to endure, the geminas have to be kept close to the agents. The two viral loads must exchange what the other lacks. Like puzzle pieces. Neither body can produce all aspects of the whole."

"So that's what makes them smell so good."

"Possibly. There's some contention, since there is no physical commonality between the geminas—at least, the ones they autopsied."

"Autopsied? Tracy—did they?"

"Yes. She was shot several times—she died instantly. There would have been very little…pain."

Well, thank God for that. "You knew all this before you—"

"No. The base nearest Felicitas is a research and records facility. Copies of certain things are held there. Very messy, and redundant, but any large bureaucracy will be inefficient. I have reason to believe…" Maddeningly, she stopped.

Cal took a deep breath. He wasn't smelling smoke; it was just the memory of the farmhouse. Realizing something wasn't right, while Tracy, her hands clasped so tightly just like Trinity's were now, looked up at him. *It's not that I'm not grateful, because I am. I just... This is a little much, you know?*

Now this woman, sitting right next to him, didn't want his help, either. It was looking like a trend. "So what records are you after?"

She took a deep breath, as if bracing herself. It made her scent that much richer, an indigo thread of decisiveness through the honeygold of her hair. Your nose could tell you everything you needed to know, really. Except how to get them to sit still long enough for you to say *Look, I just want to help, all right?*

That was pretty selfish, too. *Let me help, because it makes me feel better about being a killing machine.*

"I have no memory before waking up on the induction table. There are some things...faint flashes, but nothing more. I am deconstructing. I..." Another deep breath. "I have to know who I am, before I die."

Don't we all. "You're not going to die."

A tiny movement that might have been a shrug.

"Not if I have anything to say about it," he added, but that just made him feel even more sheepish and selfish. He checked the rearview—a state patrol cruiser was hanging back, a shark in a lazy flock of minnows, just swimming along. Not anything to be worried about yet. Neither of them had questioned the sudden sense of danger urging them out of the hotel room. It could have been paranoia, but better paranoid than caught.

And she hadn't said a word about the kiss. Was it still burning in her, the way it was all his lips could remember? She fit just right against him, too.

Complementary. That was one word for it.

"Why?" Funny, how the slightest shading in her voice could color it with thoughtful curiosity.

Just because. "Maybe I like you. Ever think of that?"

"Ridiculous."

Did she sound miffed or disgusted? He couldn't tell. "Yeah, well, that's why they call them feelings."

"Ah." For some reason, that made her uncurl a little and set her backpack down between her booted feet. "May I ask you something?"

"You just did. But go ahead." He relaxed a notch, and a little more, still keeping tabs on the cruiser in the rearview.

"Can you explain it to me? The...feeling?" Now she sounded wistful, of all things. "It will help me calculate."

"Plan your chances of getting away?"

"No." Almost inaudible under the hum of driving and air-conditioning. "How to keep you from being caught again."

There it was again. She wanted to protect him.

Him, of all people.

His chest seized up, and if he wasn't so sure the

little swarmies in his bloodstream kept the pipes all clear, he might have thought it was a heart attack. "Ah. Well. Don't worry about that, honey. Let's just figure out where to stop for lunch, all right?"

"Another milk shake?" She sounded, of all things, *hopeful*. Emotional noise, and she thought it would kill her. *Induction*. There was a lot that word could mean. Drawing her out about it could wait until after lunch.

"I think we can do that." *All the milk shakes you could ever want. Just don't get any more crazy ideas in your head about suicide missions.* He checked the rearview again. The state patrol car was gone, and a little muscle at the base of his neck relaxed. He was feeling better about this whole thing now.

He should have known it wouldn't last.

The strawberry milk shake was not quite as marvelous as the chocolate one had been. Tiny red clots of frozen fruit were faintly unnerving, she decided. Nevertheless, it was delicious and soothing, and she was almost sorry when it was gone. It satisfied her basic calorie requirements after a day spent sitting in a car, but Cal told her they would stop for barbecue in a little while, as well. At the moment, he was outside in a simmering afternoon, arms folded, leaning against the blue pickup while gas pumped into its sloshing tank.

The twenty-dollar bill he'd given her was folded

precisely in her pocket. *Get some snacks, huh? And more water. You still smell dehydrated.*

She had not bothered to protest that she was operating at reasonable efficiency, considering the events of the past forty-eight hours. She had, however, availed herself of the key to the restroom, the sleepy-eyed and heavily pimpled young man behind the counter simply glancing at her and marking her as *female* and *no trouble* before he handed it over. The key was taped to a wooden ruler, sadly battered and scarred, and after she closed herself in the bathroom's odorous but reasonably private confines, her bladder eased and her jeans rebuttoned, she examined it closely.

The marks were faded but comforting. The idea that measuring was standardized, that rulers like this were mass-produced and relied upon, was extremely soothing. To know that at least an inch was an inch, a centimeter a centimeter, was the closest to objectivity one could reach.

Unless, of course, quality control at the factories was below reasonable standards. It was the old problem of a widening perspective reducing everything to insignificance, and hence, overloading a complex machine into spinning inaction.

Trinity frowned, set the ruler and the dangling key down. Cold, mineral-hard water from the tap ran until it was reasonably clear, stinging slightly as she splashed her face.

He kissed me.

She folded the thought away. Immediately afterward, he'd looked... She couldn't find the proper word. Blue eyes dark and wondering, his wounded nose crusted with drying blood, a high flush on his cheeks. None of them added up to any expression she could name.

Even now, she was having difficulty. He was disgusted by her cold logic; she obviously irritated him.

And there was the Moritz operation.

The urge to confess was irrational, but powerful. Lying, even by omission, consumed energy.

Lying to Bronson was easy. You simply stopped speaking.

The problem now, Trinity decided, was that she *wanted* to speak. Cal had slipped off grid as soon as he could during the pursuit and gone to warn Six and Candless of the danger. Both agents had been slated for liquidation and autopsy, and Candless, too, since Bronson had by that point been losing control and trying to regain it the only way he knew how— liquidate and cut it off, seal and disinfect, with the bonus of feeling like a big man because he was giving orders.

Handing out death from on high had pleased him immensely.

She could still feel his greasy hair in her hands when she slammed his head against the table, hard enough to break his nose and render him unconscious or at least dazed for a significant period of time. Then she had guided Candless out—but the woman had refused to leave without Six and Cal. Even if Trinity had left her there, Candless would have kept searching for the two male agents until she was caught and liquidated.

They were, as far as Trinity could tell, all three the same, obeying those strange directives that had nothing to do with logic. Emotional noise made them risk mission objectives in unacceptable ways.

Of course, she had risked her own objectives by rescuing Candless—*Holly*—and for what?

Trinity raised her head, stared into the mirror. Time in the sun, however short, had brought out lighter streaks in her hair. Dye always lost its hold; maybe she should blame that on the virus, the way the color flaked off the hair shaft, little bits of camouflage shed everywhere. Forensic dandruff.

Her pupils dilated slightly. Windows to the soul, they were called.

Could you have a soul after induction? Ridiculous, to waste time on such a philosophical—

Her skin tightened. Consciousness of danger brought her swiftly upright. She listened intently, all metaphysical quandaries taking a backseat to survival. *What is that?*

There were certain sensory thresholds even the virus couldn't break. Often, in debrief, the agents spoke of instinct, and Trinity had decided it was simply calculations going too quickly for waking consciousness to latch on to. But the body knew and prepared.

A faint unsound. Fine hairs on her nape bristling. She dug in her pocket for an elastic and pulled her hair back. Scooped up the ruler and stopped by the door. The layout of the store was clear behind her eyelids; she unlocked the door with soundless, gentle fingers and pressed the lever down. Pushed the door open a fraction, peering out through the crack, easing it through the particular point where the hinges would dry-squeak. Her nostrils flared, her entire body a taut string.

Air-conditioning. Floor wax. Spilled cola dried to a sticky residue. A thread of acrid testosterone, aggression and fury spiked with a metallic tang. She sniffed, quietly, cautiously.

Drug. Methamphetamine based, male subject, sweating, high level of emotional excitement.

She pushed the door a little farther open.

The yell, when it came, was so sudden and surprising she almost twitched. "Give me the money!"

"Wha— Oh, man, okay. Okay, man. Just calm down." High, squeaky note of fear in the cashier's voice.

A robbery. Trinity sniffed again, her nostrils flaring. Too much adrenaline and an odd gritty tang to the smell.

Gunfire. The subject had fired at something recently.

The testosterone reek spiked, aggression ramping itself up even though the clerk's scent was submissive and terrified.

This will not end well.

She eased through the door, protected from sight by a rack of soda—a brief flashing memory of Tengermann falling over the endcap almost distracted her. She glided down the aisle.

A stocky back, the man wore a ski mask and a long-sleeved plaid shirt even in this suffocating heat. His jeans had motor-oil stains near the cuffs, and she smelled recent violence on him, along with a queer, brassy note. One she found she could place with no trouble at all.

Death.

The boy at the counter emptied the cash register drawer with clawed, stiff fingers. Change bounced, chiming, on the floor, forgotten. He held out a wad of paper money, shaking so hard he almost blurred. "That's it, take it."

"Don't you tell me what to do! You got more, I know you got a safe!"

"I can't open it! It's, you know, it's timed!" Squeak-breaking, the kid's voice bounced off the ceiling. Trinity glanced toward the windows—there was the truck at the pumps, and a dusty, low-slung Camaro pulled up in front of the store's glass doors, still running. An accomplice? Perhaps. Her grip on the ruler firmed, she slid forward silently in her well-broken-in boots. There were weapons on any shelf, but with the advantage of surprise, she didn't need anything other than hands and feet.

And, well, the ruler.

She was almost within range when the robber leveled the gun. He smelled blond, a light note almost vanishing under the haze of drugs, fury and whatever else was impelling him. "Wrong answer," the man hissed, and Trinity blurred forward, dropping to the floor and sliding, her foot flicking out to apply sideways pressure to the robber's knee with a swift, shattering *crack*.

The shot went wide, the clerk yelled, and the robber's scream rose and broke in harmony. *How interesting.*

Balance regained after the critical strike moment, but the man still had the gun, and the drugs in him gave him a temporary boost to reaction time. He swung wildly, and Trinty leaned back, avoiding the strike, then darted forward, her knee ramming against his temple while she lunged across his body to keep the firearm down and away. The gun went skittering wide, and there was a solid *tchuk* as she drove the ruler through the robber's outstretched hand, calculations of velocity and trajectory flooding her head.

With enough speed, you could drive a straw into concrete. It was fascinating—and disturbing—to see a similar feat performed.

The robber howled, and Trinity was over him and up in one lithe movement, the gun in her hands. A .45 ACP, good stopping power and low muzzle blast, but a larger frame. Heavy and showy, with low magazine count. Its factory specifications flashed

through her head and away, as well as the small bits
of evidence that the piece was not well-maintained.

Her mouth was dry. She considered the man
writhing on the floor. The ski mask was rumpled,
yanked up to show blond stubble and pitted acne
scars on his chin, his mouth a wet loose O and his
pierced hand flailing toward his chest, a bright star
of blood, the key jangling madly at the end of the
ruler and twinkling merrily.

Liquidate or leave?

She hesitated between the two options. Liquidat-
ing him with his own gun had a certain appeal. Did
this place have video surveillance? Footage of her
would give Division a lead.

The bell on the door jangled, a wave of blue-
tinged musk rolling in. She didn't bother to look up
from the man writhing on the floor, stabbing himself in the chest repeatedly with the ruler. She had,
she saw, driven it completely through his hand. An
excess of force, or had she simply, coldly calculated
the relative density of flesh and metacarpals?

She couldn't tell.

"You hurt?" Cal pitched the words loud enough
to break through the robber's screaming. She shook
her head, the gun steady.

Liquidate or leave? She opened her mouth to ask,
but he stepped to her side, took the gun and glanced
over the countertop at the cowering clerk, who had
urinated on himself, a sudden sharp fearful smell.

Common response, the body's reaction to fight-

or-flight hormones. Her hands dropped to her sides, combat readiness fading. In its wake, a wave of harsh, temporary exhaustion, bodily systems struggling for balance.

Cal checked the gun, quiet clicking lost under the noise. A remote expression slid over his face, closed-off and chill. Maybe it was the look he wore in the middle of a mission, or maybe he was, again, disgusted by her.

Who wouldn't be?

He waited until the robber had to stop to hitch in a breath. "Go out to the truck. Wait for me."

There was no reason not to, so she did, stepping outside into the breathless heat. A shudder passed through her. *Change in temperature,* she thought, dully. And the leftover chemical reactions, the virus eating waste products and overproduction of adrenaline. *Breathe. Necessary to oxygenate the brain during and after combat, aids decision making and...*

Calculations froze. She didn't want to perform them. There was another noise inside her head, a dark rushing. A memory trembled just under the surface of consciousness, retreated into a deathly haze.

The Camaro was running, but nobody was inside. She crossed to the shade of the pumps, calmly opened the truck's door and clambered into a ghost of air-conditioning still lingering in the cab. It wouldn't stay cool for long, though.

Her cheeks were wet. Her hands, dropped into her lap, curled into fists.

Liquidate or leave?

Standard protocol would be to liquidate both robber and witness, to cover her tracks. Disable whatever surveillance footage they had, then vanish and forget the casualties left behind.

And yet she hadn't. It wasn't that she couldn't kill; she'd shot Bronson.

It was that she didn't *want* to, and the uncertainty had crippled the smooth execution of what should have been simple, textbook. Another symptom of deconstruction?

What would she be without logic and calculation for guidance? How did normal people decide what to *do* with all this noise in their heads, their bodies, their…souls? Was that the proper word?

She couldn't tell.

Trinity came to with her forehead on the dash, breathing slowly and deeply. She didn't move when the driver's door opened. The engine roused, cool air began pumping through the vents, and she could not lift her head. If she did, he would see the damp spots.

A plastic bag crackled between them, and he dug in it as the truck accelerated onto a ribbon of two-lane highway flanked by pawnshops and trailer courts. "Here." Soft and quiet.

Cardboard. A sharp corner.

It was a box of tissues. Trinity squeezed her eyes shut, her nose full of wet stuffy heat. He drove for a little while in silence, then his hand landed softly on her back. Slid up, and a warm hard palm cupped Trinity's nape.

He drove like that for a little while, until she was able to uncurl a little. Then he took his hand away, but the heat of it remained.

"Put your seat belt on," he said, and the cab was brimful of a new silence between them.

She couldn't measure its dimensions, so she simply blew her nose and kept her mouth shut as the miles rolled by.

She wouldn't talk. Just nodded when he finally decided the numb quiet had gone on long enough.

"We're over the border early tomorrow." He peered at the glittering of El Paso's lights out the windshield, shimmering as they rose to engulf the pickup. From the south, those lights probably looked like the promised land, blurring from Juárez into the milk and honey of El Norte.

Or maybe not. Maybe from the south it looked like Las Vegas, glitter on top and dirt underneath, everyone grubbing for a worm. A poisonous, carnivorous carnival. The Chevy bounced as he cut the wheel, and the faux-adobe hotel rose up to block out the lights and all fun little imaginative thoughts.

His mouth just kept on going. "There's a place I know, over the border. Killer food, a couple cervezas, we can celebrate getting away. I'll bet you burn instead of tan, but we'll hang out by the pool. You can even have those fruity drinks with umbrellas, if you want." *I'm babbling.*

What else could he do, though? Realizing the black Camaro at the gas station door was still idling, his nape roughening instinctively and seeing her standing over the writhing would-be robber on the floor, the gun in her hands and that horrified, shell-shocked expression... Jesus.

Yet one more thing she shouldn't have had to deal with. One more thing he should have been there to handle instead.

When he cut the engine, even the radio's soft static died, and they were left with a ticking quiet full of sharp edges. He'd dealt with all sorts of responses to sudden violence—tears, shock, screaming. Trinity's staring quiet was a new one, and he found out he didn't like it. There wasn't even the sense of her listening, of quiet attention, and now he realized he missed it.

You could get used to something like that pretty quickly, a woman's soft listening. It was almost seductive.

Even slack and eye-glazed, she was beautiful. The elastic had come loose, and her ponytail was messy, a small detail, but it disproportionally bothered him. Her hands, folded together and white-knuckled, didn't move. Her backpack slumped at her feet. It was like having a life-size, breathing doll in the passenger seat.

Or a ghost.

"Trinity." He touched her shoulder, swallowing hard, and quelled the urge to shift uncomfortably. It was a hell of a time to have hormones distracting him. "Honey, you're safe. Nothing's going to hurt you."

A tiny flicker of a shrug. Well, at least that was something. Her profile didn't change.

"Hey." He polished her shoulder with his palm, the heavy white cotton button-down well washed, living warmth underneath. "You saved that kid's life, you know."

She murmured something, her lips moving almost soundlessly.

"What, sweetheart?" The sun was going down, but it wasn't getting any cooler out there. This place looked as if it had decent AC, at least. There was even a pool, shimmering blue and innocent behind a chain-link barricade, its white enamel sides probably still warm. The roof tiles, nice and red, would be baking still. He imagined again what she'd look like in a bikini, and that didn't do a single thing to help him get his mind back to business.

As graceful as she was, she'd be a good swimmer.

That thought wasn't guaranteed to lower his blood pressure, either.

A little louder now. Her lips were alarmingly pale. "Liquidate or leave?" The words were very soft; he had to strain even his virus-acute hearing. "I couldn't calculate. Too much."

"Yeah, well, I told the kid to wait for us to leave

and hit the silent alarm. He gave me a look like I was stupid. Guess he had to call the cops the old-fashioned way."

"The risk of—"

"Which is why we're crossing with a crowd tomorrow. They're too wary at night."

"Surveillance footage—"

"Honey, the cameras were dummies. Kid might even say he stabbed the robber himself, and I gave him the gun. He won't be able to remember what either of us looks like, he was pissing himself. *Literally.* So what if you were thinking about protocols and you almost pulled the trigger before you thought about it? You didn't, and that's what matters. It's like they never sent you into the field."

Her expression changed minutely.

"They didn't?" He kept feeling as if he was getting socked in the gut around her. "Oh, man. Was that your first... It can't be."

"The escape..." A little stronger now. "The escape was my first real live-combat scenario. Since then, I've simply avoided capture."

"Didn't they train you?"

"I took modified agent training so I could predict and calculate. Too valuable for fieldwork." A tiny shudder, a guitar string vibrating under aching tension. "They think a woman can't kill."

Huh. Each time he thought he'd found the limit of her bravery, she surprised him again.

"It just takes a lot more to get them there." He scrubbed at his face, almost forgetting he had the key in his palm, rubbing the warm metal across his cheek. His stubble rasped. "Your first time…it's normal. To feel this way."

"I don't feel," she whispered, but she slumped back against the seat. "I assess, I plan, I calculate."

She sounded so lost he wanted to unclick her seat belt, pull her across the center console and hold her in his lap. Stroke her hair, say something comforting and breathe her in until that fragile, tense expression faded. "Looks like you're feeling it from out here, sugar pop."

"Deconstruction." She dropped her gaze, stared at her white-knuckled hands. "I can't function. That's *dangerous*."

"You can, though." Inspiration struck. "I'll teach you. And if I can't, Reese sure as hell can. He was their golden boy, right? Low emotional noise, high mission fidelity. Right? But he was feeling the noise all the time. We can *help* you."

"I'm a danger to all—"

"Maybe. But I'm not exactly in this game to play safe, sweetheart. Come on. Let's check in and find you something to eat."

That managed to get a response. She made a small movement, as if she wanted to crumple, and he ached to catch her. *Let me in. Let me help.* But she pulled herself back into rigidity, and a quick flare of instinct told him not to attempt touching her. She was wound so goddamn tight she might shatter.

"I don't think I can." She lifted her chin a little, with that heartbreaking, transparent determination.

"Let's try." He reached into her lap, touched her knuckles. It took some doing to prize her hands apart, to stroke her delicate, capable fingers until they relaxed. When she glanced up at him, those huge dark eyes wide and her lashes matted with salt dampness, he almost leaned over and kissed her again. *Cool down, boyo. Pressure from you is the very last thing she needs.* "Okay? You can try, right?" He slid his fingers through hers, held her left hand. She squeezed, suddenly, with surprising strength.

"I'll try." A little color flushing back into those exquisite lips. Her ponytail was still loose, and fine strands of gold had worked free. A last flush of sunset filled the pickup's cab, lighting her eyes and hair, and Cal lost all his breath.

She was goddamn *beautiful*. All the way through.

I didn't expect that. God. "Good girl," he managed with numb lips. "I, uh. Yeah. Let's go check in. I would have stopped sooner, but—"

"We needed distance. Resting now increases our chances of success tomorrow. Yes." Her shoulders squared, and she set her jaw. Did she know how vulnerable she looked? Probably not.

Jesus. They have her convinced any emotion at all is going to kill her.

It made him wonder more and more about this "induction" process.

And why the other agents, all male, hadn't survived it.

It took some coaxing, but she demolished a room-service club sandwich, and the fries, as well—which she seemed extremely pleased by. He risked the steak, and while it wasn't great, it wasn't bad, either, and satisfied the requirements for a protein load to keep him—and his viral load—functioning tip-top.

Her first taste of sweet tea was accompanied with such an expression of mystified shock he had to laugh, and her slight, tentative smile in return made something in his chest blow up like a balloon. He very carefully didn't ask her any more questions, and when she eased down onto the bed, stretching out atop the duvet and not unlacing her boots, he didn't say anything, just set the tray out in the hall.

She was asleep before he shut the door again. He'd coaxed her into washing her hands and face; tomorrow she'd want a shower.

Now, *there* was a thought. Unfortunately, it wasn't the kind guaranteed to calm him down. It just wound him a little tighter, too.

A little? No. A lot. Cal leaned against the wall next to the closet, let out a long slow breath. So far, so good.

Except it's not. She's convinced she's going to die. And you, you're not a psych head-monkey. All you know how to do is interrogate and infiltrate. There was nothing in the training about how to deal with a fragile, traumatized woman who smelled like heaven and kept reaching for a gun he was very, very careful to leave nowhere near her. She didn't look so thin and tired now.

The urge to sink down on the bed next to her was overwhelming. It was about to drive him out of his goddamn mind, especially since he'd got close enough to get a mouthful of her. Granted, it was full of blood, and she hadn't said a word about it since…

Well, to be fair, neither had he. You could talk about threat ratios, induction, scenarios or the chemical composition of sweet tea, but asking a girl what she thought of you getting that close was another thing entirely. It wasn't like with Tracy, or an infiltrate target, or the Army or whoever keeping their agents supplied with a head-clearing function, like psych evals or immunizations.

The trouble was, Cal wasn't moving her smoothly through the maze, knowing when to push and when to let go, the little machine inside his head that never stopped assessing how easy other people were to affect going haywire. He didn't want her *affected*, he wanted her…

Well, *honestly*. Except that was a handicap in this situation.

The trouble was, you couldn't ever be sure if someone else really liked you or if you'd pushed them in just the right way. It was just so *easy*. Even before the virus, in those dim memories, seen through a filter of only-normal senses, it had been easy. It probably hadn't been any physical talents that got him into the program. Just that machine, the cold hard *how can I get what I want* and the willingness to follow through.

And the rage.

Funny, though, the longer he breathed her in, the calmer he felt. Unless he thought about what they'd done to her. Or what that stupid, small-time meth-head might have done to her.

It was no use. He was stepping, softly and quietly, over harsh hotel carpet. Even in the swanky places it was the same easily cleaned nylon.

She deserves more.

Tracy had, too. The world was full of people who deserved more. Pretty goddamn arrogant to think he could do anything about that.

"I want to, though." His own voice startled him. Trinity stirred slightly, turning over, crushing the pillow. She'd worked it out from under the duvet.

That felt like a small victory. Maybe next, he'd get her to sleep under the blankets. Cal took another deep, searching breath. He couldn't smell anything wrong with her. A healthy blue haze, full of the clean, beautiful tinge of a pretty woman, stress and tension draining away.

Can't save the world, Cal. You just focus on keeping her safe. Check the parking lot again.

He did. And kept telling himself, over and over again, that the right thing to do wasn't lying down next to her, no matter *how* badly he wanted to.

Until he gave up and stretched himself on the edge of the bed, listening to her breathe.

Noah Caldwell let out a long, soft breath. Bay hadn't made his last check-in, but that wasn't uncommon on live missions. The agent had spent twelve hours in a high-security ward, machines beeping and booping in surprise over his vitals, and awakened ready to execute more orders. Caldwell had skipped the medical clearance—if the man was ambulatory, he was fine. At least, so the eggheads swore, with all their talk about vectors, mitochondrial uptake, enhanced healing and the benefits of the induction process.

Speaking of eggheads...

"I'm really not supposed to," Robbie Kingswell said, blinking owlishly. "I mean, I could get in real trouble."

The red button on the desk phone was flashing. It was Control calling, but the old man could wait. Caldwell kept his expression interested and calm. "Not if you hand it over to me right now, sir. I'll take care of it." *Just give me the goddamn briefcase.*

Kingswell, a virology control specialist, had access to the vials of raw viral serum. For a few hours, he and Control had both thought Bay would need another shot of the serum to jolt the healing factor even further into overdrive. So Kingswell had been scrambled out to the base and jolted in a Humvee to the county hospital, arriving just as Bay's vitals

smoothed out. The serum, in a small briefcase cuffed
to his wrist, was unnecessary.

At least, as far as Control was concerned.

"But you don't have the *forms*," Kingswell repeated. "If I go back and I don't have the forms, I
could lose my security clearance. My job."

"No, you won't." Sweat prickled under Caldwell's
arms, along his lower back, in every crevice. It made
him long for the simplicity of just shooting someone. "It's being requisitioned. I have the paperwork
right here. You're being relieved of it. We'll send
you on vacation to thank you for coming out here
in such a hurry. Really, that showed amazing flexibility. You're to be commended."

The scientist actually clutched the black briefcase
to his chest, his eyes swimming behind Coke-bottle
glasses. He was handsome, in an unremarkable, weedy
way, though Caldwell wouldn't let a man under his
command sport a soul patch under his bottom lip.

It just looked too damn fruity, especially when
the rest of the egghead was marathon-runner lean.

"I don't know." Kingswell wavered.

Caldwell swallowed impatience. In the end, the
forms had to be signed in triplicate, but when the
scientist left, his wrist was naked and he was without
the little black suitcase. Armed guards would take
him to an airfield, and by the time the dumbass realized something was wrong he'd have already disappeared into the black hole of extraordinary rendition.

Control wouldn't like it, but Noah Caldwell didn't

give much of a shit about that at the moment. The red light on the phone began blinking again, and Caldwell glanced around the stupid little office commandeered in this crappy little Southwestern fake-adobe town. Control was sitting pretty in Virginia, while Caldwell ran around and did the dirty work, cleaning up after Control's cronies.

There was a time to let go, Noah Caldwell told himself.

It wasn't quite yet, but it was fast approaching.

How many offices like this had he sat in, with Control calling from the cushioned nest? How many times had he smoothed over misunderstandings with local law enforcement, finagled resources and got nothing but a *that could have been better, son* in return?

One time too many, goddammit.

The briefcase went under the desk; Caldwell put his wingtips on either side of it and picked up the phone. Before he punched the accept-call button, though, he dumped the forms he and Kingswell had wrangled over for the past few hours into an industrial-sized shredder crouching to his right. It chewed the paper into oblivion with a brief blurring buzz, and Noah braced himself.

"What the hell's going on out there?" Control's smoke-roughened rasp had become worse.

"Agent Bay is active, local resources are being minimally used, and all is proceeding as planned." The lies rolled smoothly off his tongue. "There's some heat from a chicken-fried Feeb agent, but he's been sidelined."

"Yeah, well, he had a friend in DC asking uncomfortable questions."

Interesting. "How uncomfortable?"

"Nothing that couldn't be handled, but I have to tell you, the investors are worried."

Of course. The all-holy investors. "It's only a matter of time before Bay brings in Three. Then the program has two stable, viable subjects. Right?"

"Let's hope so," Control said darkly. "Try not to throw any more wrenches into DC's works, all right?"

"Yes, sir." *You sonofabitch. As if stonewalling a high-ranking FBI creep is anything close to the running around I'm doing here, to protect your goddamn investors.*

He'd gotten into this whole thing to serve his country. Now Caldwell was thinking for the first time that maybe the whole heap deserved to sink beneath the waves of its own ignorance, not to mention laziness.

If you couldn't serve the good old American way, though, what else was left?

His ankles caressed the briefcase while Control nattered on into his ear. Caldwell made all the right noises, soothed the old man and finally hung up. He sat there for a long while, in the windowless office, his socks and trouser hems brushing the briefcase sides. Cold-packed and insulated, the vial inside was just waiting to unload its cargo into a syringe. Noah had studied the injection protocols; he knew what to do.

The virus made them stronger, smarter, faster, better. Caldwell was owed some recompense for his services. And when Bay brought Three in alive and well, he'd have all sorts of leverage.

Enough to get him everything he deserved.

Noah Caldwell smiled. He could, he was sure, find a clean syringe.

The dream is always the same. It is the forest, aqueous green light bathing ferns and scant under-brush, and it is peaceful because she is hiking up the hill toward her car. She's decided she will tell him no, that she's done as he wanted all her life but this one thing she will not do.

Swiping at her forehead, flushed and smiling, she hops nimbly between stones. She's always found solace in the greenness, the hush and then the chatter as the animals accepted her intrusion and went about their business. It had always been her escape from the strained breathlessness of the house, with regimented corners never out of place and regulations so tight even a stray hair is enough to earn that paralyzing stare.

Discipline, *he always says*. Make it your watchword, my dear. *The warm approval when she sometimes measures up never quite balances out the cold chill of disappointment when she doesn't.*

The military, actually, was much more forgiving. Even for a girl.

Any moment now she will reach the trailhead and see him standing next to her old but lovingly maintained Volvo. That had been her first defiance, refusing to buy a new car when he made one of his broad hints that she could surely afford better if she saved a little. She will see the soldiers, standing in dusty sunshine with full kit and live ammo, and the confusion will carry her out of the woods until they stand in a loose ring around her, and he says It's time to go now, my dear. *The objections will dry up in her throat and a lifetime's habit of obedience will make her docile until she asks* What about my car? *and one of them laughs, a short sharp cough of male amusement, and she understands too late that he hadn't really asked her to sign up for the experiment because he cared what she thought. Instead, it was a mere formality; she's going to make up for the error of not being the son he always wanted, and it's going to start now...*

She swam toward the surface of sleep; the darkness was soft, but not deep enough. The heaviness on the mattress beside her was not quite right, but it soothed her. An arm around her waist, slack and familiar. He made a soft sound, a low rumble, and the words made little sense.

You're safe, he murmured into her hair. It felt so

natural, and she tried to think of why before sleep claimed her again.

She half woke once more, when he moved slightly and his knees bumped the back of hers. There was no sense of confinement. Instead, it felt as if a heavy shield had been placed over her, enough room to breathe in absolute security. The nightmare hadn't driven her to the television, free-associating desperately to stave off the hideous bleakness of fear.

Yes. *Fear.* Feeling.

Safezone. He makes the bad go away. The thought spun slowly inside her brain, then drifted lazily away as she fell back into rest.

The third time Trinity lay for a few moments between sleep and waking, before consciousness of the sound assumed its proper importance inside her skull.

A car door slamming. Well, it was a hotel, that was common—but too heavy, too crisp, too definite for the middle of the night. Something else, roughening her back into gooseflesh, the hollows behind her knees and before her elbows prickling, sweat glands tingling as full consciousness returned with a jolt. Cal moved, too, and the sudden coolness without his steady warmth chilled her far more deeply than it should.

She sat up, reaching for the gun—again, there wasn't one on the night table. Habit, that double-edged tool. It could save your life or force you into a fatal mistake.

Cal, a tall, messy-haired shadow, drifted silently across the room to the window. "You heard that." A whisper, but definitely not a question.

Trinity nodded. Then she realized his back was to her. "Yes." The dry little word from her dry lips fell into the quiet, vanishing without a ripple.

"I don't like this." He peered carefully between the curtains, a slit left open to provide a view of the parking lot, carefully not touching them. "Hinky as hell."

"We should move." She was already on her feet. Her pillow, a crumpled pale ghost, spilled to the floor.

"Hang on. Let's just think things through." His calm was infectious, warring with the clear, undeniable instinct sparking through every nerve.

She actually shifted her weight from foot to foot, hitching her backpack higher on her shoulders, her mouth full of sleep and the syrupy bite of danger. In a few moments she would start actually *hopping* back and forth with something very much like impatience.

So she slid her other arm through the second backpack strap and headed for the door. Two quick flicks of her hand had it unlocked; she pushed the handle down silently—

"Let me." His hand closed over hers, and he pushed her back, carefully. She let him, retying the button-down around her torso with swift efficiency.

She felt…clear. Rested. So good, in fact, she found

it troubling. Was she simply losing acuity, or did his presence somehow halt deconstruction?

I'm not exactly in this game to play it safe.

How had he managed to stretch out on the bed without her noticing? Sleeping through such a thing was inconceivable for an agent. She wanted to ask, but the restlessness all over her skin mounted another notch.

Cal checked the hall, sniffed. Tensed just a little, and his own scent took on a much darker, colder undertone. His left hand stiffened, his fingers spreading, and he pushed her back even farther, his touch gentle against her breastbone.

His left hand was suddenly full of a very nice 9mm, dull finish, no extended magazine.

So that's where he hid it. Calculations sparked inside her skull. *This is very bad.*

He checked the hall again and moved, Trinity right behind him despite his obvious desire to leave her in the room. It was either chivalry or trying to keep her bottled so she didn't escape while he dealt with whatever problem was looming in the very near future.

Trinity sniffed cautiously, and her eyes widened. Male, dark haired, and with a peculiar, very familiar tang of burning metal and pain to the strong, soaking, mildly unpleasant scent.

It was another agent. And that metallic note, the burning and painful nose-rasping, was so familiar because she'd carried it herself for a few months.

It was the scent of surviving induction.

Trinity *moved*.

A quick strike upward; Cal blocked it, but her other hand twisted the gun out of his grip—he wasn't expecting trouble from her quarter. She ducked away from his grab, her reaction time much quicker than his, especially operating at full capacity now.

"Go!" she whisper-hissed, then ran, the entire world slowing down as her body called on every erg of virus-soaked speed it had access to. At the end of the hall, the door to the stairwell was opening by slow, silent degrees, and a stray current of air-conditioning had brought the scent to Trinity's sensitive nose.

There was a certain relief in acting too swiftly for second thoughts.

Sliding, carpet burning against her jeans as she hit the door to the stairs, slamming it back into the attacker with enough force to break a bone. Only a temporary measure, her left foot jammed under the lever and her shoulders providing just enough friction to stop her. He was against the door, pushing it closed, probably guessing her next move. Still, the angle was good, and she cast quick glances left and right, the terrain springing into relief inside her head. *Forty percent chance he's alone; a net would alert us too soon. Calculate likely position.*

The gun jerked up as information flooded her. She squeezed off a shot; a chunk of the door evaporated and silence was no longer necessary. She rolled aside, waiting for the reply—he didn't shoot back, simply yanked the door aside and barreled through. Black hair, wide shoulders, slightly shorter than Cal, navy canvas jacket and jeans, engineer boots that probably gave him less secure footing but also protected his ankles to a higher degree. A faint sheen on his temples, his metabolism running high, and the dust-hot night outside still clinging to him.

A perfect shot from this angle, Trinity on her back parallel to the wall and her arms braced, the gun unwavering and her whole hand tightening, *squeeze don't pull*, the shooting range and its beautiful collection of angle, trajectory, velocity spinning inside her head.

Cal arrived, striking the other agent, and Trinity's arm jerked, throwing the second shot wide to avoid hitting him. *Chances of another shot just dropped 70 percent.* Irritation flashed through her and away, so she took the next best option, her foot pistoning— the knees were easy to take out, but the other agent was already moving, ducking the strike Cal intended for his throat and taking himself effectively out of Trinity's strike range.

Stupid men. She could have solved the whole situation. Trinity pulled her knees up, threw her feet out and fish-jumped upright; Cal drove the other agent back into the doorway, the two of them deadly silent except for exhalations of effort and strike impacts, both of them fairly equally matched in speed. Cal

was taller, his reach longer, but if the other agent
had survived induction, his abilities were a question
mark at best, and—

Just as she calculated the angle least likely to
cause injury to Cal, again, he dropped his weight
and rammed forward, tumbling them both out toward the stairs. It was a positively *idiotic* move, one
no trained agent should have even contemplated.

The question of *why* he'd done so was a complex
matter she had no resources for at the moment. Was
he deconstructing, as well?

Analyze. Diving in unprepared held very little
chance of success, and even less of helping Cal in
the confined space. She still hurried through the
doorway, concrete walls and floor, metal banisters,
rolling—they had gone down an entire floor and
were now on the second landing below her. Dim
lighting, the greasy humidity of sweating concrete.
Scuffling, more strikes, bouncing around and giving
her a fairly accurate idea of the dimensions of the
stairwell. Her pulse was high and hard, her breathing
rolling in deep round swells, and she was sweating
lightly, all well within combat tolerances.

Another gunshot roared, its brief flash lighting the stairwell for a moment. No whine of a ricochet, just a soft thudding as a body poured down
the stairs. A sharp copper reek of blood, and everything inside Trinity jolted sideways, all calculation
stopped for a single tearing moment.

Oh, God. A disjointed, illogical thought, a copper tang on her tongue, her heart terrified-leaping as her pupils dilated, every edge and crack standing out in sharp relief. She clattered down the stairs, the manshape on the landing rearing up in front of her—and she caught Cal as he almost fell, his bloody hand reaching vainly for the banister.

"Jesus," he whispered. "Come on, that won't keep him forever."

"You're injured." She ducked under his arm, relief at his survival warring with an unsteady, explosive weight inside her chest.

"He got me." Strained, uneven, he almost fell over again; Trinity dragged him up the stairs. "I got him, too, though. He'd not going to walk until that heals… *Ah*." A short, coughing bark of pain. "Need another exit."

"You're bleeding too much. We have to—"

"Get *out* of here now. First aid *later*."

Of course, he picked this particular moment to be logical. Trinity hauled him upright again, her fingers curled around his belt. He still had the gun, keeping it carefully pointed down and away even when he almost toppled. Trinity took a deep breath, her legs turned back into obedient pistons, and they spilled out through the doorway into the hall they had just vacated less than two minutes ago. Small scurrying sounds all around—too much noise, the hotel would rapidly become an untenable morass of witnesses. She propped Cal against the wall, took two steps away and yanked the fire alarm handle so hard the metal tab wrenched free; she tossed it back into the stairwell and ignored the resultant whooping and braying. Cal, his face graven, stared at her, his blue eyes too dark because his pupils were dilated, too.

He looked much smaller, his left hand clamped to his thigh, blood welling between his fingers. His lips moved, and she had no trouble deciphering the words.

Get out of here. Go.

She could, she supposed. It might even be the most logical, efficient path. She might even be able to return to Felicitas and retrieve fragments of her records before she died.

Why are you helping me? Holly Candless had asked, shivering with shock, pale and rumpled.

Because I might be next, Trinity had essentially replied, but that was not the whole truth, because the truth was too frightening to bear conscious examination.

Trinity glanced down the hall, back at the stairway door, closing with majestic slowness.

First, she decided, he was going to need a tourniquet and his own backpack.

Then she was going to get him out of here.

Cal faded in and out for a little while, every small movement a spear rammed through his leg again. It had grazed bone but missed the femoral artery, luckiest shot of the week, but he wasn't feeling as lucky as he could have.

Especially since he was alone in the cab of the blue Chevy pickup, it was dark as sin, and he suspected he'd lost a *lot* of blood.

It isn't so bad. Better than Kiev. Playing catch-me with both the Ukrainians and Moscow's hatchet boys had been interesting, complex and almost fatal even for him. Time shivered, threatened to fold over and trap him in the train depot, a Soviet-era pile of concrete and rebar, his contacts gone up in smoke and the entire city a hostile zone. Then coming home, the standard psych eval and other nonsense, and Tracy's messages…*getting worried about you, Stephen, can you give me a call?*

He hadn't even told her his name. She'd died believing him Stephen Martell.

"Don't…" A cracked whisper. "Don't go." Who was he asking? Trinity had probably left him here; it was a smart move on her part. Why she'd bothered to haul him out of the hotel and into the truck, the bleeding slowing but not nearly rapidly enough, was a mystery. He'd lost the world for a little bit, then when he came back, he was in this choking absolute darkness, the passenger seat of the truck pushed as far back as it could.

Don't go.

It was ridiculous, really. The world was a merry-go-round; you just held on to your own horse and tried not to puke. Reaching out for anything else in the whirl, even someone right next to you for a few turns, was an idiot's move. You'd lose your own grip, and the machine would chew you to shreds.

Sounds. Metal clashing. He cast around for a weapon. His backpack was somewhere around here, it had to be, he could remember her grabbing it—or maybe she'd taken his gear and liquid resources, too. Had she thought he was dead, or just...

A faint edge of light appeared, snuffed out. Christ, it was dark. Where the hell had she parked him? At least she hadn't left him on the side of the road. Charitable girl that she was. He couldn't blame her— it was a smart, logical, absolutely textbook move.

His door opened, letting in a burst of stuffy air full of motor oil and rust. He struck out blindly, and she slapped the feeble punch away. "It's me." Low and husky, and her smell rolled over him in a wave. She'd been sweating a little, and the iron-tang of approaching desert dawn clung to her, as well. Gleams from her dark green eyes, her hair a softly rumpled mess, a dark T-shirt instead of the tank top and white button-down. She propped him back up in the seat, peeled blood-crusted denim away from his thigh and clicked her tongue slightly. "Good. It's closing up."

"You came back." He didn't mean to sound like a five-year-old, wondering at a magic trick.

"I had to get supplies." The slight crackling was a pair of Walmart bags. "Fresh clothes. Food, water. We're going to cross as soon as you can walk."

"Listen to you." He cleared his throat; she produced a bottle of Evian, held it to his lips as if he was a child. Blessed coolness slid down his throat. He hadn't realized he was so parched. He coughed a little when she took it away. "You don't even know where we're going."

She cocked her head, looking up at him, her fingers probing at the wound. It had closed, but it was still angry and tender, and he'd rip the fragile tissue if he moved too quickly. He'd limp, and that would make him stand out. A limping man and a very pretty woman, just the sort of pair that would stick in someone's memory. "Perhaps that's why I returned."

He opened his mouth to tell her that was a lie, but a fractional lift of one corner of her beautiful mouth socked him right in the gut. "Did you just make a joke?"

"Logic does not preclude humor." She returned her attention to the wound. "You'll have to eat, to speed the healing. I brought greens and cheese sticks. Vitamin C tablets and a jar of peanut butter, too. Those, with some sliced jicama, will give you the required nutrients."

"Great."

She paused for a moment, thinking. "Now you're being sarcastic." Did she actually sound *amused*?

"I hate greens."

"I anticipated you might. They're in liquid form."

"Oh, that's so much better." *She doesn't just smell good. This woman's flat-out amazing.*

"Or you could deny yourself the nutrients, and—"

"Hey."

"What?" She looked up again, and his left hand found the back of her head, fingers tangling in her honey hair. He pulled her forward, and his mouth met hers again.

This time there wasn't a mouthful of blood in the way. She tasted of healthy effort and darkness, that blue tinge to her scent deepening, a gasp into his mouth flavored with softness. His fingers tensed, the silk of her hair wrapping around them in a web he never wanted to struggle free of, and he could *feel* the gold in the strands. He pulled her closer, off balance, her hand landing above the wound to brace herself and the pain didn't matter, because she was right there, he was drowning in her and she'd come back for him.

Someone had reached off their own horse on the merry-go-round and steadied *him*.

She broke away, gently enough, but he tried to keep her, kissing the corner of her mouth, her cheek, her chin. Finally, her forehead rested against his, her breathing quick and light. Her pulse was galloping; he could hear it as clearly as his own, and even though he'd probably lost more blood than a man should, some parts of him had somehow found a little extra.

Her hair curtained his face. Her shoulders sagged a little. She leaned into him. For just those few moments, there was something soft in the dark, before she pulled away and began digging in the bags again. He could smell the flush in her cheeks, too, her blood rushing hard and hot.

"Trinity," he breathed.

She didn't say a word.

It was an abandoned gas station on the outskirts of El Paso, a chilly dawn breeze mouthing its corners and the concrete pad out front full of trash, broken glass and rusted hulks stripped of anything even faintly valuable. Any copper fittings had been taken, too. Cal stood aside, wishing he could help as Trinity pushed the rolling door aside a little—it had been chained shut, but the chain was rusty enough she'd pried it open, leaving an antique padlock still intact.

He hobbled through, leaning on her. The truck was too hot now to take through any checkpoint, and he wouldn't be able to run for another day or so.

Trinity pulled the door shut, carefully hung the chain to make it still seem locked and slipped into her backpack. It was cold at the moment, but the pre-dawn hush already held a promise of a day's scorch. "We have a 70 percent chance of crossing without incident."

That high? "Let me guess, it goes down the longer that other agent's alive and working our backtrail."

"Yes." She paused, tilting her head. "I should tell you…"

"Go ahead." He tested his leg again, gingerly. He could hobble. It would get easier as he moved, blood flow working into the muscles and bringing the little swarmies of the virus in to heal and repair. His throat tasted like smashed kale and the grit of jicama, but she was right—it was what his body needed to get back on track. If he was normal, he'd have bled out in the dark even as he broke the other agent with a lucky knee strike that sent him tumbling and bonecracking down the concrete stairs.

Should have put one in his head to be sure.

"The other agent. He smelled…"

For one lunatic moment he was sure she was going to say *he smelled really good*, and everything inside him turned red.

She took a deep breath. Nice of her to nurse him back to health. Cal stiffened, pushing away from the wall.

"He smelled like induction." She caught his elbow, slid her arm around him and draped his over her shoulders. "Here, lean on me. They have perfected the process."

Cal almost staggered. The relief was just as red as the sudden flare of rage. "Huh."

Oblivious, she righted him. "There's a bus stop. It's not far."

"So. That's what it smells like." Cal stood up a little straighter, tested his leg again and decided he could fight if he had to. He was probably reeking of relief, but she appeared not to notice, leaning into his side. "They did that to you?"

She shrugged. "I woke up on the table after the

procedure." She glanced ahead, steering him down a mild, sandy slope. "We'll have to cross an arroyo." She paused. "It's a beautiful word. Very precise."

"Huh?"

"Never mind." She looked down. He was too absorbed in where his feet needed to go, but he wished he could see her expression.

"You like words?"

"The right ones."

"What are the right words?"

She didn't answer. He'd probably said something wrong.

"So, uh. The other agent."

"He had to have been the one in Felicitas." She nodded and hopped slightly, shortening her stride to match his. "I thought he was you."

Well, that wasn't very promising. Was he after them because… Well, who wouldn't want her? She was beautiful, smart, and if she smelled half as good to that black-haired bastard as she did to Cal, there was going to be trouble. "Did he smell like me?"

"What? No." She steadied him, and the arroyo opened up, a yawning crack in the earth. "Here, there's a better way down." Dawn painted the east in streaks, and the faraway hum of traffic was the buzz of a sleepy insect. Gravel crunched underfoot.

"You sure? Maybe he's, ah, looking for you like I…was."

"He must be Project Beta. Increased mission fidelity, low to nil emotional noise. Whether or not he calculates remains to be seen. There are several subsidiary activations he could have instead. The research is inconclusive. Or it was—"

His head was spinning, and it wasn't even from lack of blood. "Project Beta?"

"Gibraltar was only the first stage. There were several outcome proposals. Gemini was a temporary speed bump, nothing more. Induction may halt the mutation. The research is, as I've said, inconclusive, and I can only surmise—"

"Jesus." He almost tripped, but his leg firmed. He straightened, taking his weight off her slim frame. "Who's doing all this?"

"Do you even need to ask? There have been programs ever since the fifties to build a better soldier."

"Yeah, but for what?"

"Bronson took his orders from Control. Who was, as far as I could ascertain, not a congressman or senator. But very close to several of them, perhaps? Some sort of government functionary. The Department of Defense was involved. Private companies, too."

"And we're the ones dying on the ground."

"Omelets and eggs. Control was fond of that aphorism."

"What about you?"

She shook her honey-colored head, her pretty lips pursing. "It doesn't matter."

The hell it doesn't. "Why not?"

"Deconstruction." She paused, then added more.

"Quite simply, I won't survive long enough *for* it to matter."

"We'll see about that."

"I'm not your gemina, Cal."

"You say that like you're sure. You smell *really good*."

"That could be an induction side effect. And in any case…"

"What?"

She shook her head, pressing her lips together even more firmly.

He tried again. "You really have your heart set on dying?"

All he got was a shrug. He couldn't help it, he had to try again. "Don't you feel better? Less headache, you're able to eat, you look a lot better. Your pulse, too. It's just like Reese and Holly. You have to feel it." *You have to feel something.* The emotional noise was all over her.

Even *he* could see it.

She helped him up the other side of the arroyo, still silent. Dust rose from their footsteps.

"Trinity?" *Dammit.* His leg ached. He needed another twelve hours or so before he could move quickly.

"I am *not* your gemina. The odds are simply too high." Quiet, arch finality. "Concentrate on walk-ing."

"You don't like me. Maybe it's my cologne." Maybe he could get her to crack a smile. Women, always stubborn. Her entire body all but screamed at him, his pulse and respiration following hers, that marvelous aroma of hers soaked all through him, and the heart-breaking fragility in the middle of her strength. She probably hadn't even thought twice about diving in to help that boy at the service station, and she'd come back for him, too.

"Cal." Firm and polite. "I am an anomaly, I am deconstructing, and you—and Six and Ms. Candless—are much better off without the danger I represent. Not to mention that I have… I am not entirely blameless, for your…troubles."

What the hell was that supposed to mean? "You did your job, just like we did. Holly's about the only blameless one here, but—"

"Exactly. So you agree."

What? "I don't think you—"

"Shh." Her hip bumped his. "There are civilians at the bus stop."

The stop was a sorry shack that looked made out of driftwood, even though there wasn't a sea around for miles. Wind whistled through the holes, and two old women with seamed, distrustful faces examined them both. He leaned on Trinity, who managed to make it look as if it was the other way round, and every obscenity he'd learned in the Army or anywhere else paraded through his head in a steady stream.

He couldn't even tell where he'd messed up.

* * *

Bay was beginning to doubt his own effectiveness. Twice now he had pursued the most likely avenue to his goal and been balked. Chestnut-haired Miss Frasier had vanished, and his assumption that the secondary target—the blonde Three—would lead him in her direction was, he realized, a product of shock and fuzzy thinking. He had not been medically cleared before leaving Cuartova, but as far as he could tell he was in good physical condition, even if his bones throbbed and he had to chew palmfuls of calcium supplements to fuel remineralization.

It was his mental acuity that seemed to be suffering. A steadily building discomfort pervaded the day he spent holed up in a Motel Six near the eastern edge of El Paso, chewing the calcium tabs and staring at the ceiling when he wasn't studying the laptop he'd stolen from the FBI agent who had brought Miss Frasier to Caldwell's attention.

A beautiful piece of work, top-of-the-line and turbocharged, a solid-state drive and a magsealed power cord lovingly repaired with pink electrical tape. Password-protected and full of illegal software to break, decrypt, hack and infect with abandon, it was also, most chillingly, sporting a pink Hello Kitty sticker on the top of its case.

Miss Frasier was no fool. The process of scrambling occurring inside the laptop's electronic depths could only be halted by keying in a carefully constructed series of numbers and random phrases at certain intervals. Most of the usability of the machine was gone, but before it had completely faded Bay had been able to gain access to a journal program.

He'd skimmed many of the entries and within them found clues. Three tries to guess each password, and he wasn't doing too badly. In the process, he was learning quite a bit about Fray, as she preferred to be called. Extremely intelligent, highly driven, disdainful of authority and distrustful of strangers, she saw herself very much as a crusader for justice.

It was, in short, the picture of a woman ill-equipped to deal with the ramifications of coming to Major Noah Caldwell's attention. Caldwell and Division were ruthless, and Bay himself was a finely tuned machine built for infiltrate-and-destroy. If Fray had any chance of surviving, it was with Bay's help.

The question of just *why* her survival was a priority was a difficult one, and Bay needed his resources for other pressing matters. He'd missed his first check-in, and after a few more, Caldwell would begin to wonder.

He hunched over the keyboard, counting the few minutes he had until the next code needed to be input, and a green light flashed in the taskbar. Curious, he clicked it—and realized just what he was looking at.

A few more clicks brought up a map. The location, pinging rapidly, was on the other side of El Paso, and who knew how long she would stay there?

Agent Bay rocketed to his feet. A few minutes later, the motel room was empty.

Trinity had always considered borders, international or state, mental constructs more than anything else. Still, the relief of turning a few corners, getting out of sight of the guards and letting out a long soft exhale was not inconsiderable. Cal even moved differently, body language shifting by a crucial few millimeters to match the setting—a little more hip-shot, chest out a little more, a gringo but one with some familiarity with the terrain, not a stiff *norte* tourist. Trinity rounded her own shoulders slightly, chin up but avoiding eye contact with any passerby, her backpack straps settling differently now.

"Hard part's over," Cal murmured, and she didn't bother to correct him.

The difficult part would be choosing the right moment. Once his vulnerability factor had reduced somewhat but his speed was still impaired, she could be assured of his safety *and* free to pursue her own agenda. She could, she supposed, have left him on the other side of the border; the truck had been well-hidden and he'd have survived.

Yet she hadn't. Why?

His presence halted deconstruction, but it also reduced her solitary effectiveness. Not only that, but he'd committed an almost fatal error, diving into the stairwell to keep the other agent away from her.

He thought she was a gemina, and therefore was

obeying those strange emotional directives. It was going to get him killed.

That, she had decided, was an unacceptable outcome indeed.

Cal glanced around. "Okay. This way."

"You know where you're going?"

His easy grin almost managed to cover up the paleness of blood loss. "I do, pretty girl."

"Don't call me that."

"But you are. We've got to get on the road. There's a plane to catch, as soon as I can get some document time in and find us some transport. I know someone who'll be happy to see you." The grin stretched, becoming more natural.

"Oh?" For a terrifying moment, the calculation of betrayal filled her lungs with lead—but another occurred just as quickly. "Six? And Candless?"

"Yeah. Told them I'd bring you."

"How did you—"

"Sometimes failure isn't an option, Trin."

Trin. Cal. Small words, impossibly short to carry the complexity of a human being. Yet they were said with a different shade each time, complex nuances she couldn't decode.

Cal straightened a little more. "Leg's a lot better. You were right about the greens."

Of course I was. She was tempted to say it, didn't. Held her peace as his stride lengthened a little; any onlooker would think they were a couple.

A hot flush went through her at the thought. He'd kissed her twice now, which didn't precisely bother her.

No, what bothered her was that she…liked it. More than *liked*, but she couldn't find the proper word for the sensation.

Which could be a sign of deconstruction all on its own, proceeding insidiously in the background. Cal—and Six and Candless—were morally questionable according to the authorities, but they were *ethically* correct, as far as Trinity could ascertain. Had Bronson or Control ever suffered any qualms? None that she could remember, and she had been forced into daily contact with Bronson for a significant period of time.

She almost shuddered at the memory. Control's heavily distorted voice caused its own uneasiness, easily explained as the scrambling algorithms turning the sound waves into rasping jagged discomfort.

"Did you hear me? You were right. You know?"

"Yes." *No.* Reminiscing would not help; neither would unburdening herself, except in one very specific way. "Cal…"

"Hmm? We'll drive to Chihuahua. Hole up near the airport, I'll work my magic and we'll get an early flight to the capital. From there we'll bounce even farther south."

Her unease sharpened. "You shouldn't tell me."

"Come on." He grinned down at her. Dawn, rising fast, lit the eastern horizon with gold; the rim of the sun was peering up over the covers and yawning. Street lamps began to flicker out. The light was kind to him, tinting his hair and bringing out the blue of his eyes. "Try to enjoy being free, honey. It's a nice feeling, once you get used to it."

Is this freedom? One was always constrained. She forced her face to the expression of neutral acquiescence she'd worn all through dealing with Bronson and later, in service jobs, working for a few weeks and moving on. Gathering resources, learning societal norms, perfecting her camouflage, aware of pursuit. Practicing tradecraft, finding the shadow economy, cash only and no questions. If that was freedom, it left much to be desired.

And yet. The wind, still fresh, tugged at her hair. Cal inhaled, let out a long sigh, and the relief in his scent eased the tension in her neck and shoulders. He no longer reeked of pain or stress. How did he shake it off?

She decided not to ask. There were other things to think about, plans to make. As soon as she was certain he was safe, it was over.

The altogether unwelcome and sinking thought that she might find some irrational reason not to do what she knew was necessary rasped at her. "Let's hurry, then."

It didn't take a genius to figure out trouble was brewing. She'd shut down again, that pretty face losing all expression when she thought he wasn't looking, and if he hadn't had to prep the fresh passport blanks, he would have dragged her south without waiting. A short hop to Chihuahua, another to Mexico City, a day or so in that smoggy whirl, then on to Buenos Aires, where maybe Holly could shake some sense into her. Girl talk, that sort of thing. Maybe even Reese would have an idea how to handle it, because sure as Shinola, Cal was failing in a big way.

He worked, his fingers sure and deft, glancing at her still, straight back at the window. The room was small and dusty, full of heavenly smells from the taqueria downstairs, and her hair lay across her shoulders in a shining wave. It was a shame she'd put any dye on it at all, the highlights were beautiful. Honey hair and that flawless skin of hers. The virus worked with what you had, so she must've been a stunner even before infection.

An ugly word. It reminded him of *induction*.

Cal frowned slightly, hitting the button a couple times. The flashes showed the pictures in high relief—according to these, they were Jane and Ed Rochester from Thorneville, Massachusetts. Even unsmiling in a cheap passport photo she was a beauty—a patrician nose, those cheekbones, her mouth relaxed just a little and making a man think about all sorts of delicious things. Maybe he could even get close enough to steal another kiss.

He hadn't wanted to make out this badly since—well, he couldn't remember a time, even in the hormonal flush of teenage years.

Calm down there, boy. Deep breath. Even those memories were darkened by the screen of only-normal senses. Did the others feel like waking up from the initial illness had peeled away the curtain over the world? Sharper, faster, better, more alive.

He decided he'd take a stab at guessing where the problem really lay. "So. I've got a question."

No reply, but her silence turned listening again. The fine hairs all over his body stood up, sensing her attention. He imagined her leaning over a dinner table, maybe with a glass of white wine, regarding him solemnly.

Keep your mind on your work. "You know about Tracy." He managed to make it soft, careful. "About the firefight. They sent two teams."

She turned, a short, graceful movement. Her hands dropped to her sides. Open and empty. A shading of tension all through her scent. Her weight evenly balanced, but she pitched back slightly. Just in case she had to go out the window. "Yes. One to suppress, one to capture."

Ah. "For the asset. What about collateral?" *They were sent to kill her, weren't they?*

A long pause. He stared at their pictures, the passports propped open, no longer blanks but official paperwork. The all-holy United States passport, a ticket out of trouble in many cases, getting you into even more in certain areas of the globe. All they needed was a little cure time, some open air. He leaned back in the chair, stretching. It felt good to do something relatively simple, something he knew inside and out.

"The projected chance of unacceptable information dispersal was high." Back to the robot-voice now. Her eyes were huge, dark, pupils flaring as she turned inward. *That* was how she did it—she buried it. Probably disassociated so hard she didn't even know she *had* feelings.

No wonder she was so confused.

"You calculated it, right?"

She stared at him. High color flared in her cheeks, died away until she was paper-pale.

He waited, but she said nothing.

"Jesus." They'd emptied her out and turned her into a machine. And now... No wonder she didn't want to feel anything, if that was what they'd made her do.

It made everything—her rescuing Holly, her saving them from Bronson, her trusting him and coming back to the Chevy—even braver, in retrospect.

She didn't move. Just stared at him. A small tremor slid through her. What else was she remembering? Knowing that jackass Bronson, there was probably plenty. Which brought up another thought—what had they done to her *physically*? A woman wouldn't want to talk about that, and she was shy, acted as if she'd never kissed anyone before. No memory, a sort of amnesia, and trained to follow orders because it was the Army, after all...

The idea that she might have been forced into

all sorts of things brought the red rage up again. He clamped down on it, and her eyelids dropped slightly, her gaze obviously measuring the distance between them.

"I'm not going to yell," he began quietly. "And I'm not going to hit you."

"Now you see," she whispered in return. "Thank you."

"What?" *The only thing I see is that it's a goddamn good thing Bronson's dead.* "You got us out of there. Me, Holly, Reese. You chose the right thing."

"Too little and too late. Excuse me." She scooped up her backpack and headed for the hall. His chair hit the floor as he stood too quickly, and the noise brought her up short. She flinched, and he froze. "I...I need the restroom. It's down the hall."

He swallowed hard. Now that they were comfortably over the border and she understood a few things, it was safe enough to let her out of his sight for a moment.

He forced himself to stand still. "Okay." Maybe she even needed to cry, and if she thought emotion was going to kill her—but still. Maybe she just wanted some privacy. Thinking about the program probably wasn't very comfortable, and Christ knew he had his own share of things he didn't want to talk about. "Okay. Yeah, you, um, you go ahead."

"Thank you." Almost prim. She didn't hurry, sliding past him carefully, her weight spreading evenly through every step as if she expected him to jump her.

Maybe she did.

She glanced back just once, at the door. "Cal?"

"Yeah?" There was something in his throat blocking the word.

"I mean it. Thank you."

For what? He listened to her footsteps down the hall, his eyes closed, imagining the sway of her hips. Even the stiffest woman in the world couldn't get rid of that—it was the way they were built. Whatever god or power had designed that curve knew just what it was doing.

She felt too much. The amount of sheer grit it probably took for her to go against orders, rescue Holly and turn on her handler, then vanish and set out all by her lonesome to find out who the hell she was... God.

God.

Just like Holly, who'd taken to life on the run with far more grace and courage than a man probably could. A raw civilian, and she'd still stuck to Reese through thick and thin. Reese, damn him, was a great guy.

On the other hand, there was Cal, always just a hair away from screwing everything up six ways to Sunday. Unfortunately, he was all Trinity had right now, so he had to be extra careful, gentle with her. Teach her how to handle the emotional noise, reassure her and keep her safe.

It was a good plan. Unfortunately, it wasn't until a full twelve minutes had passed that he glanced at the window and saw the crane made of burger wrapper sitting on the sill, crumpled but still recognizable.

Then Cal realized she wasn't coming back, and just what an idiot he'd been.

The prepaid cell from his backpack buzzed, sending a chill down his back. He'd almost forgotten about it, and the number was a familiar encrypted signal. Cal's finger hovered over the decline button, but he'd missed his last check, and there was no reason to make the other man worry *too* much. So he jabbed the *accept* button instead and lifted it to his ear. "Talk."

"Busy?" Reese's voice, deep and unmistakable. He sounded relaxed.

Cal scanned the street one last time. No use. She was well and truly gone. "Sort of. How's things?" He turned into the small hotel, avoided the front desk and headed straight for the stairwell to the empty, dusty room.

"Tango lessons and cervezas. The missus says hello."

"Give mine back." It wouldn't be fair to snap at the man. Cal's frustration, sharp yellow-tinged acridity, was beginning to leak out through his skin. None of the normals would smell it.

She would. But she was gone.

"You find yours yet?"

"Yup." He didn't elaborate.

The pause crackled. "And?"

"It's complicated." He unlocked the door, scanned the interior.

The crane was still in the window. She hadn't come back. Not that he thought she would, but...

Hope, the most deadly of all drugs. You could fool yourself into thinking anything was possible.

"It always is. You need backup. Where are you?"

Of course Reese would figure it out. Cal sighed, pinched the bridge of his nose. "Don't jump into the fire after the bacon, man."

"Give me a locale."

"The big J. Where else?"

"Shit."

"What?"

"She was right." The sound echoed oddly, and for a moment Cal heard a street vendor's cry in the background.

Doubly odd, because it was the same as the one from the avenue below. Cal blinked, his skin roughening instinctively, and strode across the room to the window.

Just then, a sharp rap at the door—two of them, in fact, a short pause, then another tap. *Oh, for God's sake.*

He wrenched the door open to find a familiar pair of dark eyes and wide shoulders—Reese was built broader in the beam than Cal, and shorter, though just as narrow in the hip. In a blue baseball cap, blue T-shirt and hip-length leather jacket, he looked just like a tourist, except for the calluses on his fingertips and the subtle difference in the way he stood—braced and ready for anything.

A slim, blue-eyed, raven-haired woman peered around him, and their combined scent—a heavy, golden honeymusk that rasped irritatingly through his nose—washed through the doorway. "Hi, Cal," she said softly.

Cal touched the disconnect button, and Reese did the same on his own cell. The two men studied each other for a few moments. The other agent could no doubt smell the irritation coming off Cal in waves.

Finally Reese sighed, slipping his phone back into a pocket. The tension left his shoulders. "She couldn't wait to see Trinity."

Are you nuts? Bringing her back this close to the border? Cal opened his mouth, shut it.

Holly Candless's smile widened. She'd put on some weight and lost the thin, tired look; a faint tan colored her cheekbones now. "Is he finally speechless? It's an occasion! Where…" Her face fell. "Oh. She's not here, is she."

"Disappeared three hours ago. Guess I'm not her idea of a dream date." His mouth pulled bitterly against itself, and Cal told himself he didn't care. A lie, just like so many others, and this one he couldn't even make *himself* believe.

Reese pitched his weight forward, Cal stepped back, and the new arrivals waltzed into the dry, dusty little room. The clutter of his interrupted passport work on the table, his backpack, the narrow untouched bed and the blue funk of despair coating everything. He'd just left supplies out in the open and left his backpack behind, too, frantic to find her. No use, she had too much of a lead, and his leg still ached way down deep where the slower healing took place.

Holly elbowed Reese. "Pay up."

"Later." A quick grin, but the man looked worried, a thin line between his eyebrows. "Really didn't expect to find you here."

Cal swept the door closed. "You recommended this quarter of the city. Lots of exits." *And she probably used one of the twenty you can't cover all at once.*

"You're in a really crappy mood." Reese said it mildly enough. He was maddeningly calm even at the best of times.

Cal throttled his irritation again, grabbing the crane from the windowsill and tucking it into his backpack. "Shouldn't I be?" *I'm the stupidest man on earth.* "Look, it's nice to see you both, really, but I've got to get going. She's going to get herself killed."

"Oh?" Holly folded her arms. "You think?" She didn't sound sarcastic, but she didn't sound quite helpful, either.

Whatever the hell she meant by that, Cal didn't care to stick around and find out. He sorted the passport mess with quick, efficient swipes, his backpack standing open and ready to receive.

"Don't start," Reese told Holly. "I'm not going to risk you."

"I missed the part where you were the boss of me" was her equable reply. "Cal, where did she go?"

Where else? "Pocula Flats. Military installation. Records there, she said." *I have to know who I am before I die.* "She thinks any emotional noise at all will kill her. She thinks— Oh, what the hell. I've got to get going. She's probably back over the border by now."

"Why would she go back there?" Reese stared at Holly, that worry line even more pronounced between his eyebrows. "Cal?"

"Because I screwed up," he told them both. "I'm stupid, all right? She thought I'd be mad at her because she worked with Bronson. Running intel, planning missions." *Jesus, what a tangle.* "It didn't even occur to me, but she sat on it until she did something stupid. Just like a woman."

"Hey, now." Holly's tone sharpened. "There's no need for that."

Oh, there's a need. His head hurt, a sharp spike through his temples. "You're right. I'm the stupid one here. I should have known. I should have—"

"Well, we'll go and get her back." Holly shifted her own backpack a little higher on one slim shoulder. "You know where she's going, we just hurry and we'll be able to find her. I'll explain, since you don't seem to have much luck, and then we'll—"

"I was afraid you were going to say that," Reese muttered. "Holly, baby—"

"Oh, don't you *Holly baby* me. Start figuring out why she's going to this installation. Cal, pack up. We're leaving."

"Is she always this bossy?" Cal couldn't help himself.

"You have *no* idea." Reese let out another long-suffering sigh. "Holly, do I have to remind you how dangerous it is to go back over the border?"

"You can stay here if you want," she informed him sweetly. "Come on, Cal. Let's get moving."

Fray frowned at her screen. In exactly five minutes she was due to pack it up and move on. It was always best to spread your access points, just in case the anonymizers didn't work as well as they could. Even the most productive session had to be cut short, no matter *what* exciting new thing was going down.

After all, she did *not* want to get caught again. Holding cells were atrocious, and dealing with that blond jerk Caldwell was nothing she wanted to repeat. El Paso was her last stop before the border, and she couldn't wait to have a decent margarita and some killer paella.

She had two pencils in her hair and felt for them with her left hand, her right-hand fingers tapping the numeric keypad. A few months ago, working on some cute little North Korean decryptions, she'd stuck a good half-dozen Ticonderoga #2s in her sloppy, high-piled bun and almost stabbed herself in the eye when she stumbled to bed to catch some z's. As habits went, it was a bad one, but she couldn't stop sticking them in her hair.

It helped her think. Her notebook, full of cramped scribbles in her own private code, lay open next to the laptop, and she frowned as a couple of the trace programs began returning weird numbers. They shouldn't have been doubling.

"Huh," she breathed, checking the time and tapping a few queries.

Four minutes left. She cocked her head, running down a list of *it could be* and discarding every one. Which just left her with the idea that somehow, someone had cracked her old laptop.

Great.

She immediately cut loose, hitting the killswitch for every running program and glancing up over the interior of the coffee shop and the golden flood of Southwest sunshine outside, shimmering off the cars in the parking lot. How did people *live* down here? Her lips kept cracking, no matter how much balm she put on.

The place was deserted, sleepy staff moving around, doing some desultory cleaning. In between rushes was the best time for food service, but also the most boring. Fray unplugged, popped the emergency shutdown keystrokes, closed the laptop and was just coiling up the cord when the door opened with a cheerful jingle…

And the black-haired goon walked right in, scanning the shop interior with one quick glance, his dark gaze settling right on Fray.

Her mouth went dry. She didn't think he'd fall for the "I need to use the ladies' room" trick again. Her fingers curled around the laptop case—an expensive bludgeon, but the only one she had, and now she was thinking that carrying a baseball bat around would probably be a good idea from now on. Or even a golf club. Nobody looked at those twice, but you could break someone's face in a hurry with one if you needed to.

He headed straight through the tables for her, those dark eyes fixed on her face. It was, she thought, sort of like a shark viewing something thrashing in the water. The same flat, hypnotic stare; the same even, unerring gliding. All he needed was a dorsal fin.

Fray's chair squeaked as she rose slowly, pushing it back. She gripped the laptop, wishing she had time to get her notebook and bag together before she had to clock this guy and make a run for it. Who was she kidding, though? He was *fast*, and she'd only escaped through luck last time. Luck—and a really long lead time, as such things went, and shooting the paperweight she'd snatched off a cop's desk through a big window to make a nice loud noise.

He cocked his head slightly, taking in her posture and her white-knuckled grip. He halted on the other side of the table, too far away for her to brain him.

"Miss Frasier." Quiet and firm.

Now would come the threats. Fray braced herself.

"I'm Agent Bay," he continued. "I…" His throat worked convulsively. He dropped his chin and glared at her. "I don't know what to do now."

Part Three: Caldwell's Revenge

Trinity returned to Felicitas with a band of monsoon rains. The headache returned, too, building between her temples. The only trouble with milk shakes was calculating the likelihood of tooth decay from the sugar—she wasn't sure if the virus kept *that* at bay.

Flash flooding filled the arroyos with foaming brown tea, heavy silver curtains drumming on roofs. Delivery vehicles wallowed through sheets of water. Soaked to the bone, little curls of steam rising as her body hiked temperature to keep her at peak efficiency, Trinity clung to the top of the semi's rattling trailer. Normally every delivery truck coming through would be examined by dogs and the watchtowers on either side of the gate would have a clear view of the trailer's top. However, predawn in the pouring rain, her glands buttoned down and water blurring whatever tiny threads of scent remained, she was safe enough from the canines. It was the watchtowers she had felt a little unease over, but their glaring searchlight-eyes didn't switch on. It was only the 4:00 a.m. delivery, the same one that happened every Monday-Wednesday-Friday. Since the delivery driver always stopped to fuel his rig at a certain station outside Felicitas, it was simply a question of waiting for the right moment to clamber atop the truck, clamping the magsol pads down and lashing herself to them. The resultant short ride to the installation was cold and uncomfortable, but well within Trinity's tolerances.

Last time she'd simply cut a hole in the electrified fencing, taking care not to short the circuit, and slid through. Repeating such a method was inadvisable.

Her current plan held a great deal of risk, but time constraints loomed. Above all, she had to be in and away before Cal—*Eight* could think to search for her here. He had taken the news of her perfidy rather calmly, all things considered, but Trinity could not calculate if it was the calm of shock or a more durable disengagement from anger.

In the end, it didn't matter. She should stop thinking about it and concentrate on the current mission. Once she was far enough inside the base, she could dissolve one of her few remaining pills and the sweet, cold clarity would fold over her. After she extracted what she wanted, there was no reason to stay in this part of the country anymore.

Thinking about the pills was bad, because the word *placebo* kept rising from dark corners of her brain, and *that* was uncomfortable. Much better to use any tool at hand to maximize her efficiency and worry about such things later.

When she was in the woods. If she ever reached them. *I want to see the forest before I die.* An irrational compulsion, to be sure, deconstruction proceeding, but at least she was moving.

The gate, a pane of chain-link topped with razor wire, moved sideways; the driver yelled a cheerful platitude to the gate guard, who replied in kind. More of the small talk Eight was so good at. He would no doubt infiltrate in another way—

Stop it. Pay attention.

The sound of the tires changed—base pavement was different than civilian. Trinity filed the sound pattern away for later analysis, ramping up blood flow to her right hand to bring her tingling fingers back to flexibility and readiness. Left turns were the worst; for some reason they threatened the stability of the magsol pads.

They were wonderful pieces of hardware, and somewhat illegal for civilians to possess, but she'd had the foresight to raid a cache of Division gear just after she'd made her escape.

Yet another case of planning being indispensable.

The truck heaved along, rolling through needles of stinging rain that showed no sign of slacking. Two left turns, a long shallow grade, a right turn into the parking lot, swinging out to loop around, then the semi shuddering and backing up an inch at a time, aiming its hind end at the back of the Commissary/ PX. Any other time, Trinity might well have admired the skill with which the driver piloted the unwieldy thing, but she was too busy restoring blood flow to her extremities and unsealing the magsols, covering the *pop* of their disengagement with the sound of rain and burping of the semi's engine.

The Commissary's roof angled down over the top of the trailer, and the question of dismounting from the semi was solved rather neatly by a leap over the low ledge and onto the roof. She landed in flowing water—the gutters here were sadly underserviced— and had to pitch forward against the current. A service ladder at the other end of the roof provided her with an easy exit, and before she took advantage of it she palmed a pill up to her mouth, hunching with her back to the wind so the bottle wouldn't flood.

Wet cars glimmered in the parking lot—night stockers, no doubt. Stealing a vehicle from the residential section afforded her much more of an operational window than taking the chance of a stocker going home early and filing a report.

It occurred to her that there would be an emotional reason against such a maneuver as well as a logical one—her fellow stockers, just scraping by, were stranded without their carefully nursed, rusting cars. Cynthia, the night checker, had a moderately new Nissan, and she often drove some of the other stockers home through still-sleeping Felicitas.

Trinity closed her eyes for a moment, hugging the wet shadows at the side of the PX, calling up maps of the base inside her skull. The chemical burn of the pill began in her throat and chest, and a welcome chill settled over her.

It helped her push away Cal's face, pale and set, as he told her he wasn't going to yell or hit her. Or his mouth, hot and hungry, almost greedy as it devoured hers. The comforting closeness that stilled the scrabbling machine in her head, his strong, healthy scent.

He's better off now, she told herself again, and the strange piercing sensation in her chest faded as the drug took hold. Trinity suspected it wouldn't vanish completely. Not even with the pills.

She waited for the chemical, whatever it was, to take hold completely, but before it did the discomfort mounted. Her cheeks were suspiciously warm. Deconstruction was almost total, and cognitive degradation would follow in its wake. Physical degradation might or might not, and Trinity wondered at what point she would simply take matters into her own hands.

The trees would hear a gunshot, and the wildlife

would be silent for a little while. They would return to their chattering soon enough, though.

Pill-calm settled completely. It dulled the sensation in her chest, enough so she could function.

Trinity's eyelids fluttered open. She glanced across the parking lot again, one part of her attention hearing the rattle as the semi's trailer opened and unloading began, the song of jokes cracking between unloaders and driver. The pallets would be drawn out, and soon stockers would be imposing order on the shelves. Neatening, straightening, arranging.

In a certain way, that was just what Trinity intended to do—arrange and straighten a jumbled mess in the world. First she had to find the pieces. Then she would arrange them.

After that, it was time to turn off the light, lock the doors…and leave.

It was just the same—hushed halls, rain muffled by the size of the building, a clot-thick pall of dust and floor wax. Unlike other base buildings, this one was brick, and the damp would no doubt fuel some interesting microscopic life in the baked crevices on its outside surface. Also, the basement was a haven to all manner of desert life seeking to escape the flood—scorpions in particular, Trinity surmised, and took great care in placing her feet even on the second floor.

Her nose twitched, dust irritating tender tissues. Damp footprints couldn't be helped, but this building was usually kept locked and silent, its files moldering away. The newer cabinets for Project Gibraltar were in a climate-controlled room, easy to crack if you had designed the safety protocols.

Still, she approached carefully, a doe in a mountain meadow, every hair quivering, every heightened sense alert.

Blowing dust through the gap in a glass shield over three brand-new cherrywood cabinets showed her the usual tangle of laser trip-beams. A small, unwilling smile tilted the corners of her lips up and she turned away, toward the old, rancid, leaning file cabinets that held the newer files instead. The security on those was much more sophisticated and less showy, but a few moments with a keypad and a handheld device from the Division cache narrowed down the pincode.

It hadn't changed. She thought about this for a few moments, analyzing, and punched the numbers in with a latex-clothed fingertip. Well-greased locks inside the shambledown cabinets slid noiselessly aside, and she went for the middle drawer on the right. That was where it should be.

Her own non-redacted file. The black hole yawned inside her head, a moment of unambiguous, completely illogical terror.

Are you sure you want to know? At least, comfortable in unknowing, she could perhaps think she was somehow better than the woman who had agreed to infection and induction. *We have all your paperwork on file, you specifically asked not to know...*

She eased the drawer open and began carefully riffling through the files. Failed candidates, charts full of vitals and medical language, the induction process causing fatal seizures and cortical bleeds in male survivors of the original Gibraltar infection. The other drawers were full of these, as well. Near the end would be the survivor files—they required much less storage real estate here, their lives filed separately afterward.

She found the first one, Agent A. He'd disappeared into Russia, presumed dead. B through D had coded, died of seizures on the induction table. Then familiar files, ones she'd handled classified copies of all during her attendance on Bronson's whims.

1, 2, 5, 7, 9, 10–13, all accounted for. No Three, no Four, no Six, no Eight. Had they been pulled?

Interesting. CONFIRMED: DECEASED stamped in thick red across 1, 5 and 11, as well as B through D. Agent A's file held no confirmed stamp.

Trinity breathed out carefully, softly, sliding the last drawer open.

There they were. In defiance of all logical and rational arrangement, Six's and Eight's files were in the very last drawer. After them, extremely new files of thick cardboard. *Aleph. Beta. Gamma.*

The newer iterations, male agents who could survive induction. A chill walked up Trinity's spine.

Her own file…was missing.

A hot rasping she identified as *irritation* crawled up her windpipe, just as air began soughing through the overhead vents. It should have been usual, keeping the paper properly dehumidified and at the correct temperature. Instead, a heaviness brushed Trinity's damp hair, her wet face, her wrists. She glanced up at the climate vents, the heaviness racing up her fingers and toes, and suddenly understood.

A colorless, odorless gas.

This was a trap, or a killing bottle. And she was the butterfly in chloroform.

She reeled drunkenly for the door, leaving the papers behind in their suddenly skew-morphing cabinets, but the dosage was high and her legs folded underneath her. Her breath held, lungs squeezing every usable scrap of oxygen from trapped air, she crawl-lunged for the corridor and freedom…

Nothing. Blackness.

Gone.

Two brief taps on his door. "Sir?"

Caldwell closed the briefcase lid and pushed the entire thing aside. "Come in." No trace of impatience in his tone, even though irritation filled his entire mouth with bitter metal. He'd been just about to unseal the coldpac. Once he did so, the virus would start to degrade. He only had about twenty minutes after unsealing to get it into a warm, safe environment where it could start replicating—namely, his very own corpus. "Yes?"

It was red-faced Corporal Hector, his uniform spray-starched so hard it almost crackled when he moved. "Sir. The light, sir. The light's gone off."

"Slow down, son." Caldwell folded his hands. The top of his desk was a little tacky-sticky, and he frowned slightly. Something less than shipshape around here. If he was in charge, everything would need a good scrubbing. Of course, this was the Southwest, where all the bean dip and carcinogens probably put a dent in everyone's morale. Besides, the weather was awful, and creepy-crawly critters everywhere. It was a wonder people lived here at all. "What's gone off?" He already had an idea, of course, but you wanted the lower ranks to learn to spit out information quickly and clearly.

"The light on the records, sir. We've caught someone."

Caldwell's smile stretched, pulling his lips up and back. Hector snapped to attention as he rose, but Caldwell merely linked his hands behind his back and took a moment to think things over.

"Very good," he said. "And are we adhering to protocol? The records room is sealed, completely sealed, and nobody's opened the door to take a peek?" *Because if someone has, I'll bust him back to below buckytail private and send him to goddamn Syria.*

"Yessir." Hector nodded enthusiastically. "Yes, sir. We wouldn't even know someone was in there if it wasn't for the light. It tipped ten minutes ago, turned red. The cameras were activated, and there's a shape on the floor." He swallowed, throat working. "Is it very bad, sir?"

"Not at all." He could afford to be magnanimous. "Activate Delta Team, have them meet me there. Keep the room *sealed*, Hector. Absolutely virgin until I get there, do you understand?"

"Yessir. Sealed up tight until you get there. Whoever it is, they're not moving. The gas went in, and bang, down they went."

"Male or female?"

"Can't tell through the fuzz on the monitors, sir."

Let it be her. "All right. Dismissed, Corporal, go get them on the stick and remember, I want to pop that cherry myself."

"Yessir." Another salute, and he was gone, slamming the door in his excitement.

Caldwell headed for the door himself, but he didn't leave his office just yet. Instead, he punched the lock tab and retreated to his desk, pulling the right-hand drawer out. The two hypodermics, each in plastic sheaths, guaranteed sterile, a second one bought because he believed in preparation. Belt and suspenders, as his grandpappy used to say.

Funny. He hadn't thought of the old man, with his tobacco-stained teeth and his well-oiled strap hung behind the closet door, in years. *Noah, son, the Army will make you a soldier. It's up to you to make yourself a man.*

Caldwell was about to do one better. He'd seen what these agents were capable of doing. An edge like that, deployed in the real world—the sky was the limit. Three, with her doll-pretty face and her efficient calculations, would be a very, very useful asset, once he finished with her.

Eventually, of course, he'd have to address the problem of Control. As if the thought summoned it, Caldwell's phone vibrated in his breast pocket—two short, one long, a familiar pattern. Control, wanting an update on Bay—still out in the field—and Three. Noah touched the fabric over his phone, thought about it for a moment and shook his head once. The old man could wait. When Caldwell made a report, it would be that he had Three in custody and pliable.

Agent Bay, well...

"One problem at a time," Caldwell muttered, flicking the locks on the briefcase and raising the lid. A few moments had the coldpac out from its foam nest, and he tore into it with a decided motion, shook the icy little vial inside, then readied a syringe.

The stabilized viral load had to be injected intramuscularly. Upper arm was out, and thigh was, too—not enough mass. Caldwell had read the injection protocols and planned on giving himself the highest possible dose.

It was a little ironic that in order to acquire greater speed, flexibility and endurance, not to mention neuroplasticity and a host of other benefits, he would have to drop trou.

Caldwell readied the syringe, stood up and reached for his belt buckle.

Time to become a superman.

Cal's skin was crawling. It felt strange to be back in fatigues again, after so long in civvies. And here, on a base, with high-and-tight unfriendlies everywhere and buzzing expectancy even a normal could smell riding the air, he felt naked, as well. They'd arrived last night with torrents of rain; Felicitas and the base were both armpit saunas by now. Dry heat was better; this crap felt like breathing through cotton.

"I don't like it." Reese frowned through the windshield—he was back in camo as well, and it turned out Holly was a whiz with the sewing machine he'd found, the one with embroidery function. Their patches were as perfect as could be expected on such short notice, and they'd squeaked through the gate just before lockdown came out and the MPs on duty began hand-checking every single ID.

Something was going on in this sleepy little corner of New Mexico.

What do you want to bet it's her? Goddammit, woman. Just...just stay alive. I'll handle the rest.

Yeah. As soon as he figured out what "the rest" was.

"What transport capabilities does this place have?" Reese probably already knew, but he was making sure. It was good to work with him, really—if Cal could ignore the tickle at the base of his neck telling him that he was selfishly endangering both the other agent and Holly by letting them try to help clean up the unholy mess he'd made of everything.

Stay alive, Trinity.

"Paved airstrip and chopper pad." Cal focused on the map. "She was coming in to look for records. That means, as far as I can tell, the north quadrant. It's the only place security's tight enough."

"Records." Reese nodded. "It'd be nice to get a peek at those myself."

"Why would they keep them out here?"

"Nice and dry most of the time. Ass-end of nothing, lots of space." Reese shifted in the driver's seat. Little beads of condensation touched his forehead, gleaming. His haircut was fresh, just like Cal's, and they looked like a pair of buddies just shooting the breeze, parked at the very edge of a residential section, Base housing turning its back on them. A high board fence, whitewashed to specs, kept them from being seen by any of the single-story buildings. When they started up, dust would roostertail, but until then, they were fairly anonymous. "Redundancy. Plus there's a medical facility... Huh."

Cal's ears perked. He glanced at the map again. "Right smack in the northern quad, too."

Reese tapped at the steering wheel. "Huh," he repeated thoughtfully.

"I wonder," Cal said, "if they might take her there first. They've nabbed her."

"What makes you think they've grabbed her?"

"She's not the type to warn them she's coming, and the entire base is on lockdown."

"Just checking." Reese measured off spaces on the steering wheel between his index fingers. "It's really, really likely. You realize that'll be waltzing right into the trap, right?"

"As far as they know, we're both out of the country."

"She worked with them. Would she let them know otherwise?"

It rasped against his nerves. His headache wasn't getting any better. At least they'd both been able to shave. "We worked for them, too, man."

"Point."

"And no, she wouldn't turn on us."

"She turned on Bronson."

"That's different."

"You sure?"

"If you want to leave, go ahead. Go get Holly and take her back over the border."

"She'd kill me."

"Yeah, well."

The pause that followed wasn't quite comfortable. Maybe Reese was thinking about Cal's own treachery, hunting him and Holly after Tracy's... death. They might have gotten away clean if Cal hadn't tracked them as far as Boulder before digging the small capsule out of his hip.

If he hadn't, he would never have met Trinity, though. He wondered if she had a matching scar on her hip, if she'd ever been chipped. He hadn't thought to ask.

"Cal." Reese, very quietly. "Do you have a headache?"

"Yeah." *Who wouldn't, in this weather?*

"Huh." A short, thoughtful noise.

"Why do you ask?"

Reese's shrug was a masterpiece of indifference. "Tell you later."

A blood-dipped sun slid fully below the horizon. Thunder rumbled in the distance, lightning flashes playing on far-off mesas. They'd done nuclear testing out in this part of the States, scientists with dark glasses thinking a bunker would protect them.

Later, they found out the invisible had its ways of killing you, too. The same arrogant bastards, or their heirs, had probably made the virus swimming in both men sitting in a hot car in a New Mexico sunset.

Cal waited, though every inch of his skin prickled with the urge to get out. To run. To find wherever she was, beat down any door in his way and *make* her listen to reason.

Finally, Reese slid the prepaid cell out of his pocket, hit a few numbers and let it ring twice. On the other end, Holly would know they were beginning their run. Her part was rendezvous support—she'd been determined to come with them; it took both Cal and Reese to talk her out of *that*.

Even with a full viral load, she was still a civilian.

And even Trinity, with her training and analysis, wasn't ready for this sort of fieldwork. Besides, dammit, this was a man's job.

Wasn't it? After all, what else was he good for?

Reese hung up, glanced at Cal and twisted the key in the ignition.

Showtime.

She fought to rise, to surface from the black hole, but there was a sting in her arm and a fresh wave of velvet-black, blurring sedation. The virus ate the chemical sludges, but they kept changing by degrees, and each wave required adaptation, which consumed precious time. Over and over, she rose from the swamp and was forced back down.

Tiny bits of audio filtered in.

Look at that, her blood pressure...stable, very nice...she just keeps burning it off, it's incredible... would kill a horse...give her the ket, let's see what that does...

In the middle of the confusion, medical jargon and the confused, blurred impressions of activity buzzing around her, a familiar voice.

"Don't give her ketamine, for Chrissake, what's wrong with you? Check the restraints."

They're clear, sir.

"Good. Get out."

She's going to wake up soon.

"I know, Hector. Clear the room, folks."

Are you all right, sir?

"Hector, get *out*."

Audio drained away. The chemicals burned in her veins, blurred over her skin.

Trinity. That's my name. The thought sent a wash of strength through her, and more sensation bled through the sedation—smells of disinfectant and pain, discomfort building in muscles and joints, rasping against her stiffened hair. Rainwater always did that, left sediment on strands and scalp. Gritty dust all over her as well, from the records room.

That's what happened. Gas, in an airtight climate-controlled chamber.

As traps went, it was a patient, crudely effective one. Not at all like Bronson's paper-shuffling overkill.

Bronson's dead. Where are you now?

Her fingers and toes were all present and accounted for. The virus was burning away sedatives, adapting more quickly each time since there were only so many chemical families capable of producing the required effects. Sweat beaded on her forehead, dampened her arms and legs, no energy left over for regulating it and besides, excreting whatever the virus couldn't eat of the drugs would help her regain capacity sooner.

That was a logical thought, and she clung to it. More sensory input, a confusing strobe light against her eyes, compressed bullets of scent. *Hospital. I'm in a medical facility.*

For some reason, the realization caused a cold bath of sensation, and the final wave of sedation shattered. Trinity lunged for consciousness, pulse and respiration easing, her eyelids sliding up just a little, enough to give her a limited field of vision. White glare—lights focused at her face, probably to rob her of visual input. Shallow breathing brought in a tangle of scents—illness, the rasping testosterone acridity of excited males, overheated coffee, nylon webbing, disturbed dust, her own body's metabolizing of the chemicals a sour metal undernote.

Another tang, of sweat, excitement and sickness. It overlaid a familiar scent, blond and male, and for a moment she couldn't dredge the name or face out of memory.

Had deconstruction proceeded so far? Was she finally what she'd feared, a mindless husk?

"I know you're awake," he said. A smooth Midwest accent, and now she had the face. Blond, certainly, a strong jaw and muddy hazel eyes. He'd been attached to Bronson near the end, a major's uniform and his hungry, hungry scrutiny whenever their superior wasn't in the room.

She finally found the name. *Caldwell.* His orders had been brief and to the point. He had even ordered hot showers and fresh clothing for her. Despite that, his muddy gaze had always made her...not precisely uncomfortable, but *cautious.* There was little calculation in such caution, but a great deal of instinct, and Trinity had been careful to keep her distance.

Ah. So that's who set the trap. The machine inside her head shuddered—she hadn't judged him subtle enough for such a thing, but his handling of Bronson might have been far more adroit than she'd guessed. Ironic; if Trinity hadn't shot Bronson herself, Caldwell might have made other arrangements.

And if Caldwell was behind the other agent hunting her, the one who had survived induction, he was much higher in Division's confidence than she'd initially assumed.

Each consideration passed through her brain with what felt like lightning speed, but she couldn't be sure, with the fog of sedation and the chance of deconstruction having proceeded. She remained very still, testing each limb in turn.

Restraints. She knew the feeling—the tough fabric pulled tightly at wrists, elbows, shoulders, hips, knees, ankles. One strapped over her forehead, and another over her throat, not snugged too tightly, but impossible for her to move her head from the small, shallow bowl in that end of the metal table.

Oh.

"I said, I know you're awake, Three."

Good for you. She let her eyelids drift upward another fraction. The glare stung, her tear ducts prodded into producing a trickle of hot water. *Don't call me that.* Perhaps the deconstruction had halted for a few moments, which meant she had to maximize whatever advantage she could.

I'm tied up on a table, for God's sake. I need every edge I can manufacture.

Caldwell coughed slightly. A fresh wave of necrotic illness cut through his scent, and Trinity's nose threatened to wrinkle. *Ugh. What* is *that?*

The light shining in her face clicked off, which was a relief. She tested the bonds, one after another—very little give. Which left one or two unpalatable options, if she discounted chewing through her own limbs to get away.

Funny how that suddenly seemed a viable option if the situation took a few more turns. Trinity opened her eyes.

Half-familiar shapes loomed over her. The table was slick and cold, the harsh cheap fabric of a hospital johnny slid inadequately between her skin and chill metal. Caldwell swam into focus, a tall blond man wearing a major's oak leaf, just as she remembered him. Except he was sweating, and he smelled deathly, powerfully sick. His hair was plastered to his forehead, and he grinned as if he'd just told the world's best joke and expected her approval.

The metal arms hanging above her were *definitely* familiar. This wasn't just an exam room, it was a fully equipped medbay, and a small, cold, sharp spear went through Trinity's brain. "Sir." The word was bloodless, whispered through her chapped lips. If he thought her stupid or amenable, there might be a chance of escape.

"I've missed hearing you say that." Caldwell's smile widened before he dug in his pocket and produced a crisp white handkerchief, *Sua Sponte* embroidered on its edge in red. He coughed into its embrace rackingly, and she strained to analyze his illness. It didn't sound like a common cold. "I've been chasing you all over."

Well, that answered *that* question. She studied him, trying to ignore the metal arms. A terrifying, hideous possibility had occurred to her. Surely the shapes were coincidence, and they didn't intend to—

Caldwell coughed again, into the handkerchief. He twisted the cloth around a cargo of sputum and beamed at her. "I'd debrief you, but it's not necessary. I don't care where you've been or what you've been after." His smile widened. "After a little while, you won't, either."

Her throat was too dry. It wasn't a side effect from the sedation. Her gaze flicked back to the metal arms; Caldwell turned aside and pressed a button on the console next to him. A familiar whining sound began, drilling into her bones, and the arms twitched. Delicate servomotors moved, well oiled and silent; there was a crackle and the smell of ozone.

"We've perfected the process," Caldwell said over the noise. "Just hold still. It will all be over soon, and we'll be together."

There was no avoiding the truth. He meant to subject her to the induction process again.

Trinity began to struggle.

The restraints, the table, and Caldwell took no notice whatsoever.

Two men with fresh crewcuts, fatigues and white lab coats should have been able to slip into any military hospital unchallenged, especially if they moved and even *smelled* right. Unfortunately, some brass had chewed someone out, and the MPs at every entrance were an unforgiving bunch. Secondary security was also tight, which left getting creative. The kitchen was oddly deserted for a place this size, and its back door only had one or two easily circumvented countermeasures, since there was no use in making staff sign in and out every time they took scraps to the Dumpsters. Reese popped the lock while Cal used some wire and ingenuity to tell the door sensor that it was closed, no really it was, just do your job and don't make trouble. Then it was a simple matter of shadow-moving to avoid cameras, penetrating a cadaverous, dusty kitchen.

Nobody had eaten here for a while.

The place reeked of floor wax, pain and the greasy industrial staleness of *military*, a familiar mix of sweat, bad orders and gun oil. It took him back to working for the program, coming in for blood draws, the interminable poking and prodding and tolerance tests, the endless round of psych evals. *How's your digestion? Any uncomfortable thoughts? When was the last time you dreamed? What did the dreams consist of? Urinate into this receptacle, we're going to do a cheek swab, we have tolerance tests scheduled, a full workup.*

And even before that, sitting in a dust-free office, its window looking out onto a stretch of green lawn, while a striped, starred and mustachioed bigwig tented his fingers and said *We have a special program, son.*

"Yep, smells familiar," Cal muttered.

Reese glanced at him. The man was a ghost, quiet even for an agent. Surprisingly, though, he offered a tight smile, wrinkles at the corners of his dark eyes fanning out. "I was just thinking that."

The halls around the kitchen, full of cameras and tense expectancy, were also dusty. This part of the facility hadn't been used in a while. His head ached, sharp jabs stabbing down his neck no matter how often he breathed deeply or pushed his shoulders back. "What about the headache, Reese?"

The other agent checked around the corner. "Cameras, standard pattern. Those? Holly gets them when we're not together."

Oh? "What about you?"

"I get other effects." With any other man, the comment might have sounded salacious. From Reese, though, it sounded...dangerous.

To be stable, the agent and the gemina have to exchange...one virus has what the other lacks... All sorts of things were starting to make sense now. "Oh, *man.*"

"Yeah. I spend too long away, I start getting stupid. And slow."

"Degradation. Trinity says the agents and geminas need each other to be stable."

"Geminas?"

For once, Cal had an answer. "The girls. You know, what with the virus being Gemini now."

"Oh. That other agent, you think he might get a girlfriend?"

"Dunno. Didn't stop to ask him if he had a sweetheart." But now he thought about the girl with spectacles and chestnut hair, and he wondered. "The induction might stop that, though."

"Induction." Reese shook his head a little. "Like we're lab rats." He froze, and Cal did, too.

Footsteps. A standard patrol of six, coming down the halls in order, little clicks of gear and the breathing of excited, testosterone-high meatheads. Something was *definitely* going on in here, the whole place bubbling like a poked anthill. It was probably Trinity. God knew the woman could cause havoc just by breathing.

If she was here, it could only mean she'd been incapacitated in some way.

Caught.

Just stay alive, honey.

Cal's weight dropped onto his back foot as Reese glanced back at him, a silent question printed on his face. *You ready?*

They were going to take this patrol down. Good. Cal held up one finger.

Leave one for questioning.

Reese nodded and braced himself.

The logical extension of the headaches was pretty goddamn simple. If he needed Trinity to stay stable, she probably needed him, as well. She was already so goddamn fragile, and her fears of degradation so intense... Jesus. Her pale, set face, trying so hard not to give anything away. Standing across the room, not even sure if she'd be invited to eat.

Never even tasted a milk shake before.

"Hey, Southie," one of the men around the corner said. "You wanna get some beers after shift?"

"Sure thing," another man responded, but it was

too late. Reese was around the corner, Cal was, too, and from there it was simple—strike to the throat, small bones crunching, a short kick to a knee, more bones breaking, a swipe of hot blood because Reese had a knife, its blade blackened so no betraying gleam pierced the dark. It wasn't even a contest, six men against two prepared agents.

He used to feel bad about that. Now he just wanted to find Trinity and get the hell out of this hideous little place. He used to be a patriot, and these guys were just doing their jobs, planning on going out for beers afterward.

Now none of them would.

At the very tail end of the fight, the shortest of the patrol had the wherewithal to yell, a cry choked off almost as soon as it started. A body hit the floor with a dull thud, and Cal stopped, cocking his head.

Reese halted, too, one booted foot on the patrol leader's wrist, trapping the gun down and away. He crouched atop the other fellow, one of his hands cranking the helmet back so the strap levered the chin up, his other hand clamped over the man's mouth, denying him leverage and the means to make another sound.

It came again, muffled but distinct, and Reese's eyes gleamed in the dimness. Cal swallowed hard.

"We know where she is now," Reese said softly and made a violent movement. There was a snap, the battlefield stink of death-loosened sphincters, and he stood up, his boot crunching casually on the erstwhile prisoner's wrist. "Let's go."

It came again, a long trailing howl of female agony.

Fury ignited deep in Cal's bones.

Fray exhaled softly, pulling the last jump drive out. A printer whirred into life, hard copies of the most important and damning papers about to be spat forth into the world.

It hadn't even been that hard, not when she knew what she was looking for.

The big dumb black-haired lug stood at the window, peering out into the parking lot. "I don't like this," he muttered in that weird toneless voice.

"The door's right there," she pointed out, wrapping the USB stick in a Ziploc, sealing it with practiced efficiency. "Just boogie on out if you're so offended."

That earned her a whole thirty seconds of silence, during which he turned from the office window to look at her, steadily, thoughts moving below the surface of those dark eyes. Then he turned back, staring out into the gloom of approaching sauna-humid twilight. Fray tried not to feel like a bitch, but in point of fact, she *was* one, and there was no use in gilding the lily, as her grandmother often used to remark.

It's a good thing you're smart, Nan used to remark drily, when Fray came home from playing in the woods covered in gunk and clutching jars of frog spawn.

"Why are you helping me?" she asked, for the tenth time. "I mean, you could get into serious trouble for this."

His only reply was a shrug. He didn't seem to consider taking her to his boss's office and letting her play on the electronics a big deal. The whole thing could be an elaborate send-up, but Fray didn't think so.

What she did think was that this was going to blow sky-high, and she wanted to be on a comfortable beach somewhere without an extradition treaty when it did. Which would require some careful planning and all those brains Gran was always half deploring in her darling only grandchild.

"Time to move," he announced. "Chances of capture are rising into the unacceptable zone."

Fray glanced at the screen again, a blinking red light flashing in the upper right corner. *Huh. That's weird.* "Huh." A few moments of tapping at the big clunky keyboard elicited some astonishing results. "Hey. What's Site 3B?"

He crossed the room with swift strides, with that eerie economy of motion. When he leaned over her shoulder, it wasn't like that blond douchebag trying to peer down her cleavage. Instead, a warm draft of whatever cologne he wore washed over her. Really, it was kind of pleasant.

"Pocula Flats. Part of a military installation," he said, peering past her at the screen. "Records, mostly, but a full medical suite for renditions and… other things. Some of the Gibraltar testing was done there."

"Building a better soldier, right?" She tapped at the keyboard again. "Look. It's active again, look at all this chatter. They have someone held there. This signal's heavily encrypted, it's been flashing to get through all the time, but your boss isn't picking up."

"Caldwell is not my *boss*." Was that a faint hint of annoyance in his tone?

If it was, it cheered her up immensely. "You were taking orders from him the last time I saw you, chickie-babe. Anyway, you think he's in trouble, your boss, or just not answering?"

"He has plans of his own. Control might not account for that."

"Control?"

He pointed at the flashing-red signal trying to stream through. "Him."

"Who your boss takes his orders from."

"He is not my *boss*. He was a superior officer, but then…"

"Then what?"

The big lug straightened. Fray bit her lower lip, staring at the screen. Something was happening, the traffic there had a weird pattern, and she longed to dive in and figure out exactly what—

"Three," the big guy said. "They've caught her."

"The woman you were looking for?"

"I was looking for you."

When she glanced up, he looked strange, his gaze distant and a faint sweat-sheen on his forehead. It probably would be best to get the hell away from him before he figured out he wasn't supposed to be helping her, right?

Except, for a moment, he looked a little lost.

"Well, you found me. They have her. What does that mean? Wait. Wait just a second. Three. The… Oh my. The Omega file, right? The woman who survived. *That's* why they were after her." Her head spun for a moment. "Oh, man. Man oh man, this is *weird*."

"We have to go." He'd actually turned pale. "Caldwell isn't coming back to this locale, but we have to *go*."

Fray's bottom lip ached, she was chewing on it so hard. It would be smartest to get the hell out of here, shake the big black-haired guy loose and get out of the country while the getting was good.

The picture from the screen in the police station flashed through her head. The thin woman, staring directly at the camera, working at a crappy grocery store. Maybe she just wanted to be left alone. The files held all sorts of gruesome details about the "induction" process and what it did.

They'd called her a *terrorist*. It was looking to Fray like the woman was a victim. These guys were nothing more than bullies.

Alexandra Frasier hated bullies, and had since the second grade. 3B was really close—it was the base near Felicitas, and what she was thinking was idiotic. Stupid. It wasn't worth a brain of Fray's caliber to even come up with the notion.

Brains aren't everything, honey, Gran had informed her more than once, wearily.

"Oh, *damn* it," Fray said and tapped out two swift commands.

"What?" The guy stepped back as if she'd bitten him.

"Nothing." *I'm about to do something really stupid.* "Listen, mister—"

"Bay. My name's Bay."

Bay and Fray. We rhyme. "Cool. Listen, Bay, you think we could get on that base?"

"Standard penetration. Relatively simple. The trouble is—"

Don't tell me about trouble. "Great! Give me two shakes, and we'll get going."

"What are we going to do?" He sounded like a little kid. If she hadn't seen his spooky speed and unreal strength, she would have believed he was maybe a little slow. "Tell me what to do."

"You're going to get me on that base. We're going to rescue Agent Three." Another few taps, and her back doors were securely inserted. She even took the time to deploy a nifty little program that would begin collating the databases and files she'd been roaming through and forwarding them to a few email addresses—one or two were hers, and the others were journalists for some pretty major publications. The Fourth Estate was going to have a field day with this one. "Did you think, when you woke up this morning, you were gonna be a hero?"

"No." He took the papers she piled in his arms, staring at her as if she was a lunatic. "Is that what I am?"

Don't know. "You bet. Let's get out of here."

The electrodes, well greased, clamped to her temples. Trinity strained against the restraints, trying to whip her head back and forth. Caldwell coughed into his palm, a wet juicy smacking sound. The smell exhaling out of him intensified, rolling in waves. Trinity strained, but he flipped the switch again, and the pain rode through her on the back of a lightning bolt.

Very dimly, she heard someone screaming. A familiar voice, hoarse-raw, her throat burning. The fire ripped through her, body and mind both fraying under the lash.

Pain can be controlled.

And Cal's quiet answer. *Some of it.*

Cal. She clung to the thought. At least he wasn't suffering this. He was as safe as possible, over the border, and she had even unburdened herself of that terrible weight. There was still guilt, and shame aplenty, but she had told him what she did and could leave with a clear conscience.

I want to survive.

It wasn't an option. The jolts came again, electricity pulsing and crackling while the needles jabbed into flesh and the drugs flooded her body, overwhelming the viral responses. She knew the specifics of the process—electric shocks to break certain psychological bonds, the chemicals to override others. After the preparation came the sensory-deprivation tank, then the shocks and drugs again. She had survived.

The males had not.

One did. A new type of agent. Cal, in the darkness, driving himself forward to keep the other agent away from her. Cal on guard, watching out the windows. Cal's face when the trailer doors opened. *I am here to help.*

Trinity clung to the memories, already fading under electrical assault. Harsh grinding bile bubbled in her throat as the virus struggled to keep her functioning and to eat the substances assaulting her tenuous sanity. Strobe-flickers of light, things crawling under her skin, the screams turned to harsh, broken, guttural whimpers.

Taste of frozen strawberries and sugar. *Who am I? I have to know.* Now that she was almost gone, the matrix that made *identity* fragmenting, she could see again how he folded the paper crane, deftly and quickly. It was easy once you knew how.

I never did, she thought desperately, readying herself for another wave of pain, rage, fear, electricity, chemicals.

Something was happening. Caldwell coughed, retching, bent over the controls. There were supposed to be other medical personnel watching, monitoring vitals, fine-tuning dosages. A bevy of observers. *Gentlemen, today we are going to secure ourselves against all enemies, foreign and domestic—*

That was what he had said before her first induction. Who? An older man, graying at the temples, a raspy, cigarette-roughened voice.

The next jolt of agony didn't come. Trinity's muscles cramped, some firing because they had no choice, others still locked into resistance, trying to pull against the restraints.

The *loosening* restraints.

Caldwell retched again. A fresh wave of ugliness roiled through his scent. Something was happening. It was different this time. The flashes of the old induction peeled away, leaving her shivering, muscles locking down, concentration narrowing to a still, small point. Greater strength and flexibility—she wasn't as heavy-strong as the male agents, female biology instead granting her enhanced pain tolerance, flexibility, calculation—and the ruthless feminine willingness to do what had to be done.

Liquidate or leave?

She trembled on the edge of just letting go, willing heart and lungs to cease their functioning. It was easy enough, once you were pushed past endurance.

Or she could make one final, supreme effort. Either the restraints would give, or blood vessels and muscles would burst free, and she would perhaps die anyway.

I'd rather go down fighting, she thought hazily and erupted into violent motion.

Tearing. Needles ripping free—jabs in her thighs, upper arms, a spear of ice at her throat. The nylon straps didn't give, but the one over her left wrist had been slightly improperly secured, and the application of hysterical force popped one of the metal tabs free. A quick twist, a yank, and the one at her elbow was firmly locked—but she could yank upward, bone creaking as it was subjected to horrible sideways stress, then her left arm was free. Her hand blurred across, hitting the catches on her right shoulder and elbow; her right hand slipped out of the loop, leaving a generous proportion of skin behind. Blood burst free; she tore at the tough woven fabric over her throat.

Caldwell straightened from his retching fit and let out a short, garbled cry of warning. It was useless; there was nobody in here but the two of them. Trinity surged upward, her right hand blurring out and sinking deeply into the blond man's stomach. The strike didn't have a great deal of force or leverage, but he was already in bad physical shape. Whatever he had, it made him bend over, a fresh gout of steaming vomit splattering the floor. The titanic stink ratcheted up another notch.

The straps over her hips refused to budge. Trinity yanked desperately on the catch-release, electricity crackled, and the needles moved, vainly seeking her flesh. The ones that hadn't broken sprayed or dripped chemicals, the drugs meant to overpower her viral load spending themselves uselessly. The restraint finally loosened as Caldwell straightened, his flushed, sweating face rising like a bad dream atop fatigues that had once been ironed and starched but were now sweat-soaked and spattered with other effluvia.

"Three," he croaked, "you're not supposed to do that."

He's insane. It was the only possible explanation. Trinity pawed at the catch-release, and it parted grudgingly. If she could just get her legs free—

Caldwell lunged for her, and Trinity's hand flashed up, a palm-strike meant to catch and break the nasal promontory, driving it into the brain.

He lurched with eerie, stuttering speed, and if she hadn't been so concerned with getting herself free she might have had more time for the blinding realization that he was infected, and the virus—Gibraltar or Gemini, it didn't matter—was eating him alive. Snot rimed his nostrils. The speed of his physical collapse was astounding, but he was for the moment incredibly fast.

Agent fast.

He jerked aside, the strike catching him on cheek instead of nose, and stumbled back, his hands blurring up to clap at his face. "You *bitch*!" he moaned, his mouth a loose wet round O. Trinity scrambled, the thin fabric onesie tearing. A needle jabbed for her hip, another one for where her chest would have been, servomotors whining. He had expected to run the induction on her with no witnesses, and had somehow infected himself with the virus.

Yes, she decided as her hands found the releases for her knees, he was definitely, incredibly and utterly crazy.

"You're *not supposed to do that*!" he howled and lunged for her again.

Trinity *moved*, one naked hip burning against the table's metal surface, a fulcrum her entire body turned around. Her right foot flicked, sinking into his stomach, and she grabbed at a handy metal servo-arm, this one topped with a gruesomely large needle meant to deliver a massive dose into the subject's thigh. Steel screamed, delicate machinery screeching to a halt, and she might have regretted interfering with such beautifully modulated gears and movements if the situation had been otherwise.

As it was, she finished spinning, folded her knees and got her feet underneath her on the slick table surface. Caldwell sprawled against the control console, and Trinity had to dodge another jabbing needle. The electrodes crackled, smeared with conductive goop, and the entire apparatus let forth a shuddering, grinding whine.

It was getting ready to discharge again.

How had Caldwell become infected? Did it matter? Would the infection spread? The consequences of such a thing were vast, a trembling matrix of analysis and percentages inside her aching, riven head. A deeper certainty grew underneath them as she paused, watching him scrabble feebly at the console. She'd kicked him with all the force she was able to gather, perhaps rupturing something.

It will all be over soon, and we'll be together.

Had he infected *himself*?

She coughed to clear her throat, spat to the side, an economical, efficient motion. The world spun, righted itself, and her body was a loose collection of puppet joints. Freeing herself had taken most of her strength, and now she balanced unsteadily on the edge of unconsciousness, swaying and staring at the hazy shape that was Noah Caldwell.

Who, calmly enough, his eyes glittering with fever, fumbled at his hip.

And drew a gun.

The screaming stopped, and the seething fermentation of the medical building took a deep breath, pausing before the plunge. Sooner or later they were going to decide to sweep hall by hall, and that would require both of them to get even more creative. Reese's scent held an edge now, a complex stew of smoke-laced worry. He checked the corner. "Clear."

"She's got to be down here," Cal found himself saying unnecessarily.

Reese nodded, but Cal could guess the likely chain of thought. *Our chances go down the longer we're in here. Is it really worth it?* Especially if the other man was feeling the way Cal was—the headache mounting, his arms and legs not quite moving the way they should. He was still fast, and still stronger than a normal human, but now he began to see what Trinity called "degradation." It had only been a little over thirty-six hours.

What was *she* feeling?

It made him a little unsteady, to be honest. The rage, simmering just under the surface, wanted to work free. He'd failed Tracy, and he'd stupidly allowed Trinity to think whatever she did under Bronson's thumb meant anything, and now he was about to fail her in the most basic of ways, as well. If Reese decided to cut the losses and vanish, well, Cal couldn't blame him.

It was tempting to just throw up your hands and say *I've done all I can.* You could justify it a million different ways, and Reese would be justified in a million and one. He could abort, go meet up with Holly, be back over the border and safe in two shakes.

Cold, calculated self-preservation was trained into an agent. Anything else was that unholy bugbear they wanted to get rid of.

Emotional noise.

Reese glanced at him again.

Cal took a deep breath. "You can go." He pitched the words nice and low; they wouldn't carry even to hidden microphones. "Get your girl and get out of here."

The other man shrugged, covering the hallway. Cal moved automatically into the next pocket, covering, as well; they leapfrogged once more. It was outright nerve-racking even if you were trained for this sort of thing.

That was what they couldn't give you in training. You could know, intellectually, the way your pulse wanted to spike, the way sensory acuity turned every step into an excruciating feedback loop and every inch of skin into a hypersensitive antenna.

Actually living through it, though, that was another thing entirely.

I didn't sign up for this. None of us did.

Here he was, in the middle of hostile territory, right where he needed to be confident and invulnerable. Instead, his pulse kept wanting to spike, and all he could think of were a pair of big dark eyes and her soft mouth in the darkness. How the merry-go-round had stopped, and everything in the world narrowed down to a single small, still center.

Trinity.

She'd come back for him, even though she thought he'd be furious at her for any part in Tracy's death.

It wasn't your fault, he wanted to tell her. *They put us here, we didn't know what we were signing up for. We wanted to serve, and we were told to kill.*

"We should pull out," Reese said finally, very softly. "She's stopped. You know what that means."

Generally, yes. It meant liquidation.

Cal's mouth tightened. "I'm not leaving her."

Reese, with his gun pointed down the hallway, actually rolled his eyes. "Good. I was thinking you were about to bail."

"Never." Cal showed his teeth, a facsimile of a smile, and realized it was true. Getting out of here was the safe, sane, reasonable move, since the chances of her being alive were sliding downhill every moment.

The look on her face when she tasted her first milk shake. The gold in her hair. Her hands, checking the wound, her soft husky voice in the darkness.

If they've killed her...

It almost blinded him. His body moved smoothly, mechanically, training worn into muscle memory. If he could smell the rage simmering off his skin, the other agent certainly could. But Reese betrayed no nervousness. Cool and calm, he moved ahead of Cal, stopping every once in a while to test the air.

They waited in a janitor's closet while a patrol went past, three normal men moving with what they probably thought was cautious silence. Cal's free hand turned into a fist, longing thoughts of smashing the door open and taking on all of them, then just charging forward until he found her, danced through his aching skull. The effort almost made him sweat, the close confines of the closet full of the thick scent of two agents, one a haze of stress and fury, the other's smell of calm determination beginning to fray a little.

It was a relief to get out into the halls again. It felt like forever, the ringing silence where Trinity's muffled screams used to be. In reality, it wasn't very long before they heard another sharp sound, one that stopped Reese cold and jerked Cal's head up.

A gunshot.

Reese jolted forward, but Cal was already running. He plunged around a corner, the throat of a long fluorescent-lit hallway opening up in front of him, and there was a set of sealed double doors at the end, the light overhead flashing red. *Biohazard! Containment!* Cal hit them at full speed, glass shattering and the lock snapping, and a wave of sickness and death rolled out to envelop him. His shoulder crunched with pain, even agent-strong bones rebelling, and he found himself outside a containment tent, shadows moving inside the billowing opaque plastic. A faint whiff of gunfire, the iron-copper tang of blood and burned metal of agonizing pain, he ripped the plastic aside and stumbled into the operating theater.

For a moment what he saw made no sense. A

vaguely familiar blond man with a bloody face, his fatigues covered in vomit and his patches proclaiming him a major even though he was too young. Thin trickles of blood slid down from his nose and eyes, and his cheeks were aglow with fever. The gun was steady, though, and it was pointed straight at Reese, the blond's bleeding eyes widening as he swayed sideways, hitting a huge control console with his hip.

Thick cables ran from the console to an operating table, and crouched on the table, in a torn, tattered hospital onesie, was Trinity, gaunt and feral-eyed, bleeding from several places, several metal arms attached to the table's base looming over and around her like petals. A deadly flower, and the marks on her matched the pattern.

Restraints were thrown free—she'd been strapped down, and those things had been jabbing at her. Electricity crackled, more sparks fountaining, and the burning insulation smell wasn't just gunfire. It was just short of an electrical fire in here.

The fury inside Cal mounted another notch.

She had just finished gathering herself, sinking on her haunches, and the bullet intended for her had hit the base of the table instead, sparks fountaining from the jagged hole. A layer of burning insulation was added to the simmering stew, and Cal almost gagged.

"Who the—" The blond choked on another spray of vomit. Whatever he had, it was bad. He swayed again, and Cal realized where he'd seen him—the police station in Felicitas, running the grids looking for Trinity. So he'd been military, and part of Division, too.

"Cal!" Trinity blurted, and he had time to think that she actually sounded pretty happy to see him, all things considered, before the blond man pulled the trigger.

A padded hammer struck Cal right in the gut. He folded over, his stupid body not realizing he'd been shot until he tried to straighten and the pain began, breaking every barrier the virus gave him. He staggered, his own gun rising, and the blond had turned his attention from Cal back to the honey-haired, gaunt, impossibly beautiful woman on the table, who was uncoiling to leap. Not at him, but toward Cal, to put herself between him and the danger.

God, she's amazing. Training was still with him, even though his head was very light and he suspected the virus couldn't heal a gutshot. *I don't deserve her.* Something was chewing at his stomach, its fangs sinking in, but his own gun finished its steady movement, and a great calm stillness fell over Cal.

So this is where it ends. Make it count, soldier.

He squeezed the trigger.

The blond's head evaporated, and Trinity let out a short garbled scream. She launched herself, colliding with Cal a bare second after the gun spoke, and they went down in a tangle of blood, foulness and

huge clawing agony. He heard his own voice screaming as well, a hoarse cry as the pain swallowed him
whole, and the last thing he heard was her repeating his name raggedly while she clasped his body
in her slim, iron-hard, trembling arms.

This is going to take some thought. Reese eyed
the wreckage. An almost-naked woman, a gutshot
agent, a dead body with a major's oak leaves on its
sleeves and smoke beginning to waft from the ten-
tacled nightmare of a hellish operating table. Trinity
stared up at him, her dark eyes wide and her cheeks
slick with salt water, and blinked twice.

"Here." He holstered his gun, bending, and she
made a short, sharp movement, pulling Cal's limp,
bloody body closer. "He'll probably live, if we can
get that bullet out. Do you know this place?"

She looked, for a few moments, as if she'd forgotten what English meant. Then she swallowed hard
and nodded. Her lips moved, then firmed, and she
finally spoke.

"Six." A crack-pop of electricity under the word.

A cold finger touched his nape. It'd been a while
since anyone called him that. "It's Reese, ma'am.
Let's get him up."

She examined him from top to toe. A while ago
he might not have let her, just moved to grab Cal
and get him somewhere they could fish the damn
bullet out if it hadn't gone through him. Since Holly,
though, he'd become a little more patient.

Just a little.

Cal stirred a little. It looked as if it hurt. He was still trying to fight, even in his half-conscious daze. Trinity levered both of them upright, grimacing, and her doubtful acceptance of Reese was solidified when he stepped close, grabbing Cal's arm and pulling it over his shoulder. "Let's go."

She nodded, let go of Cal's deadweight and stepped away on unsteady legs. Reese was about to say something—but she simply bent over the major's body, her quick fingers finding the gun and freeing more ammunition from his puke-splattered belt. She popped a fresh clip in, her fingers fumbling slightly, turned around and reapproached as a thin flame danced near the base of the table. She coughed to clear her throat and she was whiter than flour, as if she'd lost a lot of blood. Those dark eyes hooded, she took three steps and stumbled, righted herself, and Reese got the idea she'd keel over before they got to the end of the hallway outside.

She didn't seem to notice she was only wearing shreds of thin blue-patterned cloth; flat straps of muscle stood out underneath her skin. Every ounce of extraneous fat was gone, her metabolism burning overtime to fuel virus-enhanced muscles and healing, but even so, she wasn't as heavy as the male agents. He'd wondered why Holly hadn't turned out agent-strong; it was looking as if Trinity hadn't, either.

But she was plenty determined. Reese could respect that, even if he wasn't entirely sure she was trustworthy.

"I…" She coughed, spat to clear her throat and stepped close to Cal again, taking his other arm and heaving grimly. "I know a way out."

"We've got to get the bullet out. Unless—" He checked, as Cal began to surface, probably aware he was moving. "Well, goddammit. It went straight through him." Too soon to tell if that was good or bad luck, though.

She simply put her head down and began hauling him for the door. Cal hung heavily between them, Trinity weaved, and Reese began to think they weren't going to get out of this alive.

Because there were more shadows outside the rippling plastic, and they were probably armed.

"Halt!" someone yelled, and there was the popping zing of gunfire. Reese hit the floor, Cal going down, too, in an inglorious heap, but Trinity stood, her knees locked, and raised the gun. Did she *want* to die? Jesus.

"Get down!" Reese yelled, but she didn't listen, aiming carefully through the plastic. Now Reese could see the holes blown in it, and black smoke began to puff up from the table in earnest.

More flashes of gunfire. Trinity cocked her head thoughtfully. A smear of blood on her cheek—where had that come from? Cal groaned, Reese rolled him onto his side so he wouldn't choke on whatever came out of him, and it occurred to him again—they were going to die here.

At least Holly was safe. How long would she last without him, though?

"Friendly!" someone yelled outside, and Trinity stiffened.

It was a woman's voice.

"Yo!" the new arrival yelled again, and Reese braced himself to shoot whoever came through the plastic sheets. "Hey—Agent Three, Alice Wharton, whoever you are, we're on your side! Let's get out of here, okay?"

Alice? Reese glanced at Trinity.

Who lowered her gun, slightly. Her hair hung in a darkened mop. She wore a faint, abstract look, and the terrible gashes and punctures all over her had begun to seal. Thin threads of blood trickled down her hips, and tremendous bruises flowered all over her scrawny body.

"Alice Wharton, social security number—" The new voice rattled off a list of numbers. "My name's Fray, I'm here to help you, just don't shoot me, okay?"

Trinity lowered her gun the rest of the way. She glanced down at Reese, and at Cal, who was moving feebly.

Take care of him, she mouthed and dived forward through the plastic sheets, rolling out of sight.

Reese swore internally. Popping clatters, more gunfire, a short female cry of pain.

He was about to shake himself loose of Cal's unconscious weight and bellycrawl for the curtains when they twitched aside, and a dark-eyed, black-haired agent with linebacker shoulders glanced down at him. He had a 9mm but it wasn't leveled, and behind him was a chestnut-haired girl, her green tea and healthy female scent almost agent-strong and complementary to Black Hair's.

The young woman had Trinity's arm over her shoulder, and she was grinning as if it was Christmas and New Year's rolled into one. "God, it stinks in here," she chirped. "I'm Fray, and this is Bay. He took care of the guys out there, but we'd better get going. I figure you're on the right side, since you're all beat up and everything, right?"

Trinity murmured something, her head hanging forward. She swayed, almost passing out.

Reese let out a long breath, watching Black Hair. The agent bent carefully, just out of strike range, and offered his hand.

"Truce?" he said in a flat, expressionless tone.

Reese decided they'd better get out of there before anyone else came along to join the circus, and took the proffered hand. "Help me get him up."

"I saw they'd captured her—her name's not really Alice, is it? She's Omega. Wow." Fray bounced in the passenger's seat; Bay wouldn't let her drive. The laundry van, full of bags of clean uniforms, shuddered and jounced as he piloted it across a stretch of desert. He was certainly handy to have around, that guy, even if he was creepy as all get-out. At least she could be sure he was on the right side now. "And you, you must be other guys from the program. Which ones are you?"

The dark-haired one—Reese—doused the blond guy's nasty stomach wound with something that smelled like disinfectant and ripped a towel in half with one quick, efficient yank. "He's losing a lot of blood. Trinity, hold this down—"

"Trinity," Fray repeated. "Got it. Look, can I help or anything? That looks pretty bad."

"What's our heading?" Reese said over her.

"Southeast," Bay replied, not turning from the road. "Should be a breach point there."

"Are you sure?"

"I calculate it with some certainty, yes."

"Great," Reese muttered.

"It's the way we got in, at least." Fray unclicked her seat belt, despite Bay glancing at her. She struggled into the back, where the woman—Trinity—hovered, pale and swaying, almost naked and obviously in a deep state of shock. She kept staring at the blond man bleeding all over a pile of cloth laundry bags. "This guy's magic with bolt cutters and copper wire, let me tell you. Honey, let's find you some clothes."

Trinity glanced at her, then down at herself as if she hadn't realized she was naked. "Oh." She swayed again, and the bruises and blood all over her would have made Fray lightheaded-sick if she hadn't gulped, bit the inside of her cheek, and started digging in the bags to find something that wasn't towels.

"I think I've got it figured out." If Fray didn't keep talking, she was going to throw up, too. It looked *awful*; the other woman had been through hell. "Trinity means you're Three, right? You're Omega. Your file—wow, it's *amazing*. What they did to you was awful, and then—"

"My file?" That got her attention. She cast a glance over the sacks, pointed at one. "That one should have something. My file?"

"Oh yeah. It took some doing to get into. You know they wanted to breed you? You were the only one who survived the Prometheus process."

"Induction," Trinity said. She stopped, swaying even more than the rocking of the van called for, and might have keeled over if Fray hadn't caught her arm. Her fingers sank in—the other woman was just skin and bones, her hips high arches stretching flawless, almost-translucent skin.

"Yeah, that." Fray dug in the bag—it held uniforms, and she began yanking handfuls of cloth out. "They had a whole projected pattern—harvesting eggs, in vitro, chowder to cashews. Was that Caldwell back there?"

A glimmer of suspicion in Trinity's large dark eyes. She was beautiful, even if she'd been hitting the anorexia button a little too hard. "You knew him?"

"He had me working to track you. Nice trick with the SSN, by the way. I couldn't figure it out until I thought about algorithms."

"Yes." Trinity's eyes closed, her head dropped forward, and she jerked back into consciousness when Fray grabbed her, bracing them both against a pile of bags lashed down with nylon webbing. "Who are you?"

"I *told* you, I'm Fray." She snapped open a uniform shirt—desert camo was such a weird fabric, she had to look up how they made it. "They had me looking for you until I figured out you weren't the bad guy. The East Coast's been trying to get hold of Caldwell for a while now. That was my first indication anything—"

"Control," Trinity murmured. "Of course. Caldwell…infected himself."

"He *what*?" Reese piped up. "Was that what was wrong with him?"

"Yes." Trinity managed to button the shirt, reached for the pants—the only small pair Fray could find in the bag—and her knees folded. She went down hard, and Fray, unprepared, went down with her.

"Hold on," Bay said from the front. "This could get slightly bumpy."

The wounded guy screamed, a lonely, despairing sound, and Fray's stomach revolted. There had been actual *bullets*. Bay had even punched a guy in the face. He moved like lightning, and the sound bones made as they broke was *definitely* uncool. He was a machine, and while he'd been pretty awesome so far, Fray kept hearing those crunches, her ears still ringing from all the gunshots, and she had made up her mind.

This was too deep for Alexandra Frasier, and she was getting out just as soon as possible.

For the meantime, though, she tried to arrange Trinity so she was comfortable next to the still-bleeding man. Reese, keeping his balance with a cat's lithe grace, kept working, up to his elbows in blood. He had an assortment of medical tools and some disinfectant, and it looked as if he was doing pretty good so far.

Fray's throat burned with bile. She kept telling herself not to throw up, not to throw up, not to throw up, and the laundry van barreled through the base fencing and into the desert night.

Trinity floated in comforting darkness, only half-aware of a soft, restful voice and warmth all around her. Someone held a cup to her lips; she drank greedily. Dense, calorie-rich, sweetened milk; her body seized the nutrition gratefully. The voice was familiar, but she couldn't attach a name to its soft cadences.

"She's going to be fine." A woman's voice, sweet and throaty, a comforting layer of musk and goldenness to her scent.

"Yeah." Another woman, sounding very young, this one with a hint of brunette, caramel and green tea. "Look, it's been fun and all, but I've got to jet."

"Oh?"

"Yeah. Don't… I mean, here. This is for her." A sound of paper moving. "Reese told me she went in there to find out who she was. What they did to her…it's just, you know. It's awful."

"People do awful things."

"Tell me about it."

Trinity stirred. Her entire body ached. She wanted, of all things, a milk shake. And other things—red meat, kale, Gatorade. The list of cravings was long and specific, her body informing her of various elements necessary for her continued survival.

I'm…alive.

For how long? Who else was here? Her eyes refused to open.

"So anyway," the young woman said brightly, "I'm going to scram while the Terrible Two are out having fun. Can you, uh, tell Bay it's been real? And to take care of himself?"

"Are you sure you want to go? Seems like he's good protection."

Trinity finally found names for the voices. One was Holly Candless. The younger one was the girl from the laundry truck, the gemina with the black-haired agent who reeked of induction and pain.

Fray. What an odd name.

"Oh no," the new gemina said hurriedly. "If I

stay away from him, I don't *need* protection. Besides, I have to think about the best way of breaking the story."

"You might want to consider—" Candless was endlessly patient, but a certain inflection told Trinity it was an uphill battle.

"Are you gonna hold a gun on me?"

"That's not how I do things."

"Okay, then. I'm outie. Remember, this is for her, when she wakes up."

"I think she's getting there. Fray, are you sure—"

"See you." Quick light footsteps, an interior door opening and closing.

Trinity's eyelids drifted up. Things were a bit blurry, but she kept blinking until they cleared and found herself staring at a white ceiling while a brown ceiling fan turned lazily. Its mechanism wasn't choked with dust, and there was no yellowing tape on the ceiling where flypaper used to hang.

That's right. I left that room. She focused afresh and found a familiar blue-gray gaze.

Holly Candless, her straight black hair secured in two braids wrapped around her head, smiled. She looked positively *glowing* with health and had gained some weight. Enough that her cheeks were no longer hollow, and her essential beauty shone through.

"You're looking well," Trinity croaked.

Holly beamed, bending over the bed and helping her to sit up. "Hello to you, too. I've been wanting to see you for ages." She propped two crisp pillows behind Trinity's back, and her goldenmusk scent held no tinge of stress, anger or terror. She pushed the sleeves of a peach knit shirt up and cracked a bottle of Evian from the nightstand.

"Why?" Trinity's throat wouldn't work quite right. Holly held the water bottle to her lips, and Trinity subtracted it from the other woman's fingers, taking long even swallows. It felt *wonderful*, but not as good as food would. She needed fuel. Some manner of sponge bath had been administered, probably by Holly, but the itching and crusting all over her told Trinity she was in dire need of a shower, as well. First, though, there were more important questions to be answered. "Where are we?"

"Nogales. Safe for the moment. Reese wasn't happy about using one of his contacts here, but—"

"Cal?"

Holly's face fell slightly. A sharp stabbing pain went through Trinity's chest, and the world grayed out for a moment, came back in a rush of color and noise.

"—so he's sleeping now. The bullet went all the way through him. They were worried about infection. But the virus…well, he pulled through." Candless's slight frown deepened. "He kept calling for you."

"How did—"

"Well, it's a long story, but I had a feeling Cal would need help. And I wanted to see you again. You left in a hurry last time."

Sinaloa. "I didn't want—"

"I know. Look, you smell hungry. Let's get some food in you. I went shopping, got you some clean clothes. As soon as Cal's able to get up we'll be on our way. I hope you'll stick around this time."

"Why?" It made no *sense*. They were obeying different directives than the ones she was familiar with. They had risked themselves—or had Eight discovered he was, after all, angry at her? Was it revenge? Why would they not have left her to Caldwell's tender mercies, then?

"I *like* you, Trinity. Have you ever thought about that?"

"No." *I am not likable.* "Ms. Candless, I was there when you were brought in. I ran the percentages on that operation. I also—"

"Saved me from Bronson, and saved Cal and Reese, too."

"I wasn't going to save them."

"Oh, you said it wasn't a good percentage, but you came along anyway. Stop trying to talk me out of how I feel, all right? Reese does that sometimes. It's irritating."

"Apologies," Trinity mumbled. What did Candless *want*?

"Also," the other woman continued, "Fray left this for you. Said you'd want it." She laid the file in Trinity's lap. It was labeled TOP SECRET, CLASSIFIED, and the typed label on the tab simply said GIBRALTAR THREE/OMEGA.

Trinity's missing file. "She... Fray. Who is she?"

"A hacker, I think. Here." Candless produced an energy bar. "Start with that and the water. I'll bring up milk and some supplements, and make you some eggs. You like eggs?"

Trinity nodded, although she could have informed the woman that her only experience with eggs was the powdered kind endemic in United States Army mess halls. It would be far more palatable to simply dump protein powder into a milk shake. It would be very worthwhile to learn how to make her own milk shakes, in whatever time she had left.

"Good. I'll scramble them. The boys will be hungry, too."

"Ms. Candless—"

"It's *Holly.*"

"Holly. I...have been thinking."

"Oh?" She halted near the door smiling, a stripe of sunlight down her face.

"I am...sorry. If I hadn't helped Division, you wouldn't have suffered...what you did."

The other woman nodded, studying Trinity gravely for a few moments. "Reese thinks like that sometimes. The truth is, well, things worked out. Don't beat yourself up over it, okay? You did the best you could."

Did I? But Trinity didn't respond. She simply bowed her head, staring at her blanket-clad knees, and listened as Holly left, closing the door with a quiet click.

She touched the folder's manila outside with one fingertip. *Fray.* Very strange.

This, then, was what she had risked everything to acquire. Why, now that she had it, did she suddenly want to tear it into unrecognizable bits?

Fear. She was afraid, and had been for some time. The unsuccessful induction had jolted some things loose inside her head, electricity uncovering forgotten shoals, the drug cocktails turning reality into a blurring, twisting nightmare. One thing was clear: the first induction process had not removed emotional noise. It merely masked it, numbing the subject and removing memory instead.

Without a past, anyone could be molded into the most useful shape. A creature traumatized into numbness could even gnaw off its own limbs to escape a trap.

She'd been so sure she was initially free of emotional noise.

Doesn't look like it from out here, Cal said in her memory. Why had he come after her?

Strange. She'd thought she could rest after she held her file. With the threat of deconstruction somewhat removed, other desires surfaced.

First, though, she had to know who she had been, even if that other woman, the pre-Trinity, had been... what? A willing participant, a follower of orders, a petty tyrant?

Like Bronson? Like Caldwell?

There was always a risk.

Trinity's throat was dry. She flipped open the folder and began to read.

He woke up with the worst goddamn hangover of his life, his gut on fire and his head pounding. Someone held his shoulders, and he almost starfished, throwing out arms and legs to fend off an attack, but then he smelled her—a strong, beautiful, deep blue flood—and it soothed him as nothing else could. She was *here*, and he quieted, drinking the water in long gulps.

Next came a protein shake; it tasted awful but at least there weren't any greens in it. A slight medicinal tang—penicillin. It wouldn't kill the virus, so why were they dosing him? Was he in a hospital?

It didn't matter. *She* was here. "The fever's going down." Her voice, soft, without its usual crispness. "It's a good thing the slug didn't hit bone."

"The boys are back." Another familiar voice, a woman's, but not *her*. Cool fingers on his forehead, and Cal opened his eyes.

The light stung, stabbing and scouring the inside of his skull. The room was bright with reflected sunlight, and a few sniffs through his crust-congested nose returned a confusing palette of dust, fried food, chilies and blood. *Where the hell...*

It didn't matter, because Trinity leaned over him, holding the protein-shake bottle. Her cheeks had hollowed out, her face pared down to bone, and the thinness gave her an ethereal quality. Her honey hair fell damp against her shoulders. An edge of harsh soap told him she'd just bathed, and the clothes were new—a navy V-neck T-shirt, a pair of jeans that weren't quite broken in yet. Bare arms, dotted with rapidly fading bruises and the pink stripes of fresh scar tissue, and her expression was thoughtful, no longer blank.

Her eyes, though, were still the same, wide and wounded. Moss-dark, threads of gold in the irises— she was dusted and woven through with gold, inside and out.

She just couldn't see it.

"Stay still," she said softly.

It was her fingers on his forehead; he twitched and caught her wrist. His hand was clumsy, kitten-weak, but she made no attempt to evade him.

"Don't leave," he rasped. "Stay here."

She was about to reply, but there were heavy foot-steps, the door opened and Reese appeared.

Behind him loomed the black-haired agent Cal had hit with a car *and* thrown down several flights of stairs. It felt like ages ago. He tensed, but Trinity simply glanced at them and didn't appear to judge Black Hair as a threat.

Black Hair stopped, his head lifting. "Where is she?"

Holly appeared at the other end of the room, carrying a fully laden tray. "Good Lord, I can't believe I used to do this all the time. Hi, guys. Looks like someone's awake."

Black Hair, however, was having none of this. *"Where is she?"*

"Fray?" Holly looked supremely unconcerned. "She had things to do, she said. I think she's planning on mischief. It should be interesting—"

Black Hair took two steps toward Holly, violence prickling in the air, and Cal might have leaped to his feet if Trinity hadn't grabbed his shoulder, forcing him back down on the couch. It didn't matter, because Reese stepped sideways and dropped his center of gravity, and Black Hair stopped cold.

"I don't think you want to get nasty, friend." Reese's dark eyes were level, intent and very cold.

Black Hair subsided. "Where. Did. She. Go?"

Cal couldn't help himself. "Who? Where did *who* go?"

"Fray," Trinity supplied helpfully. "This is Agent Bay. Short for Beta. I have some questions about the induction process I want to ask him, but—"

Fray and Bay? It sounds like a sitcom. "Fray? What?"

"She hacked Division's main core." Trinity looked over her shoulder, studied Bay intently. "It appears Agent Bay was only tracking us to follow her."

"Spectacles Girl," Cal muttered. "I knew it. Complementary. This is going to be good."

"I have to go." Bay relaxed, muscle by muscle, but his expression didn't change. He kicked the door shut behind him, closing off a slice of darkened hallway, and Cal's midsection gave another twitching jab of pain.

His head throbbed, too. "Christ, can you keep it down?" His throat burned, and Trinity tried to raise the protein shake to his lips again. He kept his hand on her wrist, not quite willing to believe she was here, and alive, and safe.

As safe as she could be with Cal weak and feeling like death warmed over.

"Okay," Reese said calmly enough. "You know how to get in touch if you want to join forces, Bay. Go get your girl."

"She said something about a beach," Holly supplied helpfully, setting the tray on a rickety maplewood table. "Don't you want breakfast before you—"

"No." Bay turned on his heel, his shoulders coming back up, and halted. He cast one brief, passionless glance at Cal. "You."

I ran him over. He's probably not feeling charitable. "Uh. Hi."

"Thank you" was all the black-haired man said, before popping back out the door he'd just kicked shut.

Silence returned. "Didn't you incapacitate him?" Trinity tried to pull her wrist away, but he wouldn't let go.

"Yeah, well, that works both ways. Trinity. You're *here.*"

"Yes. You need calories." Just as calmly as if he hadn't been chasing her all over creation. "Drink this. Ms. Candl—*Holly* made breakfast. Another dose of penicillin should—"

"Don't ever leave me like that again." He meant it to sound forbidding, but it came out flat and tired instead. "Do you hear me? Don't *do* that."

"Cal…" Her face fell. "I…"

"Hi, honey," Holly said brightly across the room. "Come help me in the kitchen."

"We've got to get out of here." Reese let her pull him along, with only a token glance in Cal's direction. "I don't trust him, and Felipe's edgy."

"In a little bit. Come on." And, neatest trick of the week, she tugged him into what had to be a kitchenette. Cal vaguely remembered someone saying something about the border, and hanging between two agents while Holly and another slight female form half-carried a coughing Trinity, sand gritting underfoot and a van burning behind them, a smoking crimson star in the night.

Trinity tried to straighten; he kept her wrist. She didn't pull free, though.

"Don't." He tugged at her. "You thought I— You didn't know, for Chrissake. You aren't responsible for Tracy. You didn't—"

"I calculated." Her cheeks were pale, bloodless. She needed a few more meals and some downtime. She needed some safety and a place to relax, and *he* needed to get his arms around her, lock them tight and not let go until he got it through her stubborn, beautiful brain that she was not going *anywhere* without him. "I planned—"

"Yeah, well, I did the killing for them. We're both just as wrong, okay? *Okay?* Don't leave me. Don't do that again." His belly twinged again and he suppressed a wince. If she hared off to go do something else suicidal, he was going to have to get up and follow, even if it ruptured tissue-thin repair around his guts and they spilled out like gray noodles.

"I thought you would want…revenge." Her mouth pulled down against itself, and she looked so sad and lost it threatened to break whatever in his body was still functioning. "I thought you'd be furious."

"I am. Not at you. At *them*, can't you see?"

Her gaze dropped, and he found the strength to raise his other hand. All his limbs felt like slabs of recalcitrant beef. "Trinity." Running his callused, dirty fingertips over her smooth porcelain cheek. The scraping reminded him of just how harsh he probably sounded, just how dirty he was.

Inside and out.

A single, crystalline tear slid down her other cheek. She swallowed hard. "Fray had my file," she whispered. "It wasn't complete, but…my name was Anne. Anne Hampton. I was a medic."

Okay. The pain was coming again. What was she about to say?

She finally met his gaze again, and the raw aching in her eyes was worse than his insides burning as they healed. His body was cannibalizing its reserves, and he needed food.

But he needed to understand, and make *her* understand, first.

Her throat worked. Finally, the words came, small and stark. "I don't know who I am."

Cal let out a short, harsh breath. *Is that it?* "Okay."

She seemed to expect more, searching his face, and he was abruptly aware of how filthy he smelled.

"Who do you want to be?" he finally added and decided to tack something else on. "And don't give me any of that *deconstructing* noise again. You're going to survive, dammit. You're going to be fine."

Whatever she was looking for in his dirty, stubbled face, she seemed to find it. The thin, drawn sadness eased a little, and she leaned closer. He tried to curl up to get closer, but his stomach flared with pain.

It didn't matter because she crossed the remaining distance and her mouth was on his; he tasted her toothpaste and felt a brief flash of regret at how he smelled before most of his aches miraculously disappeared and an entirely new, pleasant half-pain appeared.

I got shot in the gut. I should have died. But he hadn't, and Trinity was right in front of him, and *God* but he wanted to prove they were both alive in the oldest way known to their species.

She pulled away, and his hands fell to his sides. The weakness was maddening.

"Just tell me what you want me to do." He tried not to let it sound as if he was begging.

The thin, pallid smile blooming on her face was worth a little begging, though. "I want you to eat. Restoring mobility and combat capability is crucial. Then…"

"Then what?"

The smile struggled, then widened, and it knocked all the breath clean out of him.

Trinity straightened. "I'll tell you after breakfast."

Six Weeks Later

"I don't like this," Cal muttered for the seventh time. "It feels off."

Trinity raised the binoculars, scanning the row of brownstones. "Fifteen percent chance of passive surveillance, if they suspect the induction process is imperfect." Tension had settled in her shoulders; she breathed in deeply, focusing out through the rain-spotted windshield. Two paper cranes stood sentinel on her side of the dash, one blue, one yellow. "It's occupied."

"Well, this is DC. Lots of people looking for a place to live." He scanned the street again, shifting a little in the seat to keep his muscles supple. There was still an angry explosion of scar tissue on his muscled abdomen, and she sometimes traced the ridges and valleys, imagining a star birthing itself. He froze when she did so, and the edge of deep blue musk his scent took on was…interesting. Equally fascinating was the result of such caresses.

He was certainly *inventive*.

The radio warbled softly, liquid streams of Chopin rising and falling. It was almost time for NPR to broadcast the news, but for now she could savor the pattern of the notes, analyzing where each would fall, and no fog of pain or distortion interfered. She lowered the binoculars, searching the street. Dripping trees, a streetlight peering through tossing leaves, cracked pavement.

"Does it look familiar?"

"Vaguely." The file had large gaps in it. Parts of Trinity's service record, part of the medical evaluations and some college transcripts remained. Dredging through public records turned up nothing but blank walls. Anne Hampton had been scrubbed from existence, and the only pieces of her left were in the slim manila folder that held a black-and-white picture of a smiling, much younger Trinity in a Navy medic's uniform, her hair much darker and the shadows of teenage acne still lingering on her cheeks.

There was no trace of teenage spots left on her now, and whatever memories she had, the second induction had scrambled them, possibly irretrievably. Even the nightmares were gone.

"Do you need to go inside?" Cal, very gently.

He thought it was too dangerous for her to be here. *They'll look for you, you're high value. We should go back over the border.*

This was the only residential address in the file. Anne Hampton had lived here, once.

They had a six-hour window. There were plane tickets waiting, fresh passports, and in a few days they would rendezvous with Reese and Holly again. *Don't make us come get you*, Holly had said, cheerfully enough, but Trinity had caught a glimpse of Reese's expression and thought it very likely he agreed in ways Holly didn't understand.

Candless was a civilian, after all.

"Trin?"

Trinity bit gently at her lower lip. It was no use. There was nothing for her here.

If she said *yes*, though, Cal would be her backup. He wouldn't like it; he thought it was too goddamn dangerous, but he wouldn't let her do it alone.

There was, she reflected, a comfort to be found in that. Funny, she had never thought of herself as *lonely*, but now she recognized the…

The feeling. Strange how you could only see its dimensions when it was no longer present. That morning, Cal had given her a pack of origami paper, with a diffident smile.

She scanned the street one more time, searching for anything that looked even remotely familiar, hoping to jog a piece of the puzzle loose. Chopin ended, and Cal touched the volume knob.

"Welcome to NPR's evening report. This is Casey Guilstrom. Washington, DC, was rocked this after-

noon by the release of a Guardian *story detailing allegations of biological weaponry research and genetic manipulation by US defense contractors, as well as assassinations and covert activities on both foreign and domestic soil. The project, code-named Gibraltar, was incredibly secret, and the anonymous whistleblower apparently sent documents to every major news outlet."*

"Holy…" Cal turned it up again. Trinity's skin roughened with gooseflesh.

"Fray," she breathed. "She did it."

"Many allegations center around one Arthur Hampton, a reclusive billionaire on the board of several defense companies in the DC area—"

"Hampton?" Cal's mouth shaped the word. His hand found Trinity's, his fingers slipping through hers. She squeezed, every inch of her gone cold.

A smoke-roughened voice, scrambled through filters. *Arthur Hampton.* Was she truly familiar with the name, or was she simply free-associating? *Not enough data.* Still, it sounded so familiar. She thought of forests, of the sun in her eyes, a slope under her feet as she hiked upward…

It was gone.

The announcer kept going. The Pentagon had no comment yet. Several other media outlets hinted at further releases. They were all scrambling for a piece of the story now. The confusion would be massive, the damage to Division incalculable.

Trinity was suddenly aware of sweat on her skin, her breathing coming harsh and short, and Cal's tension.

"Trin? Honey?"

He had her hand in both of his.

"We have to get out of here," she said.

"There could be something in there. Something that reminds you."

"We need to leave." She squeezed his hand, suddenly, as hard as she could. "We'll go to the airport early."

He nodded, but didn't move. "Are you sure? This may be the only chance we get. If you've got to go in there, we should do it now."

She hesitated for the barest of moments. "I'm sure. Let's go." *I almost lost you once.*

Was that why? Or was it fear, again, of other revelations lurking in her battered memory?

Did it matter?

She finally had an answer for that particular question. *Not if I don't want it to.*

Cal let go of her hand, but only to start the Chevy sedan and put it into gear. The windshield wipers flicked, the headlights cut a swath through desultory dusky rain. He took her hand again as he pulled out, and they passed the row of brownstones slowly, Trinity peering past Cal's profile at its blank face, windows glowing with dangerous golden light.

No, she decided. *I don't want to go in there at all.*

Something unpleasant happened there, and I don't need to know.

Instead, she reached with her free hand to take the cranes from the dash. They would go in her backpack. "Cal?"

"Hmm?" He hit the blinker, nosing out onto a slightly more traveled avenue. "Change your mind?"

"No. I just... Thank you." The words almost got lodged in her throat. The storm of emotional noise would pass. She had an anchor, and his fingers were warm and forgiving against hers. "You're...good backup." It sounded unhelpful. Awkward. There was no precise word for this.

Or maybe there was one, but she didn't have the courage to say it.

"Anytime, honey." His tone had roughened, too. "We're in this together."

Relief poured through her. He understood.

By the time they hit the freeway, the music had returned. Saint-Saëns's Third Symphony began threading through the hissing of tires on wet pavement, and the city's lights were stars. Trinity squeezed Cal's hand again, but very gently, and she found she didn't need to analyze his returning pressure. In the end, she could be whoever she needed to be, and she suspected he would still understand.

A helicopter looped overhead, aiming for the residential section they'd just exited. Trinity waited until it was past, and relaxed into the seat.

The gray sedan vanished into the gathering dark.

* * *

He stubbed out the cigarette, a little more roughly than was quite necessary. "We can regroup. The investors are there, the technology's there—"

"For God's sake, Art. Stop." The man behind the desk had a brick-red, forgettable face above a be-medaled uniform. Policy wonks and certain military grades would perhaps recognize him, perhaps not.

True power avoided the limelight.

"Sorry." Arthur Hampton settled back into his comfortable leather chair. "It just burns."

"Every other two-bit junta out there now knows it's possible. Someone will figure it out before long. Who knows, maybe this leak stole the process, too, and is selling it to the highest bidder? This is a goddamn catastrophe. Someone's got to hang for it."

"There's Caldwell." The idiot had stolen a vial of weaponized virus, meant to wipe out a loose end. He'd also sent one of their civilian scientists on rendition, and the poor egghead hadn't survived his first interrogations. Bronson's stupidity must have rubbed off on the younger man. "And a list of the usual suspects."

"I don't want my neck in the noose." The general tented his thick fingers, staring at Hampton with an unsettling, piercing expression. "And you're square in the middle of it. Why the hell did you come here? They're going to ask me questions, Art, and I don't much like the idea that I'll be busted down a few stripes or thrown to the lions over this."

"You know they won't, Stilwell. It will blow over."

"This is not blowing-over material."

"What precisely are you saying? That I'm not welcome here anymore? That I'm under suspicion? This changes nothing. Our backers are still in. We still have an edge on technique." Even though Beta had vanished, too. Probably rotting in a ditch somewhere, but you could never be too sure. Aleph in Russia, too. "We're very close."

"I don't care how close you are. It ends here, Arthur. For God's sake, look around you!"

Arthur sighed. He'd always known Stilwell had a regrettable lack of imagination, but he hadn't expected outright cowardice. "Very well, then." He reached for his briefcase, clicked it open and glanced at the man. Still sitting behind his desk, fine. "Thomas, I really hate to do this."

"I can't save you from this one. Even if we did go to school together."

"I don't need saving." Arthur snapped the briefcase closed, set it aside and leveled the gun, a too-long silhouette because of its silencer. "I never did. You, on the other hand..."

Six and a half minutes later, Arthur Hampton stepped out of Stilwell's home office. The general lived alone—his wife had succumbed to heart disease four years ago, and his children were well past college age and living on the West Coast. It was Art's opinion that they wanted to be as far away from their martinet of a father as possible, and he didn't blame them.

Thinking of children and the West Coast was... painful. But sacrifices had to be made in any cause. He understood that, probably better than any of the backers.

Stability, security and freedom were never free.

He let himself out into deep darkness. The cleaners would be by in approximately twenty minutes. He could have left this disagreeable task completely to them, but good old Tommy deserved more. Some things needed to be personally attended to; he'd learned that the hard way.

In the morning, news would break that General Thomas Stilwell had taken his own life, and the implication that he had been responsible for Project Gibraltar would spread. All the appropriate cleanup strategies were already in place.

There were other loose ends. The Gemini mutation was difficult to eradicate, but in every cloud there was a silver lining. That very difficulty made the next stage of the project much more exciting. In the labs, they were working away, creating and testing, smoothing and refining. The next generation of agents would be that much closer to perfect.

His black BMW barely purred when he roused the engine, and he drove between sleeping houses carefully, obeying every traffic law. It wasn't that he feared being pulled over; it was just his inherent neatness.

Once the agents were perfected, all the loose ends could be tidied up.

Even…even *her.*

"Sacrifice," Arthur Hampton rasped to the silence inside his car. "Security. Discipline. Control."

The last word, he mused, was the most important.

Control put away the unpleasant thoughts and turned his attention to other things—the latest round of results from the new viral looping. They were calling this new iteration Psyche. Martigan, the brilliant crackpot that he was, was almost frothing at the mouth with impatience. The human trials were put on hold for a little while, until this all blew over.

Yes, the Psyche results were very exciting. It was much better, as his mother had always said, to focus on the positive…

* * * * *

If you loved this novel, don't miss the previous suspenseful title by Lilith Saintcrow:

AGENT ZERO

*Available now from
Harlequin Romantic Suspense!*

Zoe didn't remember screaming.

Didn't remember pursing her lips or emitting the loud, piercing sound less than a heartbeat after she'd opened the door.

Didn't remember crossing over the threshold into the room, or bending over Celia, who was lying faceup on the floor.

The exquisite wedding dress her sister had taken such all-consuming delight in finding was now ruined. There were two glaring gunshot holes in her chest and her blood had soaked into the delicate white appliqué, all but drenching it. The pattern beneath it was completely obliterated.

The whole scene, which was whizzing by and moving in painfully slow motion at the same time, seemed totally surreal to Zoe, like some sort of an ill-conceived, macabre scene being played out from an old-fashioned grade B horror movie about a rampaging slasher.

And if the dreadfulness of all this wasn't enough, someone—the killer?—had gone on to draw a bizarre red bull's-eye on Celia's forehead. There was a single dot inside the circle, just off-center, and whoever had drawn it had used some sort of a laundry marker, so the bull's-eye stood out even more than it normally might have.

This can't be real, it just can't be real.

The desperate thought throbbed over and over again in Zoe's head. She'd just left Celia, what, a couple of minutes ago? Five minutes, tops?

How could all this have happened in such a short period of time?

Who could have done this to her sister?

Why hadn't she heard the gunshots when they were fired?

And for God's sake, what was that awful noise she was hearing now?

Zoe tried to see where it was coming from, but for some reason, she just couldn't seem to her head.

She couldn't even move.

The noise was surrounding her. It sounded like wailing, or, more specifically, like keening. It approximated the sound that was heard when someone's heart was breaking.

Zoe had no idea the noise she was attempting to place was coming from her.

Don't miss COLTON COPYCAT KILLER
by USA TODAY bestselling and RITA® Award-winning
author Marie Ferrarella, available January 2016
wherever Harlequin® Romantic Suspense
books and ebooks are sold.

www.Harlequin.com

Turn your love of reading into rewards you'll love with

Harlequin My Rewards

**Join for FREE today at
www.HarlequinMyRewards.com**

Earn **FREE BOOKS** of your choice.

Experience **EXCLUSIVE OFFERS** and contests.

Enjoy **BOOK RECOMMENDATIONS**
selected just for you.

PLUS! Sign up now
and get **500** points
right away!

Earn **FREE** REWARDS
Join Today!
HarlequinMyRewards.com

MYR16R

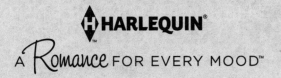

HARLEQUIN®

A *Romance* FOR EVERY MOOD™

JUST CAN'T GET ENOUGH?

Join our social communities
and talk to us online.

You will have access to the latest
news on upcoming titles and special
promotions, but most importantly,
you can talk to other fans about your
favorite Harlequin reads.

Harlequin.com/Community

Facebook.com/HarlequinBooks

Twitter.com/HarlequinBooks

Pinterest.com/HarlequinBooks